THE WOMAN WHO HUMMED

by
Marlene Walker

ISBN: 978-0-9903108-4-6

Contents

Foreward

Long, long ago my Norse ancestors would gather around the campfire to sing sacred songs and act out stories celebrating their Great Mother, Freya, the giver of life, nourishment and fertility to all creatures on earth.

Until one fateful night... a new actor stepped into the campfire light to amend Freya's story.

"I am Odin," he roared, striding around the campfire. "I am he who gave birth to Man!"

"Liar! Only females give birth!" yelled a heckler.

Odin scoffed, "You doubt me? Listen and learn!"

"Sure," cried the heckler. "Might be a laugh."

"Creating Mankind was not a laugh," Odin complained. "I had to isolate myself for nine whole days to produce the first human."

His audience laughed merrily. "Nine days? Don't you mean nine months?"

"Hah, women may claim it takes months to become mothers. But I am a god."

His audience chortled as Odin strode around the fire with his chest puffed out, boasting, "For the whole nine days, I had to hang by one foot on the Tree of Life. Ever see a woman give birth in that position?"

"To create a human life a mother has to have access to the Fount of Female Wisdom," called the heckler. "Make up your mind: are you a mother or a warrior?"

"I am both hero and heroine," Odin cried, bearing his hairy chest. "I nursed Mankind at my breast, and bravely bore the pain."

"You don't have the paps for nursing, fella!" the heckler howled.

At that, Odin swept his sword from its scabbard and drew blood from his breast. "This is how a man nourishes

1

his people," he roared.

It took centuries for that icky story to take hold with the public, but, it did-- with storytellers creating endless characters who embodied the idea that spilling blood in behalf of an all-powerful leader nourishes humanity.

Meanwhile the Tree of Life, with its roots embedded in feminine wisdom? Withered, nearly gone.

But not entirely forgotten.

~ From the MFA Dissertation of Danielle Running ~

The Old Lady is Missing

"The old lady is missing!"

That alarm sounded a few weeks after I began my engagement at Safe Haven Senior Residence. The dismaying shout was sent repeatedly down the hall from the residents' wing into the dining area where aides were setting the tables for lunch. In the adjacent common room the heads of many of the elderly folks awaiting their next meal turned as one to hear the alarming news.

Even before the word *missing* had stopped ringing down the hallway, the manager of Safe Haven, Sister Peter Mary, appeared in the doorway of her office next to the common room. I had just finished performing one of my stories for the elderly residents and I feared the nun might have emerged from her den to fire me for telling a tale not likely to please someone whose title began with the word "Sister." She had already scolded me once for my takes on the ancient myths, which I had been performing for the residents: she called them *Danielle's little fairytales.*

My fear evaporated when Sister Peter sailed past me and headed for the middle of the dining area where the aide, Lonny, was shouting, "Missing woman! Missing woman!" Sister Peter greeted him with the same facial expression worn by the sword-bearing cherubim who drove Adam and Eve from the Garden of Eden. Even though her face was inches from his, the panicky attendant kept babbling his alarming message in several different iterations.

"From her room down the hall. She's gone. Old lady who hums. Nowhere to be found. Gone off. Disappeared. Evaporated. Skedaddled like an *effing sumbitch*!"

Before he could use up the entire Thesaurus entry for "departed," Sister Peter reached out a long arm, grabbed the collar of his white uniform and brought him up so short he landed on his pillowy backside. Grabbing his face and lifting it towards hers, she hissed, "Quietly, you ass! Which lady is missing?"

Lonny could not have obeyed more promptly if the nun had been Saint Peter giving him a task to perform before allowing him through the pearly gates, and, still seated on the linoleum, the young man dutifully stretched his thick neck up towards the nun meaning to whisper the name of the missing woman in her ear. She bowed down no further than absolutely necessary to receive his message. But the aide was so agitated by the crisis and so frightened by Sister Peter he could not make a sound come from his trembling mouth. Not one to allow a rescue mission to languish because of a tongue-tied aide, the nun left the agitated fellow to pick himself up off the floor while, with a snap of her long fingers, she assembled the entire staff in an area of the dining hall far enough from the common room to prevent any of the residents whose hearing was still intact from overhearing whatever plans Sister Peter would put into motion to locate the missing woman.

As curious as any of the residents to hear who the old woman in question might be, I crept to the French windows leading from the dining room to the courtyard and folded myself in among the heavy velour drapes. I was close enough to overhear Sister Peter but was sufficiently concealed, I hoped, to avoid her notice, as I always tried to do. She looked harmless enough--from her sensible hairdo to the understated dime-sized silver cross around her neck; she always dressed unpretentiously in flared ankle-length culottes and a simple silk turtleneck jersey under a sensible cardigan. Nothing ever seemed extraneous or put-on about her, really, but she was, after all, the resident authoritarian, a breed of human that sends chills down my spine. While I stood wrapped in the draperies, admiring the calm efficiency of the woman, she turned from Lonny, leaving him on the floor gaping at her, and stood in the space between the dining area and the common room directing staff and residents with the elegance of the conductor of a major symphony. That done, she pivoted towards Lonny again, demanding, "Tell me exactly which woman you think is not where she should be?"

"The woman who hums," Lonny croaked.

"Bibi's gone?" another aide, whose name was Monte, cried in dismay.

"Her given name would have sufficed," said Sister Peter, "but, I take it Beatrice Bell is the resident in question." And, with the speed of a lizard catching a fly, she turned to Monte--whom she called Montana--and instructed him to speed down the hall of the residents' wing and ascertain whether Beatrice Bell was playing an unscheduled game of hide-and-seek from the staff. The moment Monte sped away, she swung back towards Lonny, who was trying to disappear amid the staff members standing at attention by the dining tables.

"And have you any theory, Lonsdale, as to where Beatrice Bell might be?"

Lonny knit his black brows causing them to form a bridge from temple to temple, and, to augment his mental processes, he made his hands into fists the size of cantaloupes. "Maybe she went off somewhere private to die? You know like a dog does?" Sister Peter stared at him as if he had told a dirty joke in church. He explained further. "She's old. Don't old people do that?"

Sister Peter recovered her voice. "I don't know, Lonsdale. I do know people don't casually mention it if old people do that."

It would have been impossible not to laugh at that exchange if I had not been so upset to hear that the missing woman was the woman who hums. I selfishly hoped Lonny was not correct that it was Beatrice Bell. She was my favorite senior citizen so far, and, even though I had known her for a short time, I felt I had a rare bond with her. We had even shared nicknames--a practice Sister Peter discouraged. I had told the old woman that she could call me Dani, and she had written down her nickname and showed it to me. It was the letters "B.B." So, while Monte was gone on his quest to find the woman, and while Sister Peter was questioning each of the staff members as to their last dealings with her, I listened as hard as I could for word of her whereabouts. When it became obvious that no one had seen her in the several hours since breakfast, or had even heard her humming, Sister Peter told her assistant, Gloria, to stand by to call the police. I noticed that when Sister Peter spoke the word *police*, she did so with obvious reluctance, and in a stage whisper, she called after Gloria to wait until it became clear that the woman was indeed missing before notifying the police.

When Monte returned from the dormitory wing where some old folks were still napping away their golden years, he was sweating and shaking like a devoted hound who has lost his boy.

"No sign of the lady who hums. I couldn't find her anywhere."

Looking stony as a statue of her name saint, Sister Peter inquired, "Which of our female residents are you saying is missing?"

Monte apologized, "Lonny said the lady who hums–uh Bibi--is missing, so that's who I looked for."

6

"Yes, he did say that," Sister Peter recalled without pleasure, adding,"I take it you are referring to Beatrice Bell, who is a human being, Montana, not just a stuttered note in a child's alphabet song." Sister Peter's brow was crumpled slightly with concern. That was in itself a bad sign. She did not easily fly into fantasies of doom and destruction. Diving into the well of Monte's deep brown eyes she asked, "No sign whatever? And be thinking how you'll present this to the world, Montana. Unless you know someplace else to look for her?"

With confidence, he assured her, "I swear I looked under every pillow and basket in her room, Sister Peter–and in all the other rooms along the residents' hallway. Bibi–uh, Beatrice Bell--has either left her room or has slipped Sauron's ring of power on her finger and turned invisible."

Sister looked murderously annoyed by Monte's metaphor. "What ring? Never mind. The only personage invisible around here is the Holy Spirit, and you people make me so cross-eyed sometimes I think I can even see *Him* stalking the halls."

Meanwhile, the idea that the lady who hums could have turned invisible filled me with the urge to run out at once and look for her. It was not that I felt responsible for her absence: I just thought I might have more insight into her situation than others. I had spent more time with her, I thought, than even her roommate, Bettina. But, because Monte called the missing woman by her nickname, I suspected maybe he and I might be the only ones at Safe Haven who knew her at all. It's not easy to get to know someone who only hums.

Suddenly the emptiness of the Queen Anne chair Bibi had always occupied during Story Hour seemed ominous. I pictured her, from the snowy curls bursting out of the knit cap on her head, to the sturdy tennis shoes she wore on her Lilliputian feet. Although she was as wrinkled as a winter apple, she was a pretty Dresden doll of a woman in a velour track suit. And she was so tiny I could imagine how she could be overlooked in the tumble of people, furniture and personal possessions in an old folks' home. She might have been overlooked if she crouched behind a hassock.

The moment before Lonny had shouted that the old woman was missing, I had been telling one of my stories and had noticed that there were no laughs coming from the Queen Anne chair. And she was not only the woman who hums, she was the woman who laughs. I had wondered why she had not responded as enthusiastically to my performance that day as she had done to all of the other stories I had told. As a performer who likes to get laughs, I had felt it vaguely ominous that the one person who chuckled at my tales had not been seated in the audience that day. Now that I knew she had gone missing, I found myself considering just how important she had become to me in a very short period of time. The thought of her absence made me queasy.

Just when Monte convinced Sister Peter that, indeed, the woman was not hidden under her bed or duvet or behind a window shade or shower curtain, Gloria called out from the office doorway that the police were on their way. Sister Peter grumbled through gritted teeth, "I said to stand by, not to run out immediately and hail a squad car." Then, looking around the vast dining and common room area for someone who might offer an early solution to the situation, she cast her all-seeing eye on the spot where I was trying to hide amid the draperies. She had not called me to the spontaneous staff meeting, probably because I was only a volunteer auditioning for a regular job at the home. But Sister Peter was not the sort of manager who was likely to miss an eavesdropper semi-concealed amid the drapes. And, in that moment of potential disaster at Safe Haven, when her head wheeled towards me, I could see she was about to call me on the carpet–or on the linoleum of the dining area.

Though I admired Sister Peter's seamless management skills and I desperately wanted my volunteer work at Safe Haven to lead to a paying job, I am so apprehensive about attracting the attention of authority figures that, when she cast her eyes on me, I stood frozen amid the drapes while my whole life flashed through my mind. By the time I was ten, I had learned how to make myself scarce as much as possible; for, whenever I failed to melt into the wallpaper at home, I became the family scapegoat. To avoid that undesirable fate, I learned to act as the family's comic relief. It was the same way in school: I did my work, got good grades, but almost always kept as low a profile as I could manage and expressed myself in an outgoing manner only in public speaking class, in school plays or when someone was being bullied. And in those instances I let out all the self-expression I ordinarily suppressed.

At the moment, feeling the headlights of Sister Peter's gaze upon me, I was not in an outgoing mood and longed to flee through the French windows behind me. But, even as the awesome nun bore down upon me and I prepared to meet my doom, I was alerted by a distress call from the adjacent common room area.

"Miss Danielle, Miss Danielle!"

I recognized the voice of Bettina, Beatrice Bell's

roommate and a regular member of my Story Hour audience, most of whom were still sitting around on overstuffed furniture looking dumbfounded.

"What is happening? Is this part of your story?"

Bettina was a restive soul with a thatch of lavender hair and a skin-tight pantsuit which accented legs so bowed she seemed to be riding an invisible goat. She was a kindly woman who made montages on a coffee table in the common room during Story Hour and cried at all the sad parts of the tales I told. I conveniently decided that, as an audience member, she needed me more at the moment than Sister Peter did. My theatrical instincts having smothered my congenital bashfulness, I popped out from the dining room drapes. Pretending I had not noticed Sister Peter casting her eye on me, I hurried across the open space between dining area and common room hoping to reach Bettina and comfort her before her tear-filled eyes and chuttering chin developed into some momentous weeping and wailing.

"This isn't part of the story, Bettina," I reassured her. "We're just wondering if anyone has recently seen the woman who hums. You know, your roommate? She usually sits in the Queen Anne chair near the coffee table where you make your montages during Story Hour."

Bettina turned to glare at the Queen Anne chair. "She isn't sitting there now, unless she's invisible," Bettina wheezed. "And even if she was invisible, she would probably be humming."

The woman was working herself into a state, and with Sister Peter looming nearby, I took Bettina's arm and adopted my most soothing storytelling tone.

"Sister Peter is on a quest right now to find out what's happening with the woman who hums."

"But I wanted to hear what happened in your story."

"We're in a real story now, Bettina, and our quest is to find a real life heroine."

The disconcerted woman grasped my hand and prepared to ask me some follow-up questions. But Sister Peter had endured enough of my attempts to calm Bettina and, as if wearing roller blades hidden by the cuffs of her decorous culottes, she glided towards us across the dining room floor. Without preamble, she turned her interrogation towards Bettina and the rest of my elderly, vaguely unsettled audience.

"Bettina Raye, or any of you, have you seen Beatrice Bell this afternoon?"

Those whose hearing was still sharp enough to hear Sister reacted to her question by looking around as if the missing woman might pop out from under a pile of sofa cushions. Though their heads waggled this way and that, no one seemed to have seen or heard the woman who hums since breakfast. Having garnered all the news of the missing woman available from my audience members, Sister Peter whirled on me as swiftly and smoothly as an Olympic figure skater--her culottes swirling majestically around her ankles.

"Danielle Running!" she snapped. I was surprised she knew my name, as I had not been a volunteer in her bailiwick very long and, since the day she interviewed me, I had tried to avoid her notice. My mouth went so dry I could not answer, and I viewed her approach with the natural apprehension of a half-lapsed Protestant standing in the direct path of a dignitary of the–to me–exotic Catholic Diocese. I have never been known as a great champion of authoritarian institutions, and the presence of Sister Peter seemed to imbue the place with an air of cosmic authority.

As a reluctant admirer of her immense air of command, however, I scurried to meet her oncoming eminence like a bear cub hastening to its mother's growl. I actually made a tiny curtsy as I came to an abrupt stop before her. She did not mince words.

"You know the missing woman personally, do you not?"

"You mean the woman who hums?"

Sister wrinkled her Patrician nose as if I had tossed up a handful of wet garbage in the air between us. "Use her name, please, Danielle. She is a human being, not a harp that makes noise when the wind blows through her."

"Sorry, Sister. I guess you mean Bibi."

Raising her hands to the silver wings of hair at her temples as if to block the word *Bibi* from entering her ears, Sister Peter breathed, "She is Beatrice Bell and I am Sister *Peter Mary*. Nicknames are the Devil's lingo, Danielle."

Daunted, I reverted to my family role as hapless clown."Oh! *Nick* names," I grinned nervously. "I get it. *Old Nick* being one of Satan's names."

"One of his *Nick*names," Sister Peter averred, trying to suppress a smile, and succeeding. (I suspected Sister succeeded at most things she tried.) Just now she was trying to find out something about my favorite woman among the elderly folk, and I was inclined to satisfy her curiosity, without spilling any confidences, if possible.

"Sorry, Sister. Someone told me Beatrice Bell likes to be called Bibi. I don't know why."

"Neither do I," said Sister Peter. "But I suspect the Devil does. Now, Beatrice Bell usually listens to the little fairytales you tell in the afternoon. Did she attend today?" Sister Peter gestured towards my elderly audience. "Our venerable residents do not seem to recall."

12

Remembering the musical sound of Bibi's laughter, I got a lump in my throat. Sister Peter soon got tired of trying to read my mind and tapped my hand smartly with the business end of her ever-present fountain pen. The whimsical feather on the end did not soften the blow.

"Quickly, please, Danielle, have you any brilliant thoughts about Beatrice Bell's whereabouts?"

Madly I riffled through my memory for recent contacts with the old woman, Not having anything humorous to say at the moment, I was, however, daunted by being in the close vicinity of an authority figure, and my tongue puckered as if I had just sucked on a juicy lemon. Fortunately, I was relieved of the necessity of answering her query at that moment when a great hubbub broke out at the front door.

"Danielle, Danielle Running, open this door!"

Sister Peter could not have looked more annoyed if the devil himself had summoned me. Actually, the voice was well known to me, and, unfortunately, it was not the devil. Though it might as well have been.

~ ~ ~

The Intruder at the Door

When the man began shouting my name at the door of Safe Haven, everyone in the adjoining dining and common areas stiffened as though storm troopers were about to burst in with guns raised; the building was without foyer or vestibule, and, as the front door led directly into the dining area, there was no buffer between the outside door and the person causing an uproar just beyond it. Fortunately the sturdy portal was constructed of oak and was always locked with a combination lock to prevent folks from the Alzheimers wing from taking a stroll out into a world they could not be expected to navigate with absolute safety. The upper half of the formidable door featured a window made of safety glass so thick the person on the other side of the door appeared more as the shimmering shape of a monster than an actual person. The visitor's voice, however, was dreadfully recognizable to me. And it was someone I had no wish to see at present, especially when I was in doubt about whether a major tragedy was shaping up around my favorite old lady. However, the persistence of the person causing the uproar made it impossible for me to conceal that I was the reason for his shouting at the front door.

"Why does no one answer this door?" the voice cried. "I have to talk with Danielle Running!"

To her credit, Sister Peter did not, upon hearing my name, glare at me as if I had called down some personal blitzkrieg onto the place. Instead, she motioned to her sturdy assistant, Gloria, to check out the man at the door. While Gloria chatted with my unwelcome visitor through the door's intercom, Sister Peter calmly continued questioning me.

"You are one of the few people I have seen engage

the reticent Beatrice Bell in private conversation, Danielle, so you can see why I might hope you would have some insight–perhaps without even being aware you have it–about where she might be."

"Shouldn't I...?" I asked, motioning lamely towards the loud discussion the man outdoors was having with Gloria via intercom.

"Don't worry about your friend at the door. Gloria and I will see to him."

"He's not my friend," I muttered.

"I can see that by the look on your face, dear. Now, about the matter at hand?"

Though I feared the matter of my non-friend howling at the door was something I would have to deal with before the day was through, Sister Peter's authority was such that I immediately turned my attention to the case of the missing woman. My response to the nun's interrogation was awkward but brief.

"Bibi--uh, Beatrice Bell--did not turn up at Story Hour, Sister. And I was surprised, because usually she is one of the uh...audience who laughs and seems to...you know...'get' the humor in my material. I cannot claim to have fully noted her physical absence before Lonny announced she was gone. But, I missed her laughter today. I feared the humorous elements of my story might be bombing. I'm sorry, Sister, I do try to adjust my stories to my aud...."

"A critique of your success as a storyteller will not be necessary at this time, Danielle. For now all that will be required of you is to join the search party, which will commence right now. Go. Join the hunt in the South wing. And if you know where she might usually spend time in the building, please look there first."

I cringed at the shouting and door pounding, which continued ever more loudly outside the dining room door. And, as the search party made its way down the hall to the residents' rooms, I sidled in between aides Lonny and Monte for protection–just in case the unwelcome visitor made it past Sister Peter's solid assistant, Gloria.

"Dani Running, you can't run away from me!"

When the intruder at the door shouted my name again, the group jostled down the hallway a bit faster. Lonny grumbled, "That *sumbitch* is out for blood," and shied away from me as if to steer clear of my imminent slaughter and the inevitable blood splatter. The other aide, Monte, pressed close by my side and put a protective hand on the back of my arm. I turned toward him to see what that was about, and smiled gratefully at the look of concern on his face.

"I'm hoping he won't be able to get past Gloria and Sister Peter, Monte."

"He sounds like he could walk through walls," Monte said. He did not remove his hand from my arm, and I was glad of that; hearing the man at the door call me by name was more disquieting than I was prepared to admit. I had found a place of refuge here, I thought: at Safe Haven no one from the university where I was a graduate student would be able to find me. And until my volunteer work at Safe Haven turned into a paid position, I hoped the powers-that-be at the university would assume I was sequestered in the library rewriting my thesis. As I was still fraudulently living on a grant to complete my MFA degree, it was distressing to have my ex-boyfriend trumpeting my name at the door. And, because of the circumstances of my breakup with him, it was even more alarming that it was he who had found out where I had been hiding.

Half-expecting Sister Peter to change her mind and turn me over to the man who was so cavalierly shouting my name outside her place of business, I leaned a bit towards Monte and scurried down the hall with him. It was lucky that Sister Peter had allowed me to continue searching for the old woman, because, just as we neared her room, we heard the outside door of the dining hall burst open and the intruder shout my name. The rapidly increasing volume of his cries left no doubt that he had gotten inside Safe Haven.

"Dani! I know you're here. We have to talk. Now!"

At that, Monte threw open the door to the furnace closet, and, grasping my arm tighter, pulled me inside with him and shut the door behind us. Though I was not able to enjoy the closeness at the moment, Monte was not the last person in the world with whom I would wish to be hidden in a closet. Happily, Monte was a fairly compact muscular fellow or we would never have fit together in a furnace enclosure; also, his strong grip on my arm was reassuring in case the intruder threw open the door and tried to drag me away by the hair. Meanwhile, we were as close to the furnace as I would ever want to get: I felt its presence hot on one side, and Monte's heat on the other. And I learned something about myself during that brief tete a tete in the furnace cubby: the unfortunate breakup with my exboyfriend had not left me as dedicated to a life without men as I had believed.

Turning his head to whisper in my ear, Monte said, "I don't like to pry, but, if you don't want to talk to this guy, why did you tell him where you worked?"

"If you must know, I purposely did *not* tell him where I work, or where I live."

"Damn, the guy's a talented hunter; maybe we ought to get him to help us find Bibi."

Despite the circumstance, I had to laugh. After we stifled our nervous snickering, Monte opened the door a crack so we could hear what was happening up the hall in the dining room. Apparently, two policemen had shown up close on the intruder's heels. Through the slim aperture, I could see Sister Peter swoop toward the knot of struggling men by the front door and efficiently sort out the members of the police force from my intrusive exboyfriend. Swiftly she set them upon the courses she deemed appropriate for each of them and all was quiet for a time.

Monte tilted his head close to mine and whispered to me. "If someone disappears at practically the same moment that someone else comes shouting at the door, could that be a coincidence?"

"Probably," I whispered back. I did think it probably was a coincidence, but, like Monte, I was giving some consideration to the strange conjunction of the lady's disappearance from the place where I had been trying to hide out from an untenable relationship. Although I was sure Sister Peter and the police would convince the intruder to leave off harassing me for another day, I knew him to be much subtler than his bellowing suggested. Both in his position as my boyfriend and as my immediate supervisor in the university's Drama Department, he was characteristically fine-tuned and quietly incisive.

"For the present," I told Monte, "I think the police—or Sister Peter--have protected us from the trespasser. I really want to look for Bibi now."

"Of course," he said, dropping my arm as if it had just burst into flames."Sorry to be so grabby. I thought you might be in real danger."

"Who knows, I might have been, but thank you for letting me go as soon as danger—whether real or potential–passed. I call that gentlemanly."

"Thanks," he smiled, as we emerged from the closet and rejoined the search team members who were poking about in the residents' rooms, the Beauty Salon, shower room and the laundry. We looked everywhere for the lady who hums, even in small spaces, like cubbyholes behind the shoe trees on the floors of residents' closets, under piles of laundry–dirty and clean--and under each of the twin beds in every room. I imagine another search team was combing the Alzheimers rooms in the north wing of the building in the same painstaking manner. We would have to search deeper than beneath beds and laundry baskets, however, before we would find anything even resembling a clue to the disappearance of Beatrice Bell.

When we reached the door of Room 17, Monte declared that he had already searched the woman's stuff and would go on to the next room. As I stepped into Bibi's room to see if I might find something Monte had missed, I heard the voice of my intrusive exboyfriend blaring into the residents' wing from the dining room. He was back.

"What the Hell, Danielle?" His increasingly loud voice suggested he was heading toward me as he shouted, "We have unfinished business."

Hurrying across Bibi's room, I opened her wardrobe and scrunched myself in amid the many layers of clothing. Stepping up onto a box of out-of-fashion footwear, I slipped into a heavy old coat. As it turned out, my dear intruder did not make it down the hall to Room 17, but was caught by Monte and Lonny, who helped the police escort him back to the dining room and out the front door. Still, I chose to wait until Safe Haven quieted down for the night before I crept out of the closet.

Monte had come looking for me twice, but I did not

reveal myself even to him. Oddly I somewhat resented that he too had been allowed to call the reserved woman by her nickname, and when I felt Monte riffling through Bibi's jammed-full closet, I snuggled into the heavy hooded coat as if it were a cocoon that clung to me like a second skin. And, later, when I crept out of the wardrobe, I did not shed the woman's full-length coat. It was only a long jacket on me, but it felt nice to have a bit of Bibi's clothing for company.

As I tiptoed towards the door, I gasped when someone in one of the twin beds let out a sigh. For a moment I thought it was the missing woman tucked safely in her bed. But the purple tufts of hair sticking out this way and that on the pillow revealed her to be, not the woman who hums, but her roommate, Bettina. I tiptoed past her to the hallway and, removing my shoes, padded silently past the open doors of the residents' rooms to the dining hall. Then, bending over to avoid being seen by the night cook behind the kitchen counter, I crept to the door. The nightlight over the intercom had a note I had never seen before posted under it. It said, *Do not allow a young man requesting access to our Danielle Running into the building. If he persists, call the police.*

Our Danielle Running the note said. That was comforting. The place might be *my* safe haven after all. I opened the door, peered around cautiously and slid away into the welcoming dark.

I did not go home. If my ex had managed to find my place of work, he might also have found my new apartment and could be lurking there. Instead, I stopped by a Stop 'n Sip for a bottle of chocolate milk, an apple and a box of crackers. Stuffing them into my cross-body bag, I headed to the university library.

The librarian was preparing to close up for the night, and, as soon as she left her desk to turn off the reading room lights, I snuck in, scurried to the back stairway, took off my shoes (for the second time that day), and tiptoed up the noisy iron spiral stairway to the top floor. After fumbling in the dark through the stacks to my study cubicle, I made a pallet of the chair cushions I had brought when I signed up for my cube a year before. Pushing my wastebasket out of the way, I tucked myself cozily under my desk. As my cubicle was on the east side of the building, I hoped that the dawn sun shining through the wall of dusty windows beside my desk would wake me before a janitor or fellow student discovered my hiding place. And I hoped even harder that my ex would not think to look for me in the library. He knew where my cubicle was, of course, and he knew that I ordinarily spent my time there doing research for my MFA thesis.

Hunkering under my desk, I lay back on my chair cushions and, pulling Bibi's winter coat over me, I closed my eyes and tried to forget the upsets of the day. But, as I lay in the dark, my brain cells kept playing leap-frog through my head, landing my thoughts into one remembered peril after another.

"We need to talk, Danielle," my erstwhile boyfriend, Remington (he was named after the rifle, though he was not of its inventor's family) shouted over and over as he chased me in my dreams. I feared he wanted to continue the last conversation we had enjoyed while I packed up my things before moving out of our apartment. When I heard Dream-Remy cry, "I am not a thief!" as he had that night, I woke in a sweat, panic-stricken that his cry would alert the night janitor who would come sweep me out with the dust bunnies.

Until dawn light sifted though the library's dusty windows, I hurried down the byways of my dreams pursued by Remy's voice, which was accompanied by a misty melody that drifted through my head. It was the same tune the old woman had been humming when I met her on the day I first volunteered at Safe Haven.

~ ~ ~

A New Beginning

The day I first met the woman who hums was the day I was interviewed to be accepted as a volunteer aide at Safe Haven. While I followed Sister Peter Mary toward her office like the obedient handmaid I hoped to become, she asked my name.

"Danielle Running," I said, "Friends call me Dani."

She stopped in her tracks so abruptly I actually ran into her, my nose making a small temporary dent in the back of her cardigan.

"You will find I do not hold with nicknames, Danielle."

Hoity toity, I said in my head.

As she passed before me into her office, I read the name plaque on her door. *Manager: Sister Peter Mary,* and blurted out, "What happened to *Paul?*" *Must stop making nervous jokes when in the presence of authority.*

Pausing mid-step for a moment, she made a sort of nickering sound then continued on into her office. Moving behind her desk to open her window, she said, oh so crisply, "I believe I mentioned that I find abbreviations annoying, Danielle. Were you not paying attention, or are you perhaps a bit hard of hearing?"

Obviously you're not deaf, Sister Peter, I mouthed behind her back.

She jerked her head around and gave me a look that would dry up rain before it hit the earth. I had the eerie feeling that she read my mind, or that she understood people so well she knew exactly the kind of smart remark a new recruit would make behind her back.

Despite our shaky start, she interviewed me for only about a quarter hour before congratulating me on becoming a valued volunteer at Safe Haven. She pulled a long sheet of paper out of a desk drawer, ran her finger down it, and leaned across her desk towards me.

"This place would collapse and rot away to nothing without our happy volunteers." She smiled a smile I thought looked a bit mischievous for a nun. "We who work at Safe Haven are gratified to be able to comfort some people who find the aging process not all that encouraging. I see by your resume that you are an educated woman, and I think you can understand that someone like you who is not an official part of the establishment that houses the elderly–I mean that cares for them–would seem less oppressive to them than we on the staff might seem."

If she depended on volunteers so much, I feared I had just spent fifteen minutes interviewing for a position that was never going to support me financially. And my present situation would soon become very awkward if I did not secure a living wage somewhere: obviously, I could not live on my graduate grant once it was discovered that I was no longer working on my MFA thesis in Dramaturgy. Desperation prodded me to speak up to the imposing nun.

"I was hoping, though–I mean, I thought you said, if I proved myself, I might join the regular staff--paid staff, I mean."

"Look at this list!" she cried, flashing the lengthy paper she was holding. It was long enough to inform Santa Claus who all the good boys and girls were in the entire Bay Area. "As you can see, we have such an impressive variety of little tasks that need doing around here that we will be able to test your suitability as an aide in no time."

"How long is *no time* in your time zone?" I ventured.

She smiled but only with her eyes. "Oh, a few weeks, I should think. We'll start you in the garden. The primroses lining the path need weeding."

"Primrose path?" I muttered. *"How literary."*

Sister Peter had excellent hearing for her employees' mutterings. "Hah, no!" she said. "Today, as you see on the list, is a big day for one of our elderly women. Her family is joining her for a picnic in the back garden. And it wouldn't hurt if you kept an eye on her. We do not usually let visitors hold private events here that exclude our general population, and who knows what might occur?"

"You want me to be a spy?"

"We call ourselves their *quiet guards,*" she said.

"From Shakespeare," I said. *"Have you had quiet guard? Hamlet, Act I, Scene i."*

"Very good," she almost smiled, "We are the quiet guardians of some frail people, Danielle. The woman in question is one-hundred and one today."

"One-hundred-one! Will there be Dalmatians?"

Sister Peter actually smiled with her mouth. I saw her teeth. "You are going to be such a treat," she said. Then, studying my face with a look of bemusement, she added, "I see there is an entertainer lurking inside your shy demeanor. That being the case, I have another task for you to take care of before the primroses."

She handed me a key to a numbered locker for my personal items, then led me back to the common room area where residents were waiting on overstuffed sofas and chairs for the lunch meal to be served in the adjacent dining area. "The volunteer who usually tells jokes, sings or tells stories before meals suddenly dropped out. She said something about my interfering with her *artistic oeuvre.* So, before you do the gardening, could you please dance a jig, sing a ditty or two, or perhaps recite a few of Hamlet's soliloquies for the residents? They get restive before a meal and begin milling about like a flock of geese anxious to fly south for the winter."

As I am more comfortable on stage than anyplace normal people gather, I was happy to comply with Sister Peter's wish. I had been working on some pieces for the performance element of my MFA thesis defense that I hoped might entertain the elderly audience. I did wonder if my monologues would please Sister Peter, as my *artistic oeuvre* consisted of my takes on some ancient myths meant to prove my theory about the influence of classic tales on social prejudices. I feared the prejudices my thesis took to task might be the very ones embraced by a woman of the cloth. There were no signs of religious preference around the place, however, no biblical slogans posted anywhere, and I had not been questioned about my religiosity when I applied to help out at the home. So I allowed Sister Peter to herd me to a spot in the common room where a low platform was surrounded by various pieces of plastic-covered overstuffed furniture.

Standing on the ersatz stage, I did a quick visual sweep of my audience, which appeared as a vast sea of waves of white and lavender hairdos. I could not discern which silver-haired audience member might be about to celebrate her one-hundred and first year of life, but, by the look of the oldsters, it might be a group event.

"Ladies and gentlemen, this is Danielle Running, and she is a delight," announced Sister Peter. "Please welcome her."

With that, Sister Peter disappeared through her nearby office door, and I bowed briefly in response to whatever it was the elders mumbled to welcome me.

"Did you know?" I smiled at the puzzled faces assembled before me, "That some of the fairytales we heard as children were all inside out and upside down?"

The woman seated at a coffee table right in front of me stopped tearing a glossy magazine into bits and looked up at me in disbelief.

"Yes, they were," I assured her, "I've made a little study of them and I am about to turn one of those tales right-side up and the right-way round for you."

Pandora

Once upon a time–long ago before writing was even invented–there lived a lovely girl called Pandora. She was one of those special beings just born to give to others; in fact her name, Pandora, means "All-Giver." Pandora was revered as the quintessence of femaleness and a symbol of maternal fruitfulness.

Those were the days of the first actors, folks who would act out stories for the tribe around communal campfires. They would celebrate Pandora with songs and poems, showing how she would walk among the people carrying a special pithos, or honey-vase, pouring out nature's bounties for everyone in the audience.

But. along about the time writing was invented, Pandora's story took a nasty turn. From then on, as the story goes, Pandora carried, not a pithos but just a box-- and it did not contain honey.

Pandora's fictional male guardian set a beautiful jeweled box where she could not miss it, and he told her she must not under any circumstance open it or even peek inside. It was obviously a set-up, because of course she did peek inside–as anyone would have known she would do and perhaps should do: curiosity is the jewel of the human intellect, and there would never be an accrual of knowledge among men or the creation of any infrastructure or art, if curiosity did not lead the way to finding out how things work and how they can work better.

You know the rest of the corrupted story: Pandora opened the box and out flew every awful thing imaginable: ugliness, ineptitude, disease, death, murder, war, bad haircuts and bad attitudes. And who was blamed for spilling evil into the world? Not the autocrat who baited the girl to investigate a magic box.

Instead, the pirated tale planted in the communal mind the idea that all evil derives from the quintessential female. The upshot, for us in the 21st century is that the female gender has been demonized through the age-old myth we all have heard. And if you think the bad publicity failed to change human attitudes, consider how many times in your life you've heard someone foretell disaster with the dread words, "They've opened a real Pandora's box this time!"

Though, amazingly, there are still many people who are as generous, curious and independent minded as the original Pandora. Whether they are encouraged and inspired by the stories and myths of our time to follow their best lights is a question unknown even to the wise.

~ ~ ~

The Primrose Path

While telling my tale of Pandora, I scanned the audience, wondering who might be the woman whose one-hundred-first birthday party I was about to spy on. But before I could figure out who might be a centenarian among a sea of eighty and ninety-year old faces, the lunch bell rang. Immediately the oldsters regained the sprightliness of their youth and shuffled across the open space between the common room and dining hall to have their lunch. I was putting my sling bag in the locker Sister Peter had assigned me, when one of the elderly women appeared at my elbow, murmuring "Danielle: your name is like a song."

Startled, I jumped several inches from ground zero before asking her if I could help her in any way.

"I liked your story," she said, and shyly reached out a wrinkly hand to give me a congratulatory pat on the arm. "My name is Bettina. Yours is Danielle."

"Yes," I said. "Shouldn't you be eating lunch?"

"Are you going to eat lunch?" she asked hopefully.

"Not right now," I said. "I'm to weed primroses while one of the residents' family celebrates her birthday."

Immediately I saw that I should not have mentioned the birthday party. Bettina's face transformed to one of the flowers in a Disney movie, painted with the most enthusiastic smile I ever saw.

"May I come? I love birthdays," she said.

"Sister Peter mentioned to me that this birthday party is just for family."

"All social events here are supposed to be for all of us," Bettina scolded.

"I guess this one is an exception," I explained.

"Are you family?" she persisted.

"Nope, just the gardener."

"I'm not good at gardening," said Bettina very sadly, crumpling as if an avalanche had just landed on her head. I was just wondering if giving her a hug would set a bad precedent, when a man's consoling voice came floating into our tete a tete and some vaguely remembered sweet scent came floating in with him.

"Bettina! They're dishing up strawberry jello, with real strawberries. And I know you love strawberries."

Bettina straightened up like a Raggedy Ann doll re-infused with sawdust, and, abandoning the aide who had tempted her with strawberries, she broke the elder speed record to get to the dining room, pausing abruptly to call back to me, "I make montages of gardens! You can see some hanging in my room. Number 17."

Before Bettina could take me on a personal tour of her montages, the strawberry man caught up to her and, cupping her elbow, guided her to a seat at one of the dining tables. I wished I could thank him for rescuing me from the sticky situation with the old lady, but as soon as he had seated her, he disappeared.

Standing under the archway where the residents' wing flowed into the dining area, I was wondering where I might find the primroses or the tools to weed them. While trying to work up the courage to knock on Sister Peter's office door and ask her for some direction, I caught the echo of a sweet aroma again. This time I identified it as English Leather, the aftershave whose name sounds chilly and reticent but smells warm and friendly. Leaning reflexively towards the scent, I stepped back on somebody's sneakers. Swiftly I hopped forward and spun around to apologize. "I'm so sorry. Will your foot ever recover, do you think?"

The fellow, who was misted with the beguiling

cloud of aftershave, was the aide who had lured Bettina to the dining room. He wore a white linen jacket over clean well-worn jeans, a name tag and a semi-amused look. "My foot's okay, but I haven't much hope for my left sneaker."

"How much trouble am I in? Your jacket says *Doctor*, but you could be a lawyer...or an Indian chief?"

He laughed. "None of the above. I'm a car mechanic. Or I was."

"Of course, I should have known, here amid all the cars up on hoists."

Again he laughed. I was doing better with him than I had done with my mostly-unamused audience of old folks.

"I'm on a sort of leave of absence," he said. "Suddenly I'm an aide in a care home."

"We have something in common. I've taken leave of my usual work. I'm not even quite an aide yet, but only an aide-in-waiting."

"Were you ousted from your former job for being mischievous?" he asked.

"Why would you think that?"

"That's the reason I was let go."

In case I was not supposed to chat with a handsome fellow worker, I slid into the relatively private area of the hallway. "May I ask what you did that was mischievous?"

"My boss had a big poster in his office of a U.S. president whose policies rub me the wrong way. I could not resist drawing horns and fangs on the poster's subject. Instant holiday from the car industry. May I ask what got you ejected from your place of business?"

"As it happens, my ideas were as fangs and horns to my supervisors, and, because of their negative response, I chose to step back and reconsider my career options."

"Ah, do you miss your former world as much as I

32

miss mine?" he asked.

"Oh, would you rather be home in Montana?"

He looked down at his name tag and smiled. "I'm not from Montana; I *am* Montana. My name is Spanish for mountain. Or at least that is what my mama told me. She would never let me learn Spanish, so I can't be sure. Well, I know a few Spanish songs, but I don't know what all the words mean. Anyway, my mother said someone as compact as I needed a big name and a course in muscle-building to give school bullies second thoughts. Grade school boys bullied me anyway; called me Cowboy. They thought Montana was where all the cowboys come from, I guess. So I shortened my name to Monte, which I think also means mountain, but not so flamboyantly. The manager here doesn't care for nicknames; thus, the name-tag: Montana."

"Okay, Monte," I said, "My bosom buddy Barbara divulged less personal information to me than you just did, and I knew her all my life." *Oops! Warning! Awkward moment coming up!*

"What *kind* of buddy?" Monte inquired grinning.

Yep, there it is. "Anywaaaaay," I said, "Unlike you, I don't have a name-tag yet, but my name's Danielle, call-name Dani. Love to chat with you about that later, but at the moment I need to find where the gardening tools are kept. And also, do you know where the primrose path is?"

"May I ask why you need to know?"

"Sister Peter wants me to weed the primroses."

"Uh, you should know we call her 'Sister Pete around here."

"To her face?"

"God, no. Just the staff and some of the residents. It's a sign of affection, I think. But--"

"But she wouldn't like it."

"I never had the courage to find out. So, you want me to lead you down the primrose path?" he smiled.

"Just lead me *to* it, if you would," I smiled back. I never could resist a guy who could pick up on a literary reference. Especially if he smelled good.

Monte showed me to the door leading to the back garden and the gardener's shed. Then he excused himself and returned indoors to collect one of the elderly gentlemen to give him a shave. I was left to forage in the shed for a gardening apron and some weeding tools meant for tidying primroses.

My mother was a wonderful gardener; me barely passable. But I found myself a willing one on my first day at Safe Haven. A month earlier I would have said the smell of a library full of musty old books was the most soothing smell in the world, second only to the powdery smell backstage in the university theater. But, when my life in graduate school had begun to sour, even the dust motes rising from the university theater's stage had failed to please my senses. Now, however, the scent of fresh earth drifting off the root ball of the first weed I pulled was oddly soothing. After spending a year grinding away on my thesis and trying in vain to defend the ideas I put forth in it, I was happy to perform a task located where fresh air could blast the cobwebs of academia from my mind. So, though the smell of the fresh dirt in the primrose bed was not exactly intoxicating to me, it was so comforting that I did not mind at all that Sister Pete assigned weeding primroses as my second task at Safe Haven.

Especially comforting was the fact that I could not imagine a more effective place to hide from my troublesome university contacts than in a flowerbed tucked away behind an old folks' home. And, if I were to do well at gardening and whatever other tasks Sister Pete might give me, I had the hope of employment outside academia. Also, while cultivating those primroses, I managed to keep at bay the thought that I would be living on my graduate stipend until I might earn the right to a paid position at Safe Haven.

And how pleasant it was to look up to see sunlight sifting through leafy trees and to hear fingers of wind finding their way through the branches. Why had I thought I needed a graduate degree anyway? It was not as if the academic world was clamoring for young female professors who hoped to provide a bit of insight into the social impact of storytelling on an audience. It was bad enough that the men in the Drama Department found my ideas laughable, but a rising faction of vociferous female professors had unintentionally made the male upholders of the status quo more resistant to antiauthoritarian ideas than ever. Thus, my personal relationships at the university were not likely to blossom into liaisons supportive of my values and creativity any time soon. All in all, I was feeling better than I had in some time, digging dirt in an actual safe haven. Then, while I was congratulating myself on escaping from my old life and beginning a new one, I stumbled upon another woman's story that captivated me more than my own.

I thought I espied her that first day on the concrete walkway winding hither and thither through the back yard of Safe Haven. The weediest plot of ground was a primrose flowerbed located within the wide curve in the path where a wooden bench was located. Beside the bench was an official-looking sign proclaiming BUS STOP. Sister Pete had warned me that any resident who wished to do so might safely go out the unlocked back door, happily sit on that bench and wait for a nonexistent bus while gazing at the primroses. The yard was secured with a high wooden fence and a locked gate to allow patients to enjoy waiting for public transportation without realizing they would not be able to leave the premises.

I had just moved behind the bus stop bench to work on the patch of primroses nearly overtaken by weeds when an elderly woman came tottering down the path from the back door of Safe Haven. Standing behind the bench, trowel in hand, I held my breath while watching her arrival. It was the woman who had introduced herself to me earlier. As she had not known about the garden party, she was probably not the birthday girl; also she did not look older than eighty or so. Her gait was wobbly with her awesomely bowed legs bending in various ways to propel her along, and I stood ready to rush down the path and catch her if she fell. However, she made it to the bench as confidently as if walking on jelly legs were an Olympic sport. She cheerfully asked me if the 1:10 bus to City Center had come by yet. I had not yet learned how to allow the elderly their fantasies, and I chose the white lie of least resistance.

"I'm so sorry, the bus just left."

"Darn," she said. "I keep missing it. They must have changed the schedule."

"Must have," I agreed. The disappointed look on her face was too much for me and I handed her a clump of Sweet William flowers I had accidentally snipped and kept to remind me to garden more carefully. "Sweet William?" I said offering them to her.

"You're the sweet one, not William!' She giggled, taking the blooms. "I'm Bettina. What shall I call you? Mrs. Gardener?" She laughed at her own joke.

"I'm Danielle, but you can call me Dani." I thought it best not to remind her we had met just minutes before.

"I'd better call you Danielle. Sister doesn't like nicknames. But she's not here, so you can call me Betty!" She laughed, turned towards the home, but turned again towards me. "Would you know when the next bus arrives?"

"Tomorrow about this time or a bit earlier, I think."

She nodded and, sniffing the Sweet William, wobbled back up the path. After seeing her safely enter the back door, I knelt behind the bench, and was tucking a primrose back into its bed, when I heard a hubbub coming from the back door of the home. I quickly stood; if it was another wandering patient hoping to catch the next bus, I intended to do my weeding out of sight, to avoid having to lie to an elder. But, as I paused to watch, one of the residents was wheeled out from the main residence hall with a gleeful gaggle of persons of various ages surging along in her wake. To see if I could figure out what Sister Pete would want me to report to her, if anything, I knelt to observe them through the high slatted back of the bench.

My hands hovered over the primroses while I watched the group--which I guessed was the family of the woman I had been told was celebrating her one-hundredth-plus-one birthday. A young teenage boy was thrusting the woman's wheelchair at an alarming rate along the sinuous garden pathway. Crouching behind the bench, I could see that the jouncing of her chair was making the woman's aged head bob heavily on the slender stem of her neck. I feared she would be catapulted into the air at any moment, and a tremendous urge came over me to rush to her aid and wrench the handles of her wheelchair from her careless helper. For about the thousandth time in my life, I wished I were not sometimes so shy among strangers. Why could I only overcome my bashful ways when I was on stage, or harmlessly flirting, or when someone was being blatantly bossy to someone else? Despite my shy ways, as the party came lurching haphazardly down the path, I came very close to intervening.

A colorful mass of balloons formed a jostling canopy above the approaching phalanx of persons who were apparently throwing the birthday party for their granny or, by her age, I would guess, possibly their great-granny. One of the party–a silver-haired matron–carried a tray of frosted cupcakes bedecked with a tenth of the number of candles one might expect to honor a centenarian. Another woman, with a salt-and-pepper coif, hauled a net bag of gift-wrapped packages on her back like Santa Claus.

The group's chattering and clattering caused an awful din, but, as they wended their way back and forth along the looping pathway towards me, I heard the thread of a sweet voice humming a vaguely remembered tune. Hauntingly melodious, it was clearly audible between the bursts of noise from her family. It had to be the old lady humming, I thought, because every other person in the group was gabbing boisterously about family and birthdays and parties. Quickly, I moved to cultivate the primroses directly behind the chair so that I would be fairly well hidden and would not intrude upon their celebration. The unintended result was that I was able to hear the festivities long past my intended period of gardening work. But a few feet before the party reached the bus stop bench, the teenager pushing the wheelchair gave it a wild shove up onto the skirting of stones lining the pathway, thus causing one wheel of the chair to disturb a small lizard that had been sunning itself on a stone. Laughing, the teen jerked the chair back onto the path and continued toward the bench, leaving behind a lizard which had been separated from its tail.

The old lady saw it too, and gave a cry of distress which no one in the party seemed to hear. I could tell the old woman wanted to look back to see what happened to the lizard, but her neck seemed to have lost flexibility at her advanced age. She could still hum, though, and, looking very troubled in behalf of the lizard, she changed the tune she had been humming to *Puff the Magic Dragon*. Was she humming a funerary ballad to a lizard? In case she was, I was moved to risk being noticed by the celebrants to go check on the lizard.

The site of the accident was only steps away from the primroses, but, as the woman's relatives were busy setting up the party, no one paid attention to me. I found the lizard lying beside the rock where it had been sunbathing. Most of its tail was still atop the stone, but, even as I watched it, the lizard wiggled back and forth a couple times, cocked its head to appraise me, and swiftly scampered under the nearby laurel hedge. Passing by the old woman as I moved back behind the bench, I bent close to her and quickly said, *Puff's tail will grow back; he's okay.* None of her family seemed to hear me, but the old woman did. She did not look up at me, but she looked relieved. My first good turn as an aide-in-waiting.

Meanwhile, as soon as they had reached their goal, the two matrons directed the wheelchair pusher to place Granny close beside the bench. One of the teenagers in the party got a big kick out of the bus stop sign.

"Bus stop to where, I wonder? Heaven?"

The family, in unison, laughed aloud. But the insistent humming emanating from the heart of the group ceased momentarily and the old woman lifted a lace-covered hand to conceal a subtle grimace. No one took notice of her gesture, except the gardener behind the bench. After some of the party-goers abruptly lifted the old woman out of her wheelchair and Hoopla! swung her tiny carcass onto the garden bench, the humming resumed. The old lady scarcely stopped humming all afternoon; although she seemed to like doing it just quietly enough to prevent anyone who was not paying enough attention to care that she was humming. Only one of the teenagers, who was leaning over the old woman to help lift her out of the wheelchair, mentioned it, laughing, "Auntie's wheezing like a musical tea pot!"

"Hush!" one of the matrons hissed in the girl's ear. "She can't help it."

When the old woman had been lowered into place on the bus stop bench, the silver-haired matron, whose name I would later find out was Viola, shouted in her ear, "There now! Isn't that nice, Auntie?"

Momentarily interrupting her unremitting melody, the old woman made a sound which did not sound like assent.

"They always have birthday parties out here. Did you know that, Auntie?" That was the younger of the two matrons, the one with the salt-and-pepper hair; her name, it turned out, was Rhoda. Having shouted her question at the old woman, Rhoda promptly turned away to direct two of the party to set up t.v. trays.

The old woman made another grumbling sound. It sounded to me like, "Big bother."

The bag of gaily wrapped gifts were piled on one t.v. tray, cupcakes on the other, candles were lit, and an orchid was pinned on the collar of Auntie's cardigan.

"Pin! Pin! Pin!" sang Auntie until one of the nieces

plucked the orchid out of her skin and pinned it more carefully in her collar.

The teenage girl who had pinned Auntie complained to no one in particular, "I didn't know her skin was so loose. I thought her neck was her collar!"

Quickly, *Happy Birthday* was sung, and the expression on Auntie's face might have been a choirmaster's grimace of pain at the sour notes of her ragtag choir.

"Eleven balloons for one hundred-one years, Auntie! Think of that!" warbled Rhoda. At her signal, the balloons were lofted into the sky to make their way to places where they might get tangled in telephone wires, choke animals at the zoo, or interrupt the flight patterns at the nearby airport.

To bring the celebration back down to earth, Viola raised a solemn hand to quiet the celebrants, then, knotting her fingers into a double fist at her somewhat concave breast, she began a prayer. It was a short one that many a docile Christian has uttered at one solemn gathering or other. The words *Jesus* and *should* and *grateful* were prominent, and the upshot of the blessing was that the birthday girl should thank her lucky stars (or the creator thereof) that she didn't die before she got to eat the yummy cupcakes her niece baked especially to celebrate the century of life she had enjoyed amid a family good enough to visit her on special occasions like this one though they had to drive a considerable way through horrid traffic to do so.

Having offered the family's official benediction to the woman, Viola intoned *Amen*, and the family echoed her with one voice–except for the old woman, who looked around at their bowed heads, threw her head back and quietly howled like a lonesome coyote.

A little girl standing next to Rhoda and the cupcakes took special notice of the old woman's failure to bow her head and shot her a look of severity one does not expect to see on a little girl's face. She was about six years old and was wearing a party dress with prettily embroidered flowers on the bodice, several ruffled tiers of organdy billowing from waist to knee, and a bow large enough to adorn the gift of a new car. Before the family's amens had ceased humming, the little girl, whose name was Sunday, opened her rosebud mouth and loudly scolded "Auntie" for not saying *Amen.* Then, performing an amazing rendition of the righteous tone of a fire and brimstone preacher, the girl demanded, "Do you love Jesus?"

Rhoda, who was apparently her mother, boasted, "Sunday's not afraid to speak the Truth to anyone, Auntie."

The old woman leaned towards the child, smiled and whispered, "Jesus likes *nice* children."

The child shrank away as if Granny were Evil personified and snapped, "You need to go to Sunday School!" With that, she circled around her mother and hid behind her broadest part. With a protective arm around the child's shoulders, her mother delivered a short sermon about there being only one Truth, that being that Jesus is coming.

The old woman shrugged, "Preachy girls run in the family."

Rhoda heard that and looked as if someone had thrown a family history book at her head. "I almost prefer your incessant humming, Auntie."

Her sister, Viola, hearing at least part of that exchange, bustled in between Rhoda and the old woman, crying, "Time for cake!"

Viola directed a teenager to place the tray with the

tiered cupcakes on it close to the old woman. Rhoda swiftly lit the candles and she and Viola gathered everyone close around their old relative, who, with her head down, seemed to be humming a dirge.

"Blow out the candles, Auntie!" the matrons cried.

"If you got the wind for it!" giggled one of the teenagers. The family's laughter made the candle flames dance uneasily.

The old woman extinguished the eleven candles with the breath of her unceasing song. The moment the flames were out, Viola plucked the candles from their beds of frosting. Then, Rhoda, with excessive enthusiasm, picked up the top cupcake and encouraged the old woman to eat it by smashing it into her mouth. That stopped the humming for a moment, and I had to wonder if that was what Rhoda had in mind.

While her niece cried, "Cheers," the old woman angrily pushed Rhoda's offending hand away, causing everyone to laugh at funny old Auntie. Rhoda laughed hardest of all. "Oops! Sorry, Auntie."

The old woman sat for a long moment looking frosted in more ways than one while Rhoda dipped a napkin into the bottle of water allotted to her grandaunt and dabbed at the sugary goo on her chin.

Viola officiously grabbed a paper napkin and attempted to wipe off a glob of frosting Rhoda had missed. Even semi-obscured by the slats of the garden bench, I could see the stony look "Auntie" gave her nieces.

Meanwhile, Rhoda was apparently feeling affronted by the old woman's failure to see what was funny about having cake shoved in her face. "You jerked your head just when I was offering you your cupcake. Not your fault, I'm sure. Just kind of old and shaky."

The old woman's humming abruptly ceased, and her words came out clear as B-B's shot from a gun. "Not too old to make fun of."

At that, there began a murderous mumbling and rumbling aimed at the birthday girl. "No one's making fun of you, Auntie! We're throwing you a party!" cried Viola.

"Throwing cupcakes," the old woman murmured to herself, and, reaching out to the tray holding the birthday paraphernalia, she chose a nice plump cake for herself.

Laughing as heartily as if Auntie had told a minimally off-color joke, one of the matron's husbands–I think they called him Tweedle--strode across the path to the old woman and aimed a condescending air kiss towards her head, crooning, "Oh, Auntie's just being silly." Then, guffawing, he ran at the children, who were gawking at the proceedings from the lawn on the other side of the path. "Who's for a game of Nerf football?"

At that, they all–except for the two aunts--turned away and partied at a discreet distance across the path, as if the old woman were still indoors in her bed asleep. Her nieces unfolded some garden chairs they had brought and sat across the path with their backs to the bench where the old woman sat amid the primroses. The younger ones ran around on the lawn across from the flower beds, screeching and playing a much degraded form of Nerf football in which, apparently by decree, no one fell to the grass and soiled their party clothes.

Putting a bit of emotional distance between them and herself, the old lady ate her cupcake daintily as a hummingbird feeding at a blossom. And between bites she hummed and talked softly to herself, but loudly enough for me to make out some of what she said. Once I heard her say with absolute clarity, "Oh, well, it makes a life."

I would like to have heard what she meant by that, and, ceasing weeding, I leaned against the back of the birthday bench to listen more closely to the old woman's humming and occasional commentary. Meanwhile the ladies of the party sat on their folding chairs cheering for the football players, until one of the teenage boys spiraled the ball right into Viola's chest. Viola grabbed the ball, tucked it under her arm, stood up, and declared that the game was over and everyone had won. She strode across the walk to her grandaunt, and cheerfully included the old woman in a game she would not have enjoyed at all if she had not been eating cupcakes throughout. "Wasn't that a fun game, Auntie?"

Auntie toasted her with a third cupcake. Viola did not seem to get the irony of the gesture. The old woman calmly wiped a bit of frosting off her ear left by Rhoda's careless delivery system, while the Nerf players turned down their sleeves and buttoned their cuffs, and Rhoda launched the next exciting phase of the celebration.

~ ~ ~

Wally's Wake

"And now that the birthday festivities have been enjoyed, Auntie," said Rhoda, "it is time for the other very important family event we have gathered together to enjoy today, a personal memorial for our father, your nephew, Wally Bell."

The old woman dropped her cupcake. "Today?"

Viola stepped stiffly to her aunt and brushed cupcake crumbs off the woman's cardigan. "It's not our fault that one of the most important events in Rhoda's and my life–our father's death--should have fallen so close to the day of your birth."

Even with the bench-back between us, I could tell the old woman was profoundly shocked. "Today?" she repeated. She was shaking so much I was afraid she was going to have an apoplexy and expire right there at her one-hundred-and-first birthday party. Selfishly I hoped Sister Pete would not blame me for it.

Smiling encouragingly, Rhoda leapt into the cold space caused by Viola's dismissal of her aunt's discomfort. "When the passage of one life happens just at the moment we acknowledge the moment another life in the family began, it is meant to point our attention to the life in heaven beyond this earthly life."

During her niece's lengthy speech, "Auntie" sat on the garden bench retrieving the cupcake from her lap, plucking candy Red Hots from the frosting, and placing them one by one on her tongue. Before that moment, it had never occurred to me that a person could hum with her tongue sticking out and a constellation of Red Hots melting on it.

Rhoda finished delivering her speech and turned to her grandaunt for an Amen or, perhaps, applause. Seeing that the old woman was sticking out her Red Hot-inflamed tongue at her, Rhoda smiled stiffly, bent down and pried her aunt's cupcake from her fingers, one digit at a time. Then, with a cheery judgmental stare, she unceremoniously shoved the cupcake onto a paper napkin, saying, "Don't they teach you not to play with your food here, Auntie?"

The old woman waggled her red tongue at her niece, and, looking her steadily in the eye, spat seven Red Hots in a row onto the sidewalk. I almost applauded.

Instead, I hunched down among the primroses, patting them quietly into their newly cultivated bed. From that lowly position, I could see the two nieces' heels bracketing their aunt's sneakers, which dangled between them as they lifted her back into her wheelchair. Peering around the end of the bench, I could see them wheel her across the sidewalk onto a pretty greensward with a morning-glory trellis at its apex. Rhoda cleared off the t.v. trays and plopped the bag of birthday gifts onto "Auntie's" lap, chirping, "You can open them in your room later and feel as if the family is still with you."

They carried the clean tray to the greensward, and, after placing one tray on either side of the trellis, Viola strode solemnly to stand behind the tray on the left while one of the teenage great-grand-nephews, I supposed, stood behind the tray on the right.

All the younger children in the party sat cross-legged before the trellis and the adults stood facing it as if a couple of celebrities were about to plight their troths there. Instead, Viola gave another speech. I will not bore myself by recalling it in toto, but I will report that she announced that, though Auntie's birthday was of course noteworthy, the more important celebration of the day was the family's recognition of the recent demise of the paterfamilias,

Wallace Bell, Auntie's nephew, and Rhoda and Viola's father, who was, "Please note," said Viola, "Auntie's lifelong support on this earth."

Rhoda stepped up to the t.v. tray then and added a more personal and less kindly note. "We didn't think Auntie would want to travel all the way across town to the funeral; therefore, as the family's special gift to her, we have brought the funeral to her. Great-aunt Beatrice, the memorial for your nephew Wally culminated with Leon, my nephew, your great-grandnephew, singing in his prize-winning tenor voice one of the songs our father composed. I hope you will recognize it as one of the many creations Wally Bell gifted to the world. Like all the songs folks wrote back in the day, it is of course very corny, but the interest from Father's investment of the residuals from his songs supported you and your family for generations."

While Rhoda spoke, the old woman's humming got louder and louder. It was the same tune she had been humming all afternoon, and it intrigued me more and more. I wondered why it seemed so familiar to me. Was it an advertising jingle heard when I was a kid, an old standard from the 1940's, or *Happy Birthday* in a language other than English? I had no idea, but I was about to get a hint.

Rhoda and Viola flanked a teenage boy who was wearing a white dress shirt and stiff new blue jeans. Waving their hands with the classic *Ta da!* gesture, they announced that the boy, who was called Leon, would be singing one of his Grampa Wally's favorite songs. Leon had a long shock of hair sticking up like the spines of an angry porcupine; his hairdo might have been called a Mohawk except the barber had pig-shaved the front and back of the boy's head and had left a voluminous mass of hair laterally, from ear to ear rather than from temple to nape. Could not wait to hear this prize-winner sing.

Actually, he had a beautiful voice. Even through the bench-back I could hear he was singing melodiously a sort of golden oldie lyric which began, *Lilac blossoms of pure white, shone like stars on our last night.* Then, part way through the song, the boy broke into raucous rapping that mocked the old-timey words and chopped up the graceful rhythm of the piece.

Conscientiously I had moved to another part of the flowerbed where the family could see me clearly and ask me to respect their privacy if they noticed me. They did not seem to, and I had a fine view of the birthday girl observing her family's idea of a gift for a centenarian. Seeing the look on her face and the way her quivering fingers dug at the crocheted throw covering her knees, I had the impression she felt her family was as blind to her feelings as a swarm of sociopath bats. Maybe I was projecting my own feelings on her because of my recent set-to with my little academic family--who knew my core self about as well as they knew where the nearest inhabited planet lay. But I imagined I could see welling up inside the old woman a desperate longing for the world to know her before she died, to understand what she was really feeling under all the lap robes and birthday gifts dumped on her knees. The old lady was about to give some credence to my interpretation of her facial expression.

Viola had just grabbed Leon by the sleeve and pulled him over to his great-grand aunt, trilling, "Didn't my son sing Father's song beautifully? Oh, I know the lyrics are silly and sentimental; still, I wish Leon's grandfather could have heard him."

The old woman answered quietly, busying herself by brushing cupcake crumbs from her afghan. "Could'a wakened the dead."

Viola moved closer to the old woman. "What-say, Auntie?"

Auntie looked up innocently. "Hummmm?"

Leon's young ears had not missed his great-grandaunt's critique. "She said I was too loud, Mama."

Viola showed her overlapping front teeth. "She meant just loud enough to be heard perfectly by everyone here, didn't you, Auntie? Probably even the gardener heard."

The primroses suddenly had my full attention.

"And with such expression, he sang!" Viola continued. "Leon gave the fusty old words of days gone by a new lease on life."

Auntie was not going to take that lying down. "Not the *right* fusty old words."

"Why would you say that, Auntie? He sang the right words. What is the matter with you today?" Viola demanded.

Rhoda strode to the wheelchair and clasped Auntie in a steely one-arm hug. "Aw, she can say whatever she wants. She's one-hundred-and-one years old today."

Leon produced a piece of paper from his jeans pocket. "I sang the words on the sheet you gave me, Mama. I might have changed the rhythm a little, but I sang what Grampa Wally wrote--as long as I could stand it."

Rhoda patted her nephew on the arm. "Don't worry, honey. Auntie's memory isn't what it used to be."

"If she doesn't know the words, why did she say that about me?"

The old woman spoke quietly but very firmly. "Know 'em better 'n your grampa."

"You think you know Father's song better than he

did?" laughed Rhoda.

Viola pointed a red-nailed index finger at her. "Auntie, for shame! Stealing the spotlight from a dead man, and on the day of his wake."

"Aw, to tell the truth," Rhoda shushed her sister, "I'm not crazy about Father's songs either, but the royalties put me through college. But, Auntie, over the years he gave you tons of money that might have been appreciated better elsewhere. Give the man his due, for pity sakes."

Without a word of introduction, and like a teapot announcing it was ready for business, the old woman began to sing. Her voice was thready but sweet, with a bit of a growl to give it authority.

Lilac blossoms of pure white
Shone like stars on our last night
Dropping petals soft as silk,
Blossoms sweet as mother's milk--

Beatrice Bell shed no tears while she sang, but it seemed every word was so deeply felt that she had to pause after a few lines to keep from breaking down. Her family did not seem to attend so much to the song as to the surprising fact of her singing. As for me, the melody seemed almost as familiar as the national anthem.

The family, on the other hand, stood around their aunt in her wheelchair looking like museum visitors being serenaded by an Egyptian mummy. How in the world could someone so ancient remember lyrics, or do anything at all a normal person could do? To my chagrin, the nieces quickly overcame the shock of hearing their father's composition sung by the old lady, and, in tandem, shushed her.

"Ugh!" exclaimed Viola. "I deleted that *Mother's*

milk line on Leon's copy!' Imagine such intimate words going out over the airwaves."

"I should'a cut all the lines and sung *Grunge Roadhouse* like I wanted," Leon complained.

Meanwhile, Rhoda was shouting accusingly in her grandaunt's ear. "You never told us you could sing, Auntie."

Quick to second her sister's motion, Viola piped in the woman's other ear, "Amen to that, Auntie. Not the time or place, though, dear. Today was Leon's turn."

"Goodness, where did you learn to sing like that anyway, on tune and everything?" Rhoda laughed.

"Inherited from Wally," The old woman said with tone. Tone was something her family never seemed to get.

Leon, who was eager to scold his great-grandaunt about anything at all, laughed. "My Grampa Wally was your nephew, so he might have inherited from you, not the other way round." He laughed again, just in case she failed to get his point.

Viola held up a hand to forbid his attack on his great-grandaunt. "Don't make fun of the elderly, son. They don't always have all their...."

"Marbles?" the old woman said. "*Who* inherited *whose* marbles?"

"Don't upset yourself, Auntie," Rhoda said, tucking the afghan around her great-aunt's lap. "We just don't feel the same way about the old songs as you do."

"That's for sure," Leon chortled.

Even viewed from across the lawn, the old woman's wrath was evident to me. "Son," she said to Leon, "The songs are old, not cruel."

To forestall words that might hurt her son's feelings, Viola began collapsing the t.v. trays and leaning them against the trellis. "As for me I find all these so-called golden oldies as pagan as witches and warlocks. Of course I'm grateful for father's musical career, but for myself I prefer good old Christian hymns."

Perhaps to forestall her sister from singing a hymn or two, Rhoda shoved a slim pamphlet at her grandaunt. "Look, Auntie. We were so sad you weren't able to attend father's funeral, we saved a program for you. Look at all the songs!"

The old woman opened the program as if opening a terrarium full of snakes.

"For the bulletin board in your room," laughed Rhoda. "So you won't forget you have a family."

"And sometimes I think you do forget," Viola chuckled indulgently. She reached a hand between her aunt's face and the funeral program to point out the items listed on it. "See here at the end, Father's song that Leon just sang."

That was the moment I noticed a real change coming over the old woman. She stopped humming and took the time to find her reading glasses in her bag, removing lip moisturizer, hankies and a comb before she found them. She did this with what appeared to be conscious ceremony, whether to give her time to think what she wanted to say about the program or to give weight to whatever it was she darn well knew she was going to say. When she had at last positioned her glasses on her nose, she read the program of her nephew's funeral with the intense interest of an Army general plotting precisely how he was going to bomb the enemy's headquarters to smithereens. Finally, in a voice in-held and low, she spoke--to the program, not to her nieces.

"*White Lilacs*: Wallace Bell, Composer?!"

"Because it's his song, Auntie!" Rhoda explained, "We listed John Newton as the composer of *Amazing Grace;* why wouldn't we list our father, Wallace Bell, as the composer of *White Lilacs*?"

"Hope noone remembers *me* with a lie," the old woman snapped.

Viola exploded. "Auntie! I made this program, and I did not lie about my father!"

"Sure about that?" her grandaunt said.

"What in the name of goodness do you mean?" Viola insisted.

The old woman ignored her, and, turning to Viola's son, Leon, held out her hand, palm up and said, "Music?"

Leon was suspicions of the old woman. "Why?"

"A birthday gift?" She smiled broadly for the first time that day.

Leon pulled the folded piece of sheet music out of his jeans pocket and, somewhat charily, handed it over. His great-grandaunt plucked it daintily from his hand and, before anyone could stop her, she tore it to bits. After a moment of deep shock, the group exploded.

"Auntie!" several of them cried.

"I told you she's demented!" said someone.

"After all we've done for her today!" said another.

The family was distracted for a full half-minute, venting their shock and annoyance at the old woman, which gave her plenty of time to lift the funeral program Rhoda had given her and tear it into teensy pieces as well. While her kin stood around her with mouths agape, she took hands full of paper scraps and tossed them into the air. Then, smiling for the second time that day, she pulled the edge of the afghan up from the grass, tucked it under her knees and wheeled herself down the sidewalk towards the back door.

"I didn't know she could do that," said Rhoda.

"I didn't know she could do a lot of things," said Viola.

The family watched and did not rush to help as the old woman drove the wheelchair a bit off the sidewalk into the primrose bed. This time the chair was obviously going to tilt all the way over and deposit its occupant in the turf. As sometimes happens to me in real emergencies, my shyness evaporated and I hurried to her and set her chair upright and back onto the walkway. Then I gathered up my gardening tools and followed after the wheelchair with the intention of helping her get up the ramp and through the back door of Safe Haven if need be. But Rhoda ran after me and grabbed my arm, swivelling the squarish head on her skinny neck to shout in my face."Hi! You! Gardener or Nurses' aide or whatever. Do you do hair, Miss? I mean, do you give perms?"

Fortunately, a daunting stranger who accosts me physically can give me a short burst of courage. I peered closely into Rhoda's face and raised my eyebrows at her as if to say she might have noticed I had a mop of natural curls that never needed a permanent. She did not catch my vibe. So I was pretty much forced to answer her question.

"I used to give my mother and sisters permanents. I'm afraid their reviews of my efforts were somewhat spotty."

"Could you give our great-aunt Beatrice a perm? We'd pay you a little something, of course."

"I'm not sure Sister Peter would approve."

"But, you work here, right?"

"Obviously," I said, raising my trowel in evidence.

"Do you do other jobs here as well?"

"I do whatever Sister Peter tells me to do."

"Could you do me a favor? Do us, the family, a favor, I mean?"

"I don't know if that would–"

"You might have noticed our auntie was maybe a little cold to us, or defensive–you know how old people get. We really wanted to give her a permanent. Because, well, you can see her hair looks like a flock of angry birds made a nest in it. Would you ask if she would let you give her a permanent? We have another very important family event coming up, and we want her to look nice–you know, not like a poor neglected homeless woman or something."

The old woman had wheeled herself up the ramp and was having trouble reaching the bell, so I moved to help her. Her niece grabbed my arm again and pleaded outright. "Would you ask Sister Peter if it's okay for one of the aides to give her a perm? I'm afraid Sister doesn't like us much. She said all events must be open to all residents, and we insisted on making this event a family affair."

"You didn't seem to mind my presence."

"You're just a worker of some kind. Please, you obviously like our grandaunt or you would not have rushed to help her."

"I would have helped her even if I didn't like her." I took some pleasure in saying that. The niece was not hindered by the dig.

"Can you at least ask if you, or one of the aides, can give her a perm? Preferably you, because Auntie let you wheel her along the walk without biting your head off."

Seeing that the wheelchair was about to roll back down the ramp if someone did not intercede immediately, I briefly nodded to the niece before hurrying to the door to help the old woman.

To my chagrin, Rhoda followed me into the

building and, as I was wheeling Beatrice Bell towards her room, Sister Pete appeared suddenly before us. Rhoda shoved herself into the nun's space.

"Sister, I need to ask you, would it be okay for this aide here to give Aunt Beatrice a perm? Her hair is a mess and we have an important family meeting coming up. We wanted to have it done for today's celebration, but Auntie got all hissy about it."

At that point "Auntie" wheeled her chair around to face the trio of Rhoda, Sister Pete, and, unwillingly, myself.

"No perm, dammit!" the old woman muttered, trying to hide her shaky hands in her lap.

Sister Pete bent down towards her and in a kindly voice spoke her name, then let it set for a moment before she continued. "Beatrice Bell.... Mrs. Bell, you can have a perm if you want. One of our aides can do that for you. But only if you want."

The old woman nodded. "Her," she said pointing at me. "Curls like that."

"The Lord may have provided Danielle's permanent wave," Sister Pete smiled, "But if she feels qualified–?"

She looked a question at me, and I nodded. "I'll do my best. If someone has the lotion, papers and curlers and stuff. Do they even make permanent wave kits anymore?"

"We can get what you'll need, Danielle," Sister Pete assured me.

Satisfied with the agreement, the family surged out of the hall, through the dining room to the front entrance, and, like lumpy gravy through a funnel, poured into the parking lot, chattering about football and cupcakes and possibly Jesus. Only Beatrice Bell's niece Rhoda turned around in the doorway and fought her way back to me through the jostling bodies of the kinfolk making their hasty escape from the old folks' domain. She grabbed the arm she had earlier bruised with her clutching fingers and spoke loudly in my face.

"Also, would you be able to accompany my aunt to the upcoming reading of my father's will?"

I swear I saw Beatrice Bell's white hair stand up on end at mention of the reading of a will. With a sudden burst of movement, she whirled her wheelchair towards her niece.

Sister Peter did not miss the little kerfuffle and coasted back from the door of her office as smoothly as only a nun can coast.

Meanwhile Rhoda pressed me hard to put in some extra time with her aunt. "You were so quick to come to our grandaunt's rescue in the garden today," Rhoda trilled, "and we'll need somebody to keep her supplied with facial tissues and to catch her if she falls over or anything at the lawyer's office." With that, she whirled on Sister Pete. "What is the girl's hourly wage? The family can recompense you, reasonably, for whatever time she spends while keeping an eye on Great-aunt Beatrice."

"Miss Danielle is a volunteer here," said Sister Pete, "and she is free to accompany your party if she wishes, and at whatever hourly wage she might deem appropriate,." I swear she gave me a sidelong look that said clear as day, *"Squeeze as much blood out of the old turnips as you can."*

But, preferring to glean something other than blood or money from an old lady's snarky relatives, I smiled shyly and even bobbed a little curtsy at them–the irony of which I do not believe they possessed the wit to notice. "I will gladly accompany Mrs. Bell," I twinkled, "Without recompense. As a volunteer, how could I expect more than the least that could be offered?"

Their Auntie Beatrice caught my eye and bit her lip to keep from laughing out loud at my dig at her family's ungenerous ways.

After I returned my gardening tools to the shed, I stopped by Sister Pete's office to ask if she wanted a report on the garden party. She remained absorbed in the pile of papers on her desk and just waved me away, grumbling that I should check the duty roster posted on her door for tomorrow's assignment. "For today," she muttered, "just wheel Beatrice Bell back to her room." I eased the door closed and checked the duty list: she had crossed out *garden work* beside my name and had written in, *Hair care, Beatrice Bell.*

When I turned around, I found Beatrice Bell sitting in her chair staring at Sister Pete's door. I had the impression she was waiting for me. At least, she did not object to my wheeling her back to her room, where she admitted to an exhaustion she had not revealed to her family. She even let me help her prepare for her nap. The last thing she did when her head hit her pillow was to unpin her orchid and drop it in the wastebasket beside her bed.

My next task was to help set the tables in the dining room for dinner. I also wiped down and sterilized one of the plastic covered sofas on which a resident had experienced a bathroom moment without benefit of bathroom. Then I was sent to follow one of the residents from room to room to retrieve items he was stealing from other residents' digs. (Sister Peter later told me the practice is called *shopping* in the rest home business). By the time I had convinced the fellow to stop stealing it was late afternoon and Sister Pete popped her head out of her office to ask me to entertain the elderly folks sitting around waiting for the next meal.

"You know, a little fairytale like you told before

lunch, Danielle." Then pausing for a moment, she gave me a look that seemed to combine personal admiration and official disapproval in equal measure. "But, if I may suggest, a tale a bit less iconoclastic this time." Giving me an unreadable smile, she returned to her office.

As I stepped onto the common room's stage, I wondered whether Sister Pete would approve of the *little fairytale* I was about to share with the elders, as it was my–perhaps iconoclastic--take on a classic tale about a deity who considered rape an inborn right.

~ ~ ~

Daphne

Long ago when the world was young and a hero could be brutal without suffering consequences, Apollo came upon the maiden Daphne bathing in the river. He was instantly smitten and bade her come out of the water. Knowing he was a personage of great power, Daphne obeyed, and waded reluctantly to shore. Apollo smiled and whisked away her towel, saying, "You won't need that."

"I prefer to be covered," said Daphne.

Apollo laughed, and roughly pulled her to him.

She struggled but Apollo was too strong for her. She had only her words to protect herself, and cried, "Save me, Father! I fear he will kill me."

Luckily her father was the River god, and he could save her. But he hesitated--just for a moment–torn between obeying the Laws of the Fathers and his instincts as a Father. In time, he chose his daughter and cried, "I'm coming, Daphne! I will not let anyone hurt you, though he be the Sun God himself!"

Brave words, indeed. And the loving father did save his daughter. But he arrived almost too late and, forced to take desperate measures, he turned her into a tree.

One moment Daphne was a young woman with a whole life as a person to look forward to and the next moment she was a tree. She looked down at the cherry laurel branches that once were arms, the leaves that were her fingers, the trunk that was her legs, and she cried out, "Father, what have you done to me?"

"I have saved you from disgrace," he said.

"You have saved a tree!" she cried.

"Ugh!" said Apollo, leaping away from Daphne. "I'm hugging a tree!"

"Maybe you'd feel less ridiculous if my father

turned you into a tree as well," said Daphne.

"Oh, my," said the River God, "I don't think I could bend the law of the Fathers that far."

Folding her branches close around her trunk, Daphne said, "If a woman must live in a world where her body is not hers to share or not to share as she sees fit, Father, "I think I'd rather be a tree."

As if honor would assuage Daphne's pain, poets have been crowned with laurel wreaths and called "laureate" ever since. But Daphne was doomed to be a laurel tree for eternity.

~ ~ ~

Permanent Wave

Intrigued by the woman who hummed, and eager for my first one-on-one meeting with her, I looked in on her even before my shift began. When I stuck my head into her room, my eye was bedazzled by dozens of bright flower montages taped to the walls. It was like stepping into the greenhouse of a madwoman. In addition to an abundance of wall-flowers, there were some pictures of dogs, cats, horses and other animals–all clipped from glossy magazines. And all were beautifully crafted montages of many things to form pictures of their kind: dozens of cat photos configured to form the face of a Calico, for instance. Dazed by the sheer exuberance of the display, I stood gazing at the walls for a few moments before I noticed the woman in bed.

She was lying with the covers up to her chin, staring wide-eyed at the ceiling (where there were no montages.) And she was humming. There was nothing peculiar about the way she hummed, but the fact that she was humming at the ceiling was a bit jarring. Also, it was the song she sang at her birthday party that she was humming.

Apparently I was not the only one who found the humming unnerving. Her roommate, Bettina, was lying sideways in her bed facing Beatrice Bell, with her covers wrapped around her head like a hoodie and her eyes open wide while she peered at her roomie with what appeared to be mild alarm. Or, maybe like me, Bettina was trying to work out where she had heard the tune Beatrice was always humming. It put me in mind of some of the tunes my folks used to sing around my mother's upright piano, songs like Hoagy Carmichael's *Stardust,* or Kurt Weill and Maxwell Anderson's *September Song*, melodies old but timeless.

I was standing in the doorway hoping to learn more about this intriguing woman, when I was belatedly overtaken by a fit of conscience. What if it were Dani lying in her bed with someone staring in at her? I determined then and there that, of all the many reasons I would never agree to end up in an old folks' home, having to sleep with my door open in a public residence was right at the top of the list. And, come to think of it, why were the occupants' doors always open at Safe Haven, allowing anyone who strolled by to peer inside? I supposed the management considered the loss of privacy a fair tradeoff for the constant supervision of the residents, you know, in case any of the old folks might try to run a drug ring or some other criminal enterprise from their rooms. Suddenly Beatrice's roommate Bettina's eyes shifted from the humming woman to me, causing me wonder why I was still standing in the doorway staring at two defenseless old women. I gave Bettina a little head bob of apology and hurried away to prepare the paraphernalia for Beatrice Bell's permanent wave.

Finding the place designated for hair care was not difficult, for whoever designed the layout of Safe Haven's rooms had tacked on the door a name plate optimistically engraved with the words *Beauty Parlor*. When Beatrice Bell slowly strolled into the room, she was pushing her own wheelchair back and forth in a sort of syncopated accompaniment to her humming. Though her limbs were unsteady, the whole time she was making her herky-jerky way into the *Beauty Parlor*, she held a steady sort of eye contact with me that would have spellbound a professional hypnotist. I surmised that I was about to be challenged in some way. When she reached the salon chair, she tucked her rolling chair under the adjacent counter and, with surprising agility, stepped up onto the metal footrest of the salon chair. She took some time lowering herself into the seat, staring me down the whole time, and she firmly pushed my hand away when I offered to steady her during the procedure. Having seated herself, she surveyed the comb, lotions and rollers I had laid out on a towel on the counter and nodded with apparent stoic acceptance of her fate. Then she looked up at the mirror over the counter and scowled, muttering, "Go 'way," to her image.

"How are you doing today?" I asked, sliding a towel under her chin and fastening it behind her neck.

"Hafta get better, to die."

"Sorry to hear it," I murmured."Shall we begin?" I brandished the shampoo bottle as if I were selling it.

She shrugged, spun the salon chair around, and lay back with her head over the sink.

"You've done this before," I cleverly speculated.

"Weekly washing," she snorted, then to make sure to amend her attitude about her care-givers, added, "They try to make nice." Then, as if her effort at being fair and speaking three whole sentences had tired her out, she shrugged her thin shoulders, settled back onto the neck rest, and closed her eyes.

As I combed out her snarls, I admired the immaculate white of her hair. It was whiter than snow, way whiter than clouds. It was that white that shines with glints of all the colors of the spectrum when the light hits it just so. While I was working up a cap of suds on her pink scalp, I noticed she quietly resumed humming through closed lips.

"What's that you're humming?"

"Nothing," she mumbled and pursed her lips.

"Sorry, Ms. Bell. Must be my Tinnitus kicking up."

She emitted an amused snort. "Call me Bibi."

"Okay," I said. Silence descended as I began to roll her hair up in papers and slender permanent curlers.

"Bones." She said, picking up one of the femur-shaped rollers.

"The curlers?"

"No, a hampster's thigh bone," she snickered.

Not knowing how to respond to elder humor, I changed the subject. "I'm so close to recalling the title of the tune you're always humming I can almost taste it." You would think I had not said a word. I took another tack. "Is it something about white lilacs?" I hinted. At that, she flinched slightly underneath her towel, which encouraged me to press for more information. "Somehow, when you sang part of that song in the garden at your birthday party, I recalled a book I read when I was a girl. Made a big impression on me when I was eleven. It was called *White Lilacs*." She stirred a bit. "You know the story?" I asked.

She went so quiet, I thought she had fallen asleep, or was feigning sleep to avoid conversation. I tried a new line. "Did you know there are some lilacs in the Arboretum at the edge of town, in honor of the novel *White Lilacs*?"

She shrugged. I took that as a maybe.

"Have you ever been to the Arboretum?" I asked.

She shook her head and perm lotion flew around like water from a wet dog.

"Is that a yes?" I hoped.

"No talk," she said.

Wiping up droplets from the mirror and my face, I spoke as soothingly as I knew how. "This procedure will take a while. What *would* you like to talk about?"

"Daphne."

"Daphne in the story I told?"

"No, Daphne, in the Mormon Tabernacle Choir."

Pleased to have evoked so many words from her—even if they were sarcastic--I took a big chance.

"What if *I* didn't want to talk about the story I told the way you don't want to talk about the song you hum?"

Her eyes popped open.

"Is your song too personal?" I guessed.

With a surprising burst of energy, she squared around to face me. "Trade ya something personal about my song for something personal about your Daphne story."

"Promise?"

"Pinkie swear."

"A pinkie promise is legally binding," I said.

Fixing me with an undeniable glare, she jabbed her bent pinkie at me. I hooked it with mine. Honestly, there was such a contained truthfulness about her, I would have trusted her without hooking pinkies. I tried to explain my personal interest in Daphne and Apollo while I daubed her curls with a second round of waving solution.

"My thesis advisor at the university was a brilliant scholar and a great man. His class *Opera and Classic Myth* was delicious–until he made a point of praising the morality of the character of Don Giovanni, who bore some resemblance to Apollo in the classic myth."

"Daphne!" she commanded.

"I'm getting to her as fast as I can."

She gave me a shrug and nod and I continued.

"Characters like Don Giovanni, Don Juan, Cassanova--all that ilk--Professor Milton saw them not as rapists or lying seducers, but as heroes, because, he said, 'The rapes and seductions of the innocent young virgins provide a necessary step in their sexual blossoming.'"

Beatrice Bell squinted her eyes like a gunslinger taking aim."Like Apollo!"

Lifting her head, I placed a folded towel under it so she would be comfortable while the waving lotion did its work. "When you laughed at my version of Apollo, I knew you got it."

She opened one eye. "Professor Whatsis get it?"

"Professor Milton stood at his podium in front of us impressionable students and claimed that all and sundry of the Don Juans provided a necessary social service."

"You swallow that?"

Pleased at how many nearly complete sentences the humming woman had uttered, I kept the discussion going.

"I explained to the professor that forcing a hard part of a man's body inside a soft part of a woman's body to help her blossom sexually would be like hitting her fingers with a claw hammer to enhance her sense of touch."

Bibi looked a bit amused. "He expel ya'?"

"No, he laughed at what he called my *schoolgirl sexual jitters*. Most of the men in the class laughed with him, and I think some of the women. The professor smiled with condescension and continued with his lecture. You can imagine how I felt."

"Like Daphne turning into a tree," she said.

"And I felt bewildered. How could a man with such a brilliant mind—with such an exquisite sense of poetry and humanity—how could he be blind to female sensitivity? Just thinking of it pains me."

By that time the waving lotion had done its job and I had enjoyed a longer conversation with the lady who hummed than I had dreamed of having. I began daubing her curls with neutralizer.

"It stinks."

"My personal story, or the lotion?"

"Toss up. You report him?"

"No. I froze and just sat in class silently harboring my resentment. I did go to the library immediately after class and wrote my take on the story of Apollo and Daphne. And my thesis on the impact of myths that shape social gender norms flowed from the tale of Daphne's fate."

I began unrolling and rinsing her curls as industriously as if by doing so I could scour sexism from the collective unconscious.

Taking the towel from me and dabbing her hair, Bibi chuckled. "Why not tell your stories to the professor instead of to old folks set in their ways?"

She had given me her pinkie promise to exchange stories, so, while I set her hair with regular rollers, I told her mine. "I dropped out of school."

"'Cause a guy said a fictional rapist was a hero?"

"His glorifying rape is not why I am considering dropping out of grad school."

"You said you already dropped out."

"I stopped going to classes, or to campus at all."

"Haven't caught up with yourself, eh?"

"What?"

"You quit 'cause the guy embarrassed you?"

"I quit because he did not respect my *fairytales* any more than Sister Pete does."

"Nuns prefer Church fairytales," she shrugged, "Virgin births and such."

Laughing, I finished rinsing the bones and tidying the equipment. "When I first proposed my thesis, the professor praised it, calling it revolutionary, but after I handed in my first chapter, he told me I had written a feminist diatribe. I felt betrayed."

"Ha! Young girls and their big words: *diatribe, betrayed*! If you're done with this stink, I'm done."

"Whoa, you pinkie-promised me to tell about the song you hum."

She shrugged. "Just a tune I fancy."

"Well, I fancy I'll go nuts if I don't find out where I've heard it before."

"Just made it up."

"Then why do I have a strong memory of hearing it when I was a child, as if my parents sang it when we went on long car trips on holidays? It has a mellow haunting kind of feel about it, you know?"

"Nice thought," she murmured.

"Is it an old standard your nephew wrote?"

With a snap she unwrapped the towel from around her neck. "Ha!"

"I can't put my finger on it, but wasn't the tune famous once?"

The old lady flinched at the word *famous*, and her head turned slowly--and apparently painfully--on its axis. Though I think she may have had tears in her eyes, she did not allow even one to fall. As she began breathing with what appeared to be some difficulty, I stepped back and examined her closely in the dressing table mirror.

"Are you all right, Mrs. Bell?"

"Not dying to talk about it."

"I'm sorry. I didn't mean to raise a sensitive subject. It's just, you know...." I held up my pinkie as evidence of

70

our pact.

"Done with stinky stuff?" she grumbled.

"At least let me blow-dry your hair a little. Don't want you to catch cold."

She struggled to get her wheelchair out from under the counter. "Talking depresses me."

I freed her chair from the counter and rolled it to her. "Please forgive me if I've upset you."

"*I* upset me. Talking of family songs and all."

"*Family* songs?"

She whirled her chair around to face me. "The ones your folks sang on car rides. My *nephew's* songs. Thanks for the stinky curls."

I reached for the grips on her wheelchair. "Would you like me to roll you to your room?"

With amazing strength she wrenched the chair away from me and pushed it to the doorway. "So's you can grill me some more?"

"So you can remind me where I've heard that tune you're always humming."

Wheeling her chair out the door, she muttered, "It'd be nice to become a tree like Daphne. No ears." She wheeled out the door.

For weeks, even when she was not humming within my hearing, the melody would invade my mind at unexpected times, like the famous motif by Mozart my piano teacher drilled into me when I was seven, or an ancient jingle advertising dog food (*Get Dr. Ross dog food, do him a favor!*). As the date approached for the upcoming reading of her nephew Wallace Bell's will, I spent as much time as possible with Bibi, hoping her humming would remind me where in the world I had heard the song that seemed so familiar and strangely significant to me.

~ ~ ~

The Reading of the Will

The Bell tribe rolled into Safe Haven as promised, like a noisy parade of clowns harboring ulterior motives. Before Sister Pete even knew they had arrived or any aide could stop them, they surged down the residents' hall, plucked their dear "Auntie" out of her bed, plopped her into her chair and wheeled her towards the front door babbling about the soon-to-be-read will of Wallace Bell.

Rhoda handed off the wheelchair to me in the no-man's land between the common room and the dining area, congratulating her great-aunt on her new hairdo. "Daddy would be pleased you spruced up for the occasion, Auntie!" she enthused.

Viola also bent down to bleat an encouraging word in the old woman's ear. "And, just think, Daddy's sure to have left a little something to you too."

Swiftly as hungry swallows taking flight, we piled into two of the family's cars and headed for their lawyer's office. Viola was in the front seat with her tweed-encased husband who was driving, and their tenor son Leon was scrunched restlessly between the old woman and myself in the backseat. When his great-grandaunt sniffed, I handed tissues to her across Leon's lap, when she coughed, I reached in front of him to give her a cough drop, and when we arrived at our destination, I opened my door intending to scurry around to the opposite side to help her out of the car and into her wheelchair. I had barely opened my door, however, when Leon climbed over me and popped out of the back seat with the cry, "Jesus on the cross didn't suffer like me! I got *Old* all over me!"

~

The trip back to Safe Haven after the reading of the will was not as boisterous as the trip to the lawyer's office. The characteristically unreserved Bell family had abruptly become as quiet as the grave of their paterfamilias. They all appeared shocked to the core, stunned to a level of quietude most unnatural for the Bells. Except for their great-aunt: though she never hummed from the moment the will was read till we returned to Safe Haven, she looked exceedingly thoughtful.

Sister Pete met us at the door of her establishment, and when she strongly encouraged the relatives not to come in, they silently returned to their cars. Only Leon uttered a word, and all he said was, "I don't get it! What just happened?" His parents offered him no explanation of what had transpired in the lawyer's office. Only the old woman looked into her great-grandnephew's puzzled face with an expression of deep pity. As I wheeled her to her room, she shook her head slowly from side to side, muttering, "Gonna be trouble, Wally. Big trouble.'

~

The *trouble* was that Wallace Bell had left nearly his whole estate to his Aunt Beatrice Bell and only a small fraction to his daughters and grandchildren. His house he left to Viola, and Rhoda inherited the cottage in town where Bibi had lived with Rhoda's family before she had been moved to Safe Haven. But there was no music scholarship for Leon, no private Christian school tuition for Rhoda's six-year old evangelist daughter, and no leftover funds for the brothers-in-law or their numerous get. I could see why the family was in shock, and I was concerned about what they would do when their customary uncultivated behavior kicked in again. And it did kick in, within days, though not with the whole display of the family's usual bells and whistles. Viola and Rhoda and their spouses came alone, and they came dressed all in black and enshrouded with black moods. Viola spoke first, and with remarkable restraint, for her.

"We don't know what you did to drive Daddy to make that crazy will, Auntie," she declared. She was standing at the foot of the old woman's bed while her great-aunt, lying with her head sunk deep in her pillow, stared at Viola with watchful eyes. "But you should know we are challenging the will."

Bibi remained still, a very old lady in her rest-home bed, but as she looked into her grandniece's eyes, her piercing gaze evoked a mental image of a family Titan standing ramrod straight atop a pedestal and looking down at an errant teenage girl. And she said not a word, unless you count what her eyes said to Viola's eyes.

Her grandniece looked flustered for only a second, then, turning briskly and, with the cadence of a wronged penitent, she left the room warning, "Just so's you know."

Viola's and Rhoda's husbands, in unison, appeared in Bibi's doorway like heralds to royalty, and they blared, "In the common room, *tout de suite!*" Having delivered their message, they smoothed their thin hair and fat ties, turned on the heels of their newly shined shoes and marched away.

A terse exchange occurred between Bibi and me as I

helped her dress for breakfast.

"What can I do to aid with your family business this morning?" I asked.

"Gonna get ugly," was all she said.

"Banana pancakes today. Will that help?"

"Gonna take a lotta bananas."

The family had the grace to allow the woman to choke down her pancakes before they popped up suddenly in the common room like poisonous mushrooms after a rain. Though none of Bibi's younger family members were in evidence, the presence of Viola, Rhoda and their husbands--who looked weaponized in their funereal suits-- seemed to overfill the room with Bells. I could see Sister Pete through the door of the kitchen where she was going over the menu for dinner with the cook. I hoped she was keeping an eye on the proceedings.

After I had wheeled Bibi to her usual Queen Anne chair and helped her into it, Viola stood in my customary spot downstage center on the performance platform and delivered a simple ultimatum: "If you agree to turn over to us, Father's immediate family, the inheritance he mistakenly left you in his will, we will offer you the portion that you should reasonably receive. If you accept this plan, we will not challenge the will."

The old woman giggled nervously.

Turning neon-red, Viola said, "If that is a no, we might as well go to our lawyer's office right now."

The sisters and their tweedy husbands were striding to the front door when the old woman stopped them with a statement that smacked the Bell family severely right between their narrow-set eyes.

"I'm not saying my nephew's will wasn't a surprise, because it surprised me in ways you cannot imagine–ways even I do not fully understand. But his lawyer and an accredited Notary Public swear he did write it and that they witnessed him sign the document. It says I had a primary role in the creations that earned him the money that supported him and his children. Far be it from me to question the veracity of anybody's signed testament."

This was probably the longest speech Bibi had voiced to them–maybe to anybody--in years, and Viola and Rhoda were too shocked to speak. The husbands, however, manfully stepped into the breach.

"Are you saying your own nephew lied to his family about his work, all their lives, Aunt Beatrice?"

By then Rhoda had caught her breath. "Where in heaven's name did you get the idea you had the right to say such a horrible thing, Auntie?"

"Where in heaven's name did you think your father acquired his wealth?" the old woman asked in return.

"Why, profits made from clever investments he made with the residuals from his songs are what constitute the bulk of his estate," Viola said.

"From the *family* songs, as he put it in his will. And, from the one *family* member to whom he willed the bulk of the estate he acquired in his lifetime you might figure out which family member had something to do with the writing of *his* songs."

Rhoda looked uncharacteristically thoughtful, but Viola laughed out loud. "Are you claiming you co-wrote our Father's songs?"

Rhoda began to catch on. "You're saying father was sort of a plagiarist?"

"I'm saying songs were my only babies in this life."

"What do you mean songs were your babies?" Rhoda demanded.

The old woman who had mostly hummed for maybe decades transformed before our eyes into a little old lady reminiscing garrulously at a family gathering. She sat quietly in the overstuffed chair, looking at no one, her head cocked to one side as if listening to a song piped in from the past, and she talked.

"We sang together around my piano from the time your daddy could hum. He was like a son to me, and oh, how we could harmonize. He said he loved the songs we sang in my parlor, and the way he sang them proved it was true. Then one day, to my surprise, he was a grown young man who had more ideas about what to do with a song than singing it with his old auntie. He said he wanted to promote them, commercially. He did that, and he was good at it. Only, he said, no one was buying songs by or about women's lives so he shared them with the world under his name. That was back in the day, and he was probably right. He paid me some to make it right. And he paid himself and his children the lion's share."

The facial expressions of those gathered around Bibi's chair ranged from disbelief to amazement and back again. Rhoda was the first challenger to find words.

"Well, Auntie, he took payment for making the songs the great success they were in their time. I'm sure he rightly wanted to credit you with whatever small part you might have played in their creation–for encouraging a young fellow making up songs on your piano and all. I wouldn't object to your getting whatever the usual percentage is for being an inspiration, or for use of your piano–being as you're family."

One of the husbands stepped up to the old woman, and, looming over her, put some muscle behind Rhoda's suggestion. "You said you sang together for years, Auntie. Maybe while he was composing, you threw a word or a note in here and there. You deserve a buck or two for that."

"He did arrange the songs we had sung together when he was a boy and he performed them in public."

"Arranging, composing: what's the difference?" Viola asked, "See, he really did write the songs."

The old woman's head was bowed, but she glared up through her brows. "My babies."

"I'm sure you had great affection for the songs you and your beloved nephew shared, Auntie," Rhoda explained as if to an underachieving kindergartner. "But that doesn't make the songs your babies. I had a sweet baby called Sunday. Viola had a talented baby called Leon. You had a beloved nephew called Wallace Bell. But a song can't be a baby."

"Rhoda's right, Auntie," Viola exclaimed. "Singing together isn't making a song."

"Singing your heartache is what makes a song," her great-aunt snapped.

Rhoda sat in the chair next to her aunt, and, with a saccharine smile, said, "You know, Auntie, I think it's possible you made up a jingle or two way back when. Possibly our father heard you sing them and later remembered them when he was composing. Like in the middle ages, when art works were created communally. Cathedrals were built by multiple artists, and God got the credit, not the individual architects and builders. It sounds like you may have contributed to our father's songs with a...charitable Christian spirit."

Appearing to warm to her sister's effort, Viola strolled toward the old woman and sat in the chair next to her and opposite Rhoda. "But even if by some fluke a songwriter like Father might absorb a musical phrase or two from someone else, Leon tells me that, nowadays song writers are constantly borrowing from other composers' songs. It's called creating a mash-up. Whoever performs a song in public owns it, actually. Maybe it wasn't done that way in your day, Auntie, but that's the way it's done now."

Rhoda jumped up to add to the avalanche of arguments cascading down on dear old Auntie. "And, if the songwriter accidentally picks up a scrap of a melody from a blood relative, well, it's all in the family, isn't it?"

"She's right," her husband crowed. "Anyway, there are no new ideas under the sun."

"So says the man who never had a new idea," Bibi murmured to her folded hands.

"Beg pardon?" the man demanded, looming over the back of her chair.

"Auntie" had been listening with increasing consternation to the family's claims, but when Tweedy towered over her ominously, she hoisted herself up from the Queen Anne chair and, with surprising abruptness, shifted her body to her wheelchair.

"The mind can create art on its own, son. Can't take that from me."

She pointed her wheelchair towards the hall leading to her room, but the husbands, in tandem, blocked her way.

"No one wants to take anything from you, Auntie," said Rhoda catching up to the men.

"We're offering you your fair share," said Viola, scurrying to affirm her sister's words.

"Fair, ha!" the old woman cried, urging her chair towards her room. The quartet challenging her maintained their blockade of the hallway, but she made an end run around them to the open French doors, rolling out into the courtyard before they could prevent her.

The sisters and their dutiful spouses boxed her in between the peach tree and the picnic table and I could not get to her through them. Running back inside, I looked for Sister Pete in the kitchen but did not find her. Returning to the courtyard, I found the four members of the Bell clan peppering the old woman with more denials of any part she might feel she had in their father's compositions. Seeming to crumble under the barrage, she murmured *My babies, my babies* as her white head dipped lower and lower towards her lap and Viola complained, "A song is not flesh and blood, Auntie."

Rhoda seconded her motion: "Viola and I are closer in blood to Wallace Bell anyway and are meant to inherit the fruits of our father's work."

The husbands chimed in, Rhoda's husband

growling, "Whatever ladylike bits you may have invented, your nephew, Wally, undoubtedly formed a stronger invention to encompass it. Being a man, he was acknowledged by society to be in control of the creation and had to dress up any little thing you wrote and present it as his, as the mainstay of the family."

Viola's husband added, "A man is paid to be the face of his family members, because they are weaker than he is."

Bibi took one more stab at getting her grandnieces to understand her pain. "Don't make me say he flat-out stole from me. Don't make me think that." Then, having uttered those words with declining breath, she let her head fall almost to her lap. I tried to force myself past the two men to free her from them, but making a barrier of their clasped arms, they shoved me away from her. With a cry I fell backwards onto the patio flagstones, and when I turned back towards the Bell family, I saw Viola's husband standing with one of his very large shoes pressed against the footrest of the wheelchair and his imposing body standing over the old woman like a two-hundred-fifty pound avalanche perched on melting snow on a hot Spring day. Determined to help her, I pushed myself up from the flagstones, but at the same time, I saw Sister Pete levitate on the other side of the Bells.

Somehow she had made her way from the kitchen to the courtyard and, rising up like a Colossus emerging from the sea amid a frenzy of sharks about to feed on a hapless porpoise, she bellowed, "Desist!" With startled cries, the family shrank away from the angry nun, who then read them the riot act with daunting biblical quotations to back up her many appropriate moral pronouncements.

Bibi sat silent in the eye of the storm. And when Sister Pete judged she had chastened the visitors sufficiently, she reached down, released the chair's brake and wheeled her elderly charge to her room.

The family reclaimed its dignity by rearranging its loosened collars and rumpled hairdos, then, striding from the courtyard via the French doors, they bled across the dining hall and exited Safe Haven into the parking lot. Their cars could be heard roaring away, spitting gravel and laying rubber as if their drivers had thought they were a sure thing in the Indy 500 but had lost.

As I followed the nun and Bibi back to her room, I thought about the Bells. Certainly they had been somewhat daunted by their stubborn grandaunt and by a nun in full feather. I feared they would not be daunted for long, but it was some time until the Bells could regroup and descend upon Bibi again.

Then, before they had their ducks in a row, she mysteriously disappeared, leaving the inhabitants of Safe Haven in a muffled uproar. I would often imagine I glimpsed her racing down the residents' hallway in her wheelchair trilling her favorite tune. But between one meal and the next she had become the invisible woman, evaporating as instantaneously as the first snow falling on warm cement. Only the memory of her voice humming her favorite tune and the haunting question of its provenance remained as evidence of her existence. ~ ~ ~

Searching for Bread Crumbs

The day the old woman went missing, I searched everywhere I could think of, more than once. Often I would find my fellow aide Monte searching for her alongside me. Together we tramped through the shrubbery in the backyard, calling out *Bibi Bell* so often Lonny said we sounded like a *sumbitchin' carillon.* I scolded him for joking under the sad circumstances, until Monte reminded me that Bibi would have found the jest funny. After scouring the back yard of Safe Haven, we agreed Bibi had to be indoors, if she was still on the property at all.

When Monte joined the other searchers who went looking for clues in the Alzheimer's wing, I went back to Room 17 to sift through her things one more time. I suppose I hoped I might uncover among her belongings a map of her itinerary with a big red "X" marking her destination. I found no map, but I did notice a few anomalies in her room. For one thing, her cane was there, big as life. Though the centenarian did not ordinarily use it to prop herself up, she usually had it with her. She would wheel herself around in her chair, and, when it got stuck in people traffic, she would wave it back and forth in front of her to shoo away interlopers. But now her empty wheelchair sat at the foot of her bed, and her cane was hanging on the handle of the closet door. Though at times I had seen her exhibit surprising strength, I wondered if she could go far without either one of those items.

While I was checking out her cane, I noticed something unusual in Bibi's clothes closet. Behind the sliding cork-covered doors hung the wardrobe of a lifetime.

I had kidded her that her garments bulged so plentifully out of the wardrobe door they seemed about to explode into the room and bury the residents in woolens. She told me that when her nieces moved her into Safe Haven, they had stuffed the tiny closet with every stitch of clothing she owned–even pieces she had not worn in the past twenty years. She told me, whining in a dead-on imitation of her older niece Viola's put-upon tone, "We have no room to store all your things in our modest homes, Auntie." To me, Bibi had added sarcastically, "No room in your home to store *Auntie* either."

Strange that she had not packed a bag before she disappeared from Safe Haven; for I could find nothing missing from her closet or dresser drawers. I did notice that there was something on the floor of the closet I had never in all my visits to Bibi's room seen there. Her tennis shoes had been offhandedly tossed onto the floor of the closet instead of neatly lined up beside her bed where they always were when not on her feet. I stood transfixed by the sight of the woman's cast-off sneakers. Bibi might have been inscrutable, but she was neat as a pin in her manner, her actions, and her dress. She even polished her tennis shoes. What could have caused her to treat her favorite item of apparel in such a careless manner? Had someone else tossed her shoes into the closet? And, wherever she was, what was she wearing on her feet?

While I was pondering that question, Monte suddenly popped up behind my left shoulder. "Find anything interesting?" he asked.

Hearing his voice right behind me, I jumped as if I

had been caught doing something mischievous with Bibi's shoes. Hurriedly I picked up a wool scarf that had fallen to the closet floor and held it up in front of Monte's face. "Could this be a clue?"

"I don't think she ever wore that, Dani. Do you think someone else dropped it here accidentally?"

As I have a spotty record in assessing trustworthiness in men, I was still not prepared to share with him my guesses about the old woman's disappearance. So I ignored his question and asked, "How do you know whether or not she ever wore it?"

"She's my favorite old woman since my *abuela* died. I keep close track of her," he said.

"You didn't keep track of her closely enough, apparently, or she would not be lost. Oh, I'm sorry," I hastened to add. "About your grandmother, I mean. Do you have any idea where she might be?"

"My grandmother is in Heavenly Grace Cemetery. Sorry, bad joke—you meant Bibi. But I've been thinking about my *abuela* so much since Bibi disappeared. My granny was a *bruja*, a witch in the Mexican village where my mother grew up. She used to eat mushrooms or something and dance around a campfire chanting in some sort of arcane language. She called it *código*, a code through which she channeled answers to questions posed by the villagers. I could almost wish she had taught me *código*. Maybe I could use it to find Bibi. I can't, but I *am* the kind of guy who notices things. And what I noticed about Bibi today was that she missed Story Hour for the first time since you arrived on the scene."

"Is that all you noticed about the woman you keep *close* track of?" I asked. I wondered what he would make of the cane, the wheelchair and the shoes.

"I notice all sorts of things. Aides observe."

"As opposed to me, I suppose you mean. Please, tell a lowly volunteer what sorts of things you observe; I want to become an aide too one day."

Monte smiled, "To tell the truth, I noticed nothing unusual in this room, or in the whole south wing, or in the Alzheimer's wing either. Well, actually, everything's a bit unusual there. I did find a note written on a toilet tissue roll in one of the Alzheimer's resident's bathrooms and read it with great excitement, thinking it might be a secret note Bibi left about her destination. But it was clearly written by another resident, in ballpoint pen on the toilet paper roll: *Why did I come into the bathroom? Oh! Never mind.*"

I had to laugh, which seemed to relieve Monte. "Look," he said, "you're the best volunteer we've had at Safe Haven since I got here. But, I'm not surprised you didn't totally trust me right off, since you are so secretive about your own life."

Not one to appreciate near strangers forming opinions of me, I blurted out, "Hey, here's a secret about me you haven't noticed. I just dropped out of college and have not even told the college."

"Wow. I can certainly keep that secret," he said, adding, "and so, likewise I think you can keep this secret: I am an aide to Sister Pete in more ways than one. To help her promote the good image of Safe Haven, I am writing a special piece for Safe Haven's twenty-fifth anniversary."

"Writer? You told me you were an auto mechanic."

"I was. And, before my boss let me go, he had me make flyers and write advertisements for his garage. I worked my way up the food chain to write automotive articles for car magazines and the local paper. Fast forward to my boss showing me the door and me subsequently becoming a rest-home aide. Then, when I found out that one of Safe Haven's residents had disappeared a year or so ago and was found living in the wild, I saw a possible opportunity to kick-start a career as an actual journalist. I asked Sister Pete if I could write an article about it. She said yes, I think because the coverage in the local paper about the escaped Alzheimer's resident made Safe Haven look like a heartless warehouse for oldsters–which, as you know, it is not. She seemed eager to have an article published to counter the bad publicity with a report about how that man and all the residents here at Safe Haven are alive, safe and livin' the dream. Now that another of her charges has disappeared, I can't wait to hear what miracles of publicity Sister Pete will want me to perform."

"You must be really hot to find Bibi under an overpass or something ASAP, to provide the optimal deus ex machina for your story."

"Oh, I imagine the police will look in such obvious places to locate her," he smiled. "I'm sure we'll be hearing helicopters overhead at any moment. But Bibi is not just any old person, she's definitely not obvious, and, if she's hiding, she will find ways not to be seen by a helicopter."

"I agree –if she's hiding on purpose."

"Right, and I'm guessing that she, or whoever took her, would have left clues among her belongings, but I haven't found any. I've been wondering if she may have hinted where she was going to any of her associates here at Safe Haven. You, for example," he said, turning to me suddenly, "You seem to have made fast friends with Bibi in your short time here. I can't help but wonder what you talked about together. She leave you any billet-doux with clues?"

"No billet-doux. I hardly think she would have left me any love notes. It takes people longer than a few weeks to love me."

"That surprises me," he muttered. "What did you and Bibi talk about then?"

"Just how she wanted her hair done–stuff like that. She never mentioned her personal belongings, you know, clothing–scarves and such."

"Then why are you still standing there in her open closet door, Dani?"

I slid the closet door closed. "Her clothes remind me that she might be outside somewhere, wandering around without this wool scarf in the gathering chill of early evening."

"Right," Monte said, striding towards the door. "I've looked at every single object in this room and nothing points to the path an elderly lady would have taken, let alone a special lady like Bibi. I'm going to search the rest of the place for her with a fine-tooth comb."

As soon as Monte left, I found myself regarding the wool scarf in my hands. *Something about her clothing.* I turned back to the closet and noticed a lavender slip of paper stuck with a push pin to the cork door of the closet. It was half-obscured by the now brown orchid Bibi told me was pinned up there on her birthday by her niece.

"Aunt Beatrice!" the niece had complained, "You can't throw the beautiful orchid we bought you for your birthday in the wastebasket!"

Bibi had told me that when Rhoda was pinning the

dried posy to the cork board, she cried what looked to be real tears, but Bibi said she suspected they were only for the money her niece had spent on the posy. Remembering Bibi's humorous depiction of her niece crying crocodile tears made me take special notice of the paper semi-concealed by the orchid. I remembered noting before that the paper had nothing but music notes inked on it by hand. I took a wild guess that the flower concealed something about the woman's humming.

Though I am not what could in any sense be called a musician, I had enough piano lessons as a child to read music after a fashion. I stared at those black wing-footed ciphers and was amazed to hear myself hum the melody they memorialized. The notation seemed identical to the tune she and her great-grandnephew sang the first time I met her on the day of her one-hundred first birthday party. A peculiar notion occurred to me regarding some odd connections among things I had observed with regard to Bibi: her incessant humming, the fact that it was her humming song that she sang at her party, and that the song's melody seemed familiar to me. What struck me most, however, was the shock she expressed at the way the song was listed in her nephew's memorial program. Was her reaction connected to the heated family discussion after the reading of the will about her possible contribution to her nephew Wally's songs? I concluded that her mysterious disappearance might have something to do with music, and that the *something* in question might be discoverable via the bit of music pinned to the cork board.

Who was I kidding? Me, obviously. I was not going to find the lady who hums by following slips of paper or musical notes like breadcrumbs. What actual means might I use to hunt for her when I had no real idea of how perhaps demented old ladies might plan to disappear? I sat on the foot of Bibi's bed trying to sift through whatever store of useful knowledge I might own. I wished I could call up some premium hunting wisdom or some cipher for finding lost females. However, as I have neither experience as a hunter nor training as a code-breaker, I thought that an education to become a park ranger or a fireman would have suited my goal better than the degree in Dramaturgy I had been pursuing. A knowledge of plot, character and theme was all I had at my disposal.

~ ~ ~

Parsing the Code

Hours went by with no sign of the old woman coming to light. My penchant for drama caused me to fear an abduction for ransom was afoot or some other dastardly plot concocted by someone who preyed on elderly women. Though she was a quietly scrappy old lady, I did not see her surviving long without some knowledgeable care-giver around her. And where might she be forced to walk on those tiny feet without her shoes? Of course, she might have gone off on her own. Or, maybe she turned demented overnight. She did seem unsettled by her family's claims to an inheritance, but I thought it unlikely that she would suddenly go totally bonkers and run away from home. And, though I was ill-equipped to find lost old women, I somehow felt responsible for her well-being, and an urge to do whatever it would take to find her lay on me like a Homeric quest.

So worrisome was the old gal's absence that I volunteered more hours at Safe Haven than Sister Pete required of me. I ran the giant potato masher for lunch so I could casually question the kitchen staff. Unfortunately, I gleaned no clues from them. Sister Pete had sent a team out to search the neighborhood for the old woman, but, despite my heroic impulses to circle the earth looking or her, I was not ready to take my search outside Safe Haven. For all I knew my ex might be lurking behind the neighbor's hedge or a local trash dumpster waiting for me to poke my nose out the door. Since he had appeared at Safe Haven demanding to see me, I had left the building only at night. I would creep mouse-like to my car, which I always deceitfully parked a block away. Until I had found some evidence inside Safe Haven of where Bibi might have gone, I would not wander around outside looking for her, lest instead of my finding her, Remy might find me.

Thus, every time I saw Bibi's roommate Bettina busy in the common room making her montages, I snuck back into Room 17 to take yet another look. I had recalled that, amid all the doodads on Bibi's dresser, there was a nicely carved music box missing its winder, remnant of a more elegant time perhaps. As small as it was, it was large enough to hold the bits of jewelry Bibi brought with her to Safe Haven: a school pin with an animal mascot I did not recognize, a pair of pierced gemstone earrings, and a silver brooch shaped like a tree with tiny seed pearls for blossoms or fruits.

Something about *tree* sparked my interest and I decided to take a closer look at the pin. But, when I pulled it out of the music box, I found it was stuck to the velvet lining on the floor of the container. And when I tugged at the pin, the velvet came free of the box revealing a folded paper hidden beneath it. There was writing on both sides of the 4 x 6 piece of onionskin paper; it was a freehand rendering of some musical notes. It took only moments for me to recognize the same series of notes that I had found posted on the cork board on her closet. That seemed pertinent. Sitting on her bed with my feet where her tennis shoes ought to be had brought me no revelations via osmosis, so I put the tree pin back in the music box and hid it under the afghan at the foot of her bed for possible later reference. Then, grasping the onionskin paper, I began to compare the music, note for note, with the scrap of music from the closet door. Feeling like Sherlock Holmes' dumber cousin, I glanced back and forth at the notes on the two papers as if they could speak to me.

Actually, they could speak to me in a way, because, on the paper from the box, Bibi had scribbled some words beneath the musical notes. Her penmanship was so minuscule, however, it seemed intended to be rolled up inside a capsule and left in a secret mail drop for a fellow spy. I knew it would take some time to decipher the teensy lyrics, but, the few words that were legible took me a ways towards making out the rest. Also, I noticed that at the bottom of the song, in elegant, old-fashioned longhand, these words were written: *Music and lyrics by Beatrice Bell.* I would call that an *Aha!* moment. And it was Bibi's signature. I recognized it from her written menu requests.

Assuming it was her song and that the lyrics might be useful clues about Bibi's life, I figured I might guess why she hummed it all the time–and why she had been upset when her great-grandnephew sang it at her birthday party. But, though it was looking to me like Wally Bell actually did leave the bulk of his assets to her for a good reason, how might the song yield clues to her disappearance? If the family had come to believe Bibi had indeed composed the songs her nephew had claimed to have written, had they been inspired to hide her away until they cleared up the confusion about the matter of authorship? Although the Bells were chock-full of bluster, surely none of them would steal her inheritance by getting rid of her. Never having seen an actual murderer, however, I did not know what one looked like. I thought they probably looked like anyone else, which is what the Bells looked like.

Examining the paper from the music box further, I noted that the title of the song was not written in cryptic penmanship; it was clearly labeled in Bibi's hand in big beautiful cursive letters WHITE LILACS, two words which also appeared throughout the text. And, calling on my long-neglected music lessons and my sense memory of Bibi's

94

humming, I was confident that the notes on the two papers recorded the same melody Bibi incessantly hummed. Also, Bibi and her great grandnephew Leon had good voices, and the tune I had heard them sing was lodged clearly in my head. Thus, I convinced myself that the words and music on the paper from the music box definitely belonged to the one Bibi and her great-grandnephew Leon had sung on her birthday.

The fact that the song had been posted in one place in her room and hidden away in another seemed a bit devious, which suggested to me that delving into the words memorialized on the two papers might offer some hint about motivations that led to the old woman's disappearance. Thus, studying the few legible words, while recalling her and her great grandnephew singing in the garden, I managed to put together the beginning stanzas of the song. After a few minutes, I was able to sing them aloud, although I felt a little sad to be singing her song when she was not there either to hear it or to sing it herself.

As if we'd never have a care,
We breathed the dewy perfumed air
Of the lilac tree above
As if its limbs could shield our love.

I should not have sat with my back to the open door while trying to sing the words to myself; for I had just begun singing the second verse, when I was interrupted by a voice demanding, "How do you know that song?"

Turning to defend myself by hand-to-hand combat if necessary, I saw that it was only Monte, my favorite nosy aide at Safe Haven. He was standing in the doorway with an amazed look on his face as if he had just happened upon

Venus rising from her seashell at an inappropriate place and time. With the excess of caution I had developed in my last relationship with a man, I quickly pocketed the slip of paper with the white lilac song scribbled on it. If Monte noticed my move to hide the paper, he was too much of a gentleman to demand to see it. He did ask to know what I had been singing so loudly that he had recognized it easily from the hallway. "I've been hinting to Bibi for weeks that I'd love to hear the words of the song she's always humming. How did you get her to do it?"

Caught red-handed, I had to say something to him, and, to tell the truth, I was somewhat relieved that it was only Monte who discovered my very speculative detective work. "Her family accidentally goaded her into singing a bit of the song at her party," I admitted. "That's what I was singing, from memory," I added, prevaricating a little bit.

"Good memory. Sounded exactly like Bibi's favorite humming song," he said. He sat in Bibi's wheelchair and began casually wheeling it back and forth the way men do with anything that has wheels. "What moved you to sing it just now?"

"It was a funny hunch I have."

He stopped wheeling for a second and stared at me, expecting that I would naturally share my hunch with him. Though my recent romantic failure had left me feeling cautious about trusting a man I liked, I was so desperate for help decoding Bibi's song that I impulsively uttered, "I had the wacky idea that the words of the song might suggest where she might have gone,"

He grinned. "You're trying to decode a song a very old woman happened to hum in an old folks' home?"

"Got a better idea?" I snapped. So much for building trust.

"This old woman is over one-hundred years old," he kindly explained. "She could just have wandered off trying to recapture some memory she's lost."

"Have you ever known her to utter a single word that did not indicate a mind sharp as a spike? If there is one thing I'm sure of it's that she did not wander off."

"Yeah," he admitted, "I have gotten close to the wily old curmudgeon, and I don't think she wandered anywhere."

I nodded. "I'd like to be as sharp as she is when I'm a hundred."

He tilted his head and gazed at me curiously for a moment, then wheeled close to me. "Why do I not find it amazing that you are thinking that far ahead, at your age?"

"Something about the woman makes me think of my life as a whole, not just as days *in* a life."

"I get that," he nodded, adding, "To tell you the truth, I'm feeling kind of panicky about the strange lack of clues to Bibi's disappearance. So, I wouldn't mind going over the words of the song with you. If they were written in code, I may be able to help decode them."

"You wouldn't *mind* going over the song with me? Or, maybe you will publish them in your article on Safe Haven escapees?"

"If Bibi isn't found, no article is going to convince potential residents this would be a safe haven for them."

Though I was still suffering from the last time I shared an idea with a man, I had never known Monte to do anything morally slapdash or dishonest, so I was fairly certain he had not granny-napped Bibi in a fit of loneliness for his deceased *abuela*. "Okay, maybe working together to transcribe the song we might unearth a clue."

From Bibi's bedside cabinet, I grabbed a ballpoint

pen and the hand-out with Safe Haven's daily menu on it.

Monte wheeled the chair to the side of the bed and read over my shoulder as I wrote the title and lyrics of *White Lilacs* on the back of the menu.

'Neath the lilac tree we laid,
Where our wartime vows we made
Our life together lay ahead,
By spring you would return, you said.

He chuckled, "*White Lilacs?* Lilacs are purple."

"Not always; they can be lavender, pink, or, my doubting friend, white."

"But lilacs grow on bushes, not trees," Monte said."

"My gramma's lilacs grew tall as trees," I said, feeling defensive about accepting help from someone so unfamiliar with lilacs.

Monte shook his head and began turning the wheelchair in circles while gazing around at Bettina's montages, which filled the walls with splashes of color as if Jackson Pollack had whirled around in there, wet brushes in both hands. "Maybe the flowery walls confused you about the song's lyrics."

That made me mad, and, sharply, I said. "Bibi was not confused, I'm sure, when she sang the song at her birthday party. I clearly recall that she *and* her great-grandnephew Leon sang about a white lilac tree.

"I'll allow you the lilac tree," Monte said. "And I'd guess the white lilacs mean something like innocence or purity. But why is she always humming about white lilacs anyway?"

"Perhaps the third stanza–which Bibi's great-grandnephew sang in a clear voice only a few feet away from me–will spark your de-coding talents."

The season would new changes bring
And pairs of winging bluebirds sing,
The winds of peace would softly blow
The lilac petals white as snow.

While Monte absorbed that information, I wrote the verse on the back of the daily menu.

"I stand corrected," he said. "Sorry to have doubted you. Having Bibi disappear has left me feeling a bit untrusting."

"I know the feeling," I said.

"But what are the changes she expects in the spring? Why does she look forward to peaceful winds? And how does any of that suggest where she is? I must not have inherited my *abuela's* talent for translation, because I don't see how Bibi's favorite song could lead us to her."

Edgy from watching him do wheelies in Bibi's chair, I grumbled, "Perhaps this will refresh the memory of your shaman heritage." I whipped the slip of onionskin out of my pocket. "I pieced together the first three verses from hearing them in the garden. Maybe we can translate the rest from Bibi's handwriting."

He studied the paper. "Believe it or not, I can sort of make this out. When I work in the Safe Haven kitchen I have to translate the residents' shakily handwritten dinner requests."

He grabbed the pen and, with my help, wrote out the lyrics of the remaining stanzas. For a full minute, we sat there staring at his generous cursive script before I copied the musical notes from the music box paper beside their corresponding words. Monte began to hum. "Sing it with me," I said, holding the music up between us.

"I don't read music," he said.

"We both know the song Bibi hums by heart, and I have just enough knowledge of music notation to be sure this is that song."

"How will singing the words help us decode them?"

"That's how your gramma the *bruja* did it, isn't it? Chanting around the fire to find answers to problems?"

Monte laughed, "You think Bibi dances around campfires and has left a code telling us where she has gone?" He resumed wheeling the chair around and around the braided rug at the foot of the twin beds. "I don't believe for a minute that anyone can find clues by dancing, chanting, or by performing any other sorcerous ritual." He stopped rolling for a moment and reconsidered. "But I do believe what my *abuela* said: *It might not be magic but if it gets you where you need to go, it might as well be.* I have the feeling if my *abuela* were here, she could figure out how to find the old gal. I'm not so sure you and I can do it. She had centuries of *bruja* tradition going for her, but I feel as lost as I fear Bibi is right now."

"So much for magical code-breaking," I complained tossing the menu aside.

Monte slumped in the wheelchair. "Have you ever gotten a little lost in your life, Dani?"

"What?"

"I was wondering if you've ever felt as lost as I do. As an aide who was supposed to be watching over her, I feel responsible for Bibi. As her friend, I just feel lost."

"Recently I ran away from all I knew and loved, Monte, so what do you think? Right now I'm just fumbling around trying to find my way. You going to sing with me or not? Come on, tradition's got to start somewhere. Make your *abuela* proud."

Monte shook his head and laughed, "I don't have to dance around a fire like she did, do I?"

"Only if singing doesn't work."

Reluctantly, Monte hauled himself out of the wheelchair and stood beside me. We held the menu up between us and sang the part of Bibi's humming song we had just transcribed.

For, though your fate brave songs may tell,
Dear, ere the silken blossoms fell,
You played your little part in war,
And perished on a distant shore,

Monte turned a pale shade of green. "Oh, God, it's about Bibi's husband."

"That's what I thought," I exclaimed. "I think the white lilacs and all the purity and innocence tell the story of their wedding, before he went to war."

"Yes, he must have gone to war." Monte said.

"That's what the song says to me. They wed just before he left. It was in the spring, because that's when lilacs bloom. Maybe they had them at their wedding. Maybe in her wedding bouquet or a floral crown."

"You've thought this through," Monte smiled.

"Most of it occurred to me as we sang it."

Monte had a singing voice Leon would have envied, and a flair for harmony. Singing is not my best performance skill by any means, but I thought we sounded good together.

We were singing through the first verse a second time, with an ear for helpful hints for locating old ladies, when Monte suddenly jumped up and ran from the room crying, "Mr. Holmes' bath! He gives me hell when I'm late. Hold that thought!"

I did hold that thought, long after he left. I was listening to Monte singing in my head as if the power of a Mexican *bruja* could be conveyed to me through her grandson. I was hoping for some time-honored mantra or prayer for tracking lost souls to reveal itself to me. When that failed to work, I sank down in Bibi's wheelchair and waved her cane back and forth in front of me, trying to envision her sitting in it plotting her escape from Safe Haven. The thought that came to me was not a mantra; it was the echo of Monte's words: *Haven't you ever gotten a little lost in your life, Dani?* Those words and the song Monte and I had just sung were poking around in my brain as if looking for their composer when I was suddenly struck by the similarity between the tree pin and Bibi's lyrics. I do not have Hamlet's ability to tell the difference between a hawk and a handsaw, but, in the blink of an owl's eye I can spot similarities between two seemingly disparate things. I felt around under the afghan for Bibi's music box and took out the tree pin. I believed I was on the verge of decoding the possible meaning of the white lilacs when Lonny stuck his large head into the room and barked, "Sister Pete says haul your ass to the common room and tell one of your fairy tales. The oldsters are getting restless as cows in the barn mooing to be milked."

Furtively I shoved the tree pin into my pocket. "Very pretty metaphor, Lonny," I said, following him down the hall to the common room to calm the residents with one of my refurbished fairytales.

~ ~ ~

Artemis

Long ago there lived a very important personage called Artemis, a heroine in some of the oldest stories known to us. She was very woodsy, and always wore a jerkin embroidered with a beautiful tree. It was the Mother Tree, universal image of a basic human archetype, Protectress of all Life: a mother nurturing her baby.

And Artemis had skills to back it up. She had an incredible knack for tracking any living creature who was lost, hurt, captured, or in some sort of jeopardy. When she heard a fawn crying in the woods, she found it, followed a blood trail leading to the fawn's wounded mother, healed injuries the doe had suffered by arrow, knife or spear, reunited doe and fawn, and returned them safely to the forest. You might say, Artemis was the chief animal rescue service of the ancient world.

Until...some new tale-tellers turned Artemis's original story upside down. The symbol of the nurturing mother tree was stricken from her story, and, instead, a bow and arrow became her symbol. Instead of rescuing and healing woodland creatures, she was thenceforth portrayed as hunting and killing them.

As a result of the bastardization of her story, Artemis' role as healer was replaced with her opposite type, represented by Artemis' twin, Apollo, who slaughtered the priestesses in her temple. And, as a result of the revised tale, callous Apollo, not Artemis, became the traditional symbol of healing, and, even today he is known as the god of Medicine.

The Moral of this story: A creative person is like a tree of life, providing fruit and shelter beneath her boughs. A human with a bow and arrow is just a weapon of Death.

~ ~ ~

The Huntress

While I was telling the myth of Artemis with her nurturing tree aegis, I was thinking of Bibi's white lilacs. Right on cue Bibi's tree pin sprang open in my pocket and pricked me on the thigh. Probably a coincidence, but, as Monte's *bruja* might say, *It might not be magic but if it gets you where you need to go, it might as well be.* Therefore, as soon as I had taken a perfunctory bow and my hungry audience had scurried to their dinners, I headed out the backdoor to the garden and sat on the bus stop bench where Bibi had sung about white lilacs. I was wishing I could recall her aura there and thus conjure some magical guidance the way Monte's gramma did by dancing around the village bonfire. But the only iconic female power that occurred to me was Artemis, finder and protectress of lost creatures. Would that I could invoke my inner Artemis spirit and think like a wise woman of mystical wisdom in order to find Bibi.

Sitting on the bus stop bench trying to imagine how to do a little conjuring dance, I chanted in various iterations *Artemis, by your sacred tree, where might our friend Bibi be?* Immediately I was embarrassed to have pretended I might invoke an intuitive talent for finding a lost woman, and, blushing with the knowledge that I was no *bruja,* I slumped on the imaginary bus stop bench wishing a real bus would come along and save me from my helpless state.

And a sort of vehicle did come along, in the shape of another high-flown tidbit of knowledge I recalled, the fact that ancient kings derived wisdom from Artemis. Although I have not one trait a king might claim, and though I object passionately to autocracy in general, I sat on the bus stop bench in a proper meditation pose and wished for the wisdom due a king. With palms cupped on my lap, I sat there and demanded to the bland sky, "Artemis, give me wisdom now!" I received zero assistance from the old goddess, but, suddenly, an ominous voice intruded upon my fanciful musings.

"Artemis? What about Artemis?" It was a voice of authority--a sound always bound to make me leap out of my skin--and it was coming through the laurel hedge right behind me. No need to turn to see who it was. No one else in the place had a voice so big, so resonant, both in sound and sense.

"It's just me, Sister Peter," I apologized, "I was rehearsing one of my fairytales."

"You already told the Artemis story before lunch," she reminded me.

How was I to come up with an excuse for attempting to evoke the pagan Artemis, and to a titled Christian, and in her place of business? Caught with my hand in the metaphysical cookie jar, I blurted out the truth. "I was afraid you would think I'm quite the sinner, chanting like a pagan in Safe Haven's garden."

"Never mind, Danielle," she sighed. "After all, in the 4th century AD the Church re-dedicated her shrine to the virgin Mary."

"Whose shrine, Sister Peter?"

"Artemis's shrine."

"You heard *all* of what I was saying?" I crossed my arms over my breasts to disguise anything I might have in common with Artemis, such as the nurturing pagan spirit of motherhood.

Sister Pete saw through me as if I were a girl made of glass. "A mother is a mother is a mother," she murmured. "Your Artemis; my Mary. Both inspire us to create, to nurture and to rescue, when need be." Then Sister

Pete's shoulders slumped and she bowed her head in what looked like an uncharacteristic surrender to helplessness or hesitance. "This is the lowest point of my life, Danielle. It hurts me that Beatrice Bell is out there somewhere. And the world is about to find my weak spot. I have lost two old persons now. That is two more than anyone is allowed. And all I can do is to hope the police will locate her soon with their nosy helicopters." She turned quickly and pleaded with what looked to me like feral desperation in her eyes, "I would like it so much better if Beatrice Bell could be found by one of us, before the police find her and the media reveals my inability to keep her safe." With stunning familiarity she clutched my hands. "Moments ago, I prayed to the Holy Mother for rescue. Now, I'm grasping at straws, talking nonsense with a girl I hardly know, a girl who savors stories about spirits who walked the world before my savior was even born. I can only suppose I'm telling you this because, despite your whimsy, there's a peculiar sort of steadfastness about you; you obviously care about the missing woman. And I've been thinking about your little fairytales, Danielle. They suggest a natural confidence about timeless matters I don't fully understand. Do you hear what I'm saying? I know your Artemis is the protector, the rescuer, the huntress, and, though my Mary has taken her place, if you have some arcane knowledge unavailable to me, I would not blame you if you attempted to use it to find Beatrice Bell. We probably need raw intuition now more than fancy helicopters, and I have to say that–without too much fear of losing your chance of a permanent job here--I cannot prevent you from looking for our lost lamb wherever your instinct, or off-brand spiritual practice might suggest you look for her. Without assurance or authority, I feel compelled to say, we need a huntress."

Somehow her uncharacteristic vulnerability and hesitant manner made me feel stronger and more sure of myself, and I blurted out, "Then, would you mind sharing what Beatrice Bell's home address was before she came here, Sister Peter? I promise I won't break in and riffle through the belongings of the present owners."

"Beatrice Bell used to live in one of her nephew Wallace Bell's houses, did she not, with his daughter Rhoda, her husband and little girl? Can you tell me how that might help locate our missing centenarian?"

"Just a silly hunch probably–call it a *huntress* thing–that she might return to her family home. It's all I've got at the moment."

Abruptly Sister Pete straightened her spine up from a bowing parenthesis to an upright exclamation point. "Just do not do anything too silly, please. In my experience, media folk can smell an unfortunate rest-home incident as a bloodhound smells--well--blood. Anything any of us do when such a disaster strikes today can magically appear as a headline in the local media tomorrow."

As if she had never mentioned the name of a pagan goddess or suggested Artemis's powers might even slightly resemble the Virgin Mary's, Sister Pete glided up the garden path and reentered Safe Haven. Suddenly her mention of Artemis seemed to have been an illusion, and my recently acquired self-confidence was suddenly not optimal for launching a missing persons inquiry. If I found Bibi, Sister Pete had said, I *might* not lose my chance of employment; but if I did *not* find her, would I find myself without either my university stipend or a job at Safe Haven? A chasm of possible unemployment seemed to gape before me. And all I actually had to sanction my search was a tune in my head and a silver brooch shaped like a tree.

Still, I followed Sister Pete to her office, where she silently dropped in my hand a slip of paper with Bibi's former address on it. I gave her one of my guilty lapsed-Protestant curtsies as a promise to do what I could, and strode with pretended daring out the front door. But the moment sunlight hit me in the face, I slunk back behind the doorpost. I could not have felt more vulnerable if I had been hit with a spotlight down stage center without a clue what my next line was supposed to be. The possibility that Remy was lurking nearby caused me to grab the doorknob as if it were a lifeline, and I was about to hurry back inside Safe Haven when I heard a shout from across the street. Automatically turning my head, I saw a young woman perched on the curb pointing an accusatory finger at me.

"Hey, Man-hater!" she cried. "I snuck a peek at your infamous thesis on Daddy's desk."

It was the daughter of Professor Milton, my academic advisor. Her sharp-edged girly voice pierced its way into my brain and extricated from my memory the nasty tiff the professor's freshman daughter had roped me into at a department cocktail party her father had hosted at his apartment.

~

The evening had progressed as departmental cocktail parties tend to do. When the literary puns and glib theatrical references among the party-goers were reaching their apogee, Professor Milton gave me a beckoning eye from across the room. I allowed a vague smile to paint my lips, while my eyes tactfully glazed over and found a more welcome departmental personage to latch onto. Subtly detaching myself from Remy, I moved towards the friendly face of the department secretary, Paula, who was always good for a laugh at the expense of departmental politics. But the professor's daughter suddenly placed herself directly in front of me like a bouncer challenging an unwanted customer at the door of a popular club. She was all girly curves stuffed into a cream colored dress fashioned from some expensive fabric I could not even name. Her hairdo was from another century, her manners were from film noir.

"I hear you're one of those women who think Shaw is a killer playwright and Shakespeare is a crumbling has-been," she spat. "Don't you even care that your kind of thinking will be the end of theater?"

Remy was clearly amused by the woman's vitriolic wit, and slyly moved to stand behind her left shoulder where he could watch my response. "I adore both Shaw and Shakespeare," I smiled. "I think in some instances they understood women better than some women do."

Remy chuckled when she crowed, "*Some* women lack understanding, that's for sure. "You don't even know that Feminism is dead, you poor thing." Thus spake the faculty brat.

"I don't call myself a feminist. I'm an egalitarian," I explained, as if to someone whose opinion I valued. "There *are* females who are not egalitarians in that they consider values commonly called masculine to be superior to anything considered feminine."

She drew her plump chest into a huff. "If you're trying to insult me, it won't work; I know who I am."

"Yeah, I think I know who you are too," I confided. "But I won't tell."

Remy was not looking as pleased with my attempts to defend myself as he had been at the woman's attempts to ridicule me. He hooked his arm through mine, and guided me towards the door, whispering, "That's Professor Milton's daughter!"

"That makes sense," I chuckled, as he dug my jacket out of the pile on the foyer bench while continuing his commentary about my dialogue with the anti-feminist girl. "She had an article published in the *Post* about the feminist cancer in current literary criticism. Only a freshman, and she's *published!"*

Oooo, be still my beating heart!

Remy hurried me out the door as if he feared the professor would throw us over his knee and spank us.

"What's the hurry?" I asked as we took the elevator down from the professor's apartment.

"Sometimes you defy belief, Dani. Didn't you see that Professor Milton wanted to talk with you?"

"I see him enough in class, thanks. Was my ignoring his invitation to chat any excuse for you to grab me like a silver-back gorilla and drag me away?"

Remy changed stratagems. "Do I need an excuse to be alone with my girlfriend while the night is still young?" He smiled slyly, slipping his hand under my coat.

"Are you sure you weren't just afraid if I didn't scamper across the room to chat with the host when he lifted a finger, it would reflect badly on you?"

"I'm not afraid," he assured me, looking as clenched as if I had accused him of farting in company. "I would like to know, though, why you gave our mentor the cold shoulder?" While Remy scolded me, he slid his other hand under my coat and began petting me like a house cat.

"Professor Milton and I disagreed on the cultural implications of a critical interpretation of a certain dramatic character."

"Big words for what I must assume was a bit of a

110

literary tiff," he cooed in my ear. "What was the character?"

"Don Giovanni."

Remy laughed, "Are you getting carried away with feminist theory again? You wanted the work to be about *Donna* Giovanni, I suppose?"

"Good heavens no! Quite the opposite!"

"What's the opposite of gender-swapping?"

"Gender-banging."

"What does that mean?"

"Just a joke between me and Professor Milton."

"A joke that makes you unable to deal with him?"

"Oh, I'm dealing with him."

"How?"

"Via my thesis."

"You think your thesis advisor will like that?"

"I can't wait to find out."

"Shouldn't I know about this? He is bound to think I am involved."

"Why?"

"Because we live together. Because we are together. Because--look at us petting in the elevator--there's some overlap between us."

"I'd say that love involves a sort of overlapping, but not in our work."

"I'm not in the mood to figure out what that means. I am very much in the mood to overlap, though." To make his point, Remy slid his hands around to my chest and breathed into my hair.

When we reached our apartment building and reached our floor, Remy stuck his size 11 brogans in the door to keep the elevator in place while we did a bit more overlapping. Then, entwined with one another, we made our way down the hall crabwise. Once inside, we were still fueled by a pleasant Chablis Professor Milton had served at the party. At the time I was so enamored with Remy, I did not realize that the little fuss caused by the professor's daughter was only the first round in the disagreement about *overlapping* that would KO our romance.

~

The momentary flashback of the encounter with the professor's daughter had suspended my consciousness briefly, but then the razor-sharp sound of the voice of the professor's daughter shooting across the street directly into my ears returned me swiftly to my present predicament.

"What a load of pagan crap!" she hooted. "Gonna bring your coven to your thesis defense and have them cast a shaman's spell over the panel?"

The girl was dressed like the Prom Queen on her day off, as were her three girlfriends, who tittered in a princess-like manner at her jibes.

If anything could have torn me apart from my safe haven at the moment, it would be the firestorm of anger that girl lit in me. I was this close to charging across the street and using her cashmere sweater to wipe up the sidewalk, with her in it. Being bullied would sometimes free my cautious tongue, but in this case my rage left me tongue-tied. Still, I bolted across the street, planted myself solidly twelve inches from Miss Milton's face, and pointed two hex fingers at her eyes while making the guttural hissing sound I thought a witch would make. I guess I played the role pretty well, because she dropped her books and she and her pals ran down the street squealing. One of the more gratifying moments of my academic career. And, as long as I was already outside, I felt safe enough to stay outside for a time. Humming Bibi's favorite song on the way to my car, I thought I might just be the insightful huntress Sister Pete had suggested I become. After all, it was not impossible that there actually was a white lilac tree growing at the house where Bibi once lived. And who knows, after her struggle with her family, she might have sought comfort in the scent of her favorite flower.

~ ~ ~

A Scary Voice Mail

Within minutes I realized I had used up a good deal of energy trying to transform my brain into a divining rod tuned to old ladies. I was so tuckered out that I was willing to risk going home to my apartment. At home I could eat, shower, take a breather, and pack my sling bag with whatever supplies I might need on my hunt to locate Bibi.

As Remy had discovered where I worked, however, he might have found where I now lived as well. To thwart any attempts to track me, I drove to my new apartment via what I thought were devilishly circuitous pathways. All the way, I kept a sharp eye on my rearview mirror in case Remy managed to tail me. Fortunately, for the purposes of spotting his car (if not for purposes of aesthetics), my exboyfriend's car sported the distinctive grill of a vintage Ford Edsel. (When he bought that junked car and had it restored to its original gawkiness, I should have known our relationship could never thrive.)

The maze-like itinerary I followed through town to my apartment kept me on the road about four times longer than usual, and I had plenty of time to second-guess my plan to search for a woman who hummed more than she talked and who remained mysterious even when she did talk. For one thing, searching for a white lilac tree was not the sort of fact-based research I had been trained for in grad school. I slid my hand into my jeans pocket and pulled out the silver tree with the seed pearls. Holding it up to catch the light, I sighed. It was only the shadow of a clue, if that.

While I was looking away from the road to return the silver tree to my pocket, a light shining in my mirror revealed a car traveling close behind me. And it could not be confused with any other make or model: if a car could be said to have a facial expression, the ridiculous oval chrome

114

moue of Ford's tribute to corporate son, Edsel, did. Still miles from home, I took a slightly illegal left turn through a yellow light, sped up my aging Toyota to its modest limit; and, as soon as the lights disappeared from my rearview, I turned sharply into a Safeway parking lot, shot out the other side, drove around the block, and doubled back behind a sedan following the Edsel.

Though I am not exactly a race car driver, I was pretty proud of eluding Remy, and the adrenalin rush from successfully evading my own personal stalker renewed my feeling that I might actually succeed in my quest to find a centenarian. She might be as elusive as a lost chord in a neglected masterpiece, but, who knows, I might find her at her former home curled up like a lost kitten under a white lilac bush. I continued to follow my crazy route home, criss-crossing town so many times I halfway expected to meet myself in the town square.

Truly exhausted by the time I snuck in my side door, I drank a pint of ice water, fell on the couch, and enjoyed the bliss of a mindless nap. I was so worn out, I did not even check my answering machine. Later I would wish I had. When I woke, I showered, letting cool water pound on my head until I felt somewhat energized. I slapped some cheese between two slices of sourdough, ate an apple and drank a Diet Coke, which perked me up some more. Then I packed in my sling bag the food I had on hand--cheese, hummus, a packet of veggie sausages, the rest of the sourdough loaf and some dried apple chips--along with wet wipes, lip moisturizer and eye drops. Lawrence of Arabia carried less in his pack when he set off across the Sinai. I then dressed myself as warmly as if I were planning to search for a Yeti in the Himalayas, and, finally, I stuffed Bibi's size 3 sneakers into my pack.

Before stepping out the door to begin my fanciful search, I peered every which way out the windows to make sure Remy was not hiding behind a bush waiting to pounce. That scarifying thought caused me to wonder at myself again. What was I doing, setting out to rescue an old lady I hardly knew when I had a massive problem of my own from which to rescue myself? I stayed my hand on the doorknob. *No sense running around looking for lilac bushes if the object of my search has already been found.* With reason (or cowardice) as my guide, I delayed my rescue mission once again, seizing on the sudden excuse that I should call Safe Haven and ask if Bibi had been found. Before I called, I checked for phone messages.

"Danielle, I need to talk to you," said my voice mail.

Hearing Remy's voice, I scurried away from the phone, catching my foot in my couch-afghan's yarn and falling on my backside. Scrambling to my feet, I pasted myself flat against the wall. How had Remy found my new phone number? *He could be outside my door right now.*

I had doused the kitchen light when I checked out the window for lurkers, but suddenly I realized the living room light was illuminating me cowering in my own home. Diving to the floor and hunkering down behind my one overstuffed chair, I tried to think things through. While Remy's voice rumbled on and on, I covered my ears and tried to imagine how he could have found my phone number. *I should have moved to Idaho.* Even though Remy had been prevented from directly contacting me at Safe Haven, he had caused a stir there. And, even more troubling, my last meeting with him in person had caused emotional pain to him and physical harm to me. I was afraid to poke my nose out the door.

While I agonized about what to do, the string of messages from Remy kept playing on my machine, evoking memories of our break-up that I preferred not to recall. The disjointed monologue ran from angry threats, through demands to talk about our relationship, thence to pleas for a second chance, and then to what could only be called impassioned love notes, a new tone for Remy. Finally, there was a poem read in Remy's gorgeous baritone, lines Richard Lovelace might have written in the 17th century when love, though lusty, was way prettier than Remy's amorous anger.

Though I had no wish to recall our last night together, I had no choice but to listen to his demand to chat. And the sound of his voice reciting his poem liberated the memory of the night I walked away from Remy and from the university. For long minutes I huddled behind my cozy chair wrapped in the afghan my mother had crocheted for me, remembering how Remy and I had gotten into the mess we were in.

~ ~ ~

A Near Thing

It happened one night when Remy and I had made love until our satin sheets were twisted around us and we were lying on the rug with our entwined feet up on the edge of the bed and our one pillow beneath our heads on the rug. I was in that lovely after-haze of love, just drifting into the first level of sleep, when Remy began to talk. His voice, always deep, always soothing was nudging me off the banks of consciousness into the River Lethe when something he said woke me with a start.

"That was sweet," he murmured. "Reminds me of something that has been taking shape in my mind. A one-woman play. You would be good in it." He said it would be a spin-off of a particular Chekhov play on the department reading list. He was saying one scene in that play would make a perfect Noh play. "It's all in my head," he sighed. All I have to do it write it down. I could get it produced in the department, I know. It would be beautiful, poetic, the heroine's brief words sailing softly as a snowy egret onto Chekhov's rustic scene, speaking the Russian playwright's words within the divine frame of a simple Japanese setting. What a magical merging of genres my Noh play will be."

Shaking, and not with cold, I untangled the sheet and wrapped it around me. "That's too much overlapping," I whispered.

"What are you talking about?" he laughed. Standing, he threw the pillow onto the bed. "You have to agree it's a great idea."

"Yes, the idea of making a Noh play of that particular Chekhov scene where all the joy and sorrow of his heroine were born *is* a fine idea–a concept I shared with you week's ago. I described my idea in minute detail to you, including the words 'sailing softly as a snowy egret.'"

"My dear!" he scoffed. "Who's the one overlapping here? I myself have just told you the idea."

"I have proof," I said, striding across the floor to fetch my copy of Russian plays from our bedroom bookshelf. I pointed to the title page of the play in question where I had sketched out the idea weeks before. He said nothing to my claim of proof, made no further protestations that he had come up with the idea and no accusations that my proof meant nothing. Being the soul of rectitude, he could of course never have taken credit for something that was not rightfully his. He just lay down and rolled away to the far side of the bed–taking our pillow with him–and seemed to go to sleep. It occurred to me that he might be faking sleep; how could I ever again know for sure if he was lying, now that he had stolen an idea from me?

So agonized by the thought that someone I loved could absorb a creative idea I had produced, I had to talk with him about it. How did he come to think the idea was his own? How did such a transfer of thought happen between lovers? I lay beside him, claiming a small corner of our pillow, and spoke my questions quietly to him.

"Please, let's talk about what just happened. I know you wouldn't intentionally steal anything from me–or from anyone–but I could use an acknowledgment you made a mistake, even if you made it unconsciously."

He rolled over and tore the pillow from beneath my head. "You call me a thief and you want to chat about it?"

"I know you're not a thief. But do you think borrowing a creation from someone close to you is okay because tradition whispers in your ear that it must be so?"

Remy rolled away from me again, and lay still. Not a twitch of his fingers or a furrowing of his brow in response. I began crying over how forlorn I felt.

"I love you, Remy. If I agree to meet you in the middle, can you explain to me how this mix-up happened? Maybe we could share credit–you know, produced by you and conceived and written by me?"

Finally he rolled back towards me and embraced me. In his most amorous voice he said, "I love you too. You know that. You're inside me. You're part of me. So everything you create is part of me too."

Shocked, I pulled away from him. "You mean you *know* you took the idea as your own even though I came up with it?

"No, silly," he laughed. "An idea of yours would be mine, because you are part of me."

"If you mean I'm part of you like a leg or a kidney, I suppose you believe when I'm urinating, you can take credit for my pee?"

He leapt out of bed, taking the pillow with him. "If you're going to be crude, I'll sleep on the sofa."

"Don't worry," I said. "I'd rather sleep where I'm known as a person, not a creative organ inside a man."

He huffed out of the bedroom, and I started packing my things. I was just tightening the strap around one of my suitcases when he peered around the door frame. His anger flared up the moment he saw what I was doing.

"You can't be leaving," he said.

"I have to, Remy."

"I can't let you leave."

"Why not? Am I not a free and individual person?"

"Within my protective care, yes."

"Really, and who's to protect me from you?"

He sneered. "Why, do you have someone special in mind for the job?"

"Oh, I don't know, maybe the police–since your

rage is scaring me."

"You *have* been seeing someone else!" he said with dazzling certainty.

I shook my head and tried to say no, but he socked me in the chest before I could get the word out. Courage was knocked out of my body with my breath and I collapsed on the floor.

Remy was quivering. "You are the most maddening woman in creation," he said, as if it were an apology.

"Please let me leave," I gasped.

"No! Now *I* want to talk about this too." For emphasis, he threw the larger of my two suitcases across the room, shattering the full-length mirror on the closet door. It was a thick beveled mirror, old fashioned and meant to last. Never before that night had I seen him do something so violent. I was icy with fear. He was filling the doorway, my only escape route. "Why is this happening?" I whispered, backing away from him.

"Because you are stubborn and crude and you are poisoning our relationship." He grabbed my shoulders and lifted me to my feet. "How could you call me a thief?"

"How could you not try to understand I have a right to my idea?" I squeaked.

He threw me on the bed. "I do understand. Because it's *my* idea!" he shouted, knocking a hole in the bedroom door with his fist. The thought that I was less solid than the door he destroyed with one punch passed through my head. He gathered himself together as if about to explode with the moral outrage of a man betrayed by someone in whose loyalty he had vested all his trust: he glistened with rays of anger like an enraged porcupine bristling with fiery quills.

Happily, just then, the police came pounding on our apartment door. The neighbors had heard our heated disagreement and called them. Before Remy could shoot quills of fire at me, the police entered our bedroom. Remy's blazing rage did not disappear in their presence, but he masterfully turned on the charm of a man who felt rightfully indignant at having his honor insulted. Taking one long step towards me, he gathered me in his arms, like a bale of hay or a boxing bag and grinned, "We were just horsing around. I guess she got scared. Some mares do."

One of the policemen was very young, and his expression was nothing like you see in the movies or on television: his chubby face was so full of concern and compassion for me I imagined it would spill out of him and happily infect Remington. While his partner returned to their car to take a call, the kind officer stayed with me while I re-packed the bag Remy had thrown at the mirror. Then he escorted me past my boyfriend and out of the apartment. The police drove me to a motel and helped me carry my belongings inside. They asked if I wanted to file a complaint, but I did what many women do in such cases, I said no. I hoped it was my maiden–and I hoped only–voyage on the sea of domestic abuse.

~ ~ ~

Now, cuddling my afghan and remembering the well of loss that had opened up between Remy and me that night, I sobbed until I was sweating with the effort. I threw off the afghan and snuck out from behind my cozy chair long enough to wash my face over the bathroom sink. Shuddering at the awful memory of the last words Remy had spoken to me while our heads shared the same pillow, I looked in the bathroom mirror to make myself accept the reality of what had happened between us. Meanwhile Remy's phone messages kept ringing in my head, bringing to mind the look of outrage on his face the night his fist made a hole in the oak door. I was curled in a quivering ball in a corner of the bathroom when the phone rang and a new message blared through my home. With the suddenness of a thunder clap, the anger I had felt at Remy's attitude toward me returned in full force. Leaping up, I ran into the living room and shouted my answer at the machine. "You think your mind is real and mine is not."

Honestly I did not know if Professor Milton and I could work through our differences about my thesis, but I certainly could not return to the department he chaired as long as Remy was there. But, if I failed to find the old woman, Sister Pete might not employ me. Then I would be forced to return to the university. I realized the only way I could do that would be if I finalized the end of my relationship with Remy in a way he could understand and accept. While I was mulling over the possible answers to that life-and-death quiz show, the phone rang again. I startled so extravagantly I slid under the phone table and crouched there tangled in the phone cord while I listened in horror to the latest alarum.

"I'm not going away, Danielle," his gorgeous baritone crooned. "You might as well let me in."

Is he here now! In the driveway? On the porch? I could not make myself get up and peek between the blinds. Remy's voice crooned on, in his most musical tones. *I found out your phone number; I will find out where you live.* That sounded as if he had not found my apartment yet! The huntress had evaded him!

Though the knowledge that he was looking for me weighed like a velvet-covered anvil on my heart, the need to go looking for a lost old lady flared up again. I may not be safe, but someone should be.

~ ~ ~

Athena
*You have probably heard of Athena, the ancient
virgin goddess of Athens who was such a force of nature
she created herself. The Parthenon was her virgin-temple,
where she was revered for her legendary creative power.*

*Until....some men rewrote Athena's life story,
claiming she was born from Zeus's, head--as if he had
conceived the idea of her in his brain.*

*Apparently those who took over Athena's story
meant us to believe that Zeus gave birth to her out his ear
or some other convenient hole in his head, and she lived as
an organ outside him capable only of persuading the public
to embrace his authoritarian values. That faux depiction of
female wisdom as a product of a man's brain has rolled on
and on over the centuries promoting a notion of inequality
of creative power between the sexes. One has to wonder
what Athena thought of the idea that she had no talent not
imparted by a male, and that she must be guided by a man
who would be publically dominant over her forever.*

~ ~ ~

Caught in a Cul-de-sac

Crawling out from under the phone table, I sternly reminded myself, "I've got an old woman to find." I did not feel as grandiose as I might sound: I was shuddering with dread of the day I would have to deal with my ex. But, I reminded myself that the fear of a controlling boyfriend was not as crucial as the concern that a very old woman was possibly outside on a chilly night, without her favorite footwear. I thrust my arms into the coat I had stolen from Bibi's closet, pulled a knit cap over my curls, and, grabbing my sling bag, ran out my side door before I could think twice about it.

Being a very clever sneak, I had parked my car two blocks away to baffle my bitter boyfriend. Sneaking through some strangers' backyards, I retrieved it and, within minutes I had located Bibi's former home. It was a quaint cottage with dingy white siding, sky-blue window shutters and a semi-neglected look. As Sister Pete had told me Rhoda and her husband still lived there, I did not stride up onto the front porch and ring the bell. And, in case Rhoda and the gang were present, I was not about to barge in to see if they had kidnaped their great-aunt and had her tied to a chair. The cottage's windows were dark, though, and I was hopeful the occupants were not home. I stood at the foot of the sagging wooden porch trying not to imagine a stern six-year old girl might burst out the front door at any moment and pelt me with Sunday School pamphlets. All remained quiet, however, and conditions seemed excellent for clandestine activities that night: the nearest streetlight was broken, and I allowed myself to believe I might poke around the yard seeking a white lilac bush.

After making a circuit of the property, however, I was seated on the well-worn slats of the steps, gazing at a lovely unkempt front yard dimly lit by the shattered street lamp. The landscaping featured a rose lattice drooping by the porch, two tall firs, a sad willow, a decrepit apple tree, a wildly propagating hazelnut copse, and a flowering plum that was unlikely ever to flower again. For a moment I was excited when I spotted a butterfly bush whose blooms I knew would be conical and purple in season. However, I knew the shrub could only fool someone who had read a description of a lilac but had never smelled one.

After peering under every branch and frond in the yard, I had not stumbled upon one elderly person snoozing under a shrub. Artemis and her iconic blossoming tree seemed worlds away from me here; not one lilac, white or otherwise, was there to be seen. Why had I imagined for one moment I could dredge up some antique arboreal emblem and code-talk my way to finding a local elder? Was intuition really even a thing? Remy could be right, I might just have an overactive imagination.

The murmuring of Bibi's song was still nosing around in my mind though. *Lilac blossoms of pure white shone like stars on our last night.* Recalling Bibi's *White Lilacs,* I glanced again in the direction of the butterfly bush, in the unlikely case Bibi had mistaken it for her favorite flowering shrub. *Of course not, idiot!* The poor drooping thing stood near the tallest fir in the yard, too close under the evergreen's canopy to have received all the nourishing sunshine it needed for optimal development--even as a fake lilac let alone a real one. Still, the fir had dropped needles for years creating a nice thick coverlet over the whole yard. I imagined even a fragile elderly person might rest comfortably on such a bed.

Then a tantalizing wisp of wind must have passed through the yard, because I imagined that the swing hanging from a fir branch had moved almost imperceptibly. My hackles rose as I stared hard into the darkness where a drift of fir needles lay between the swing and the butterfly bush. Had I overlooked Bibi hiding in the scrub behind the fir tree when I checked before? Just as I was hauling myself to my feet to take one more look under the butterfly bush, I heard the classic snap of a twig in the direction of the tree swing. Though the wan rays of the crippled street light did not reach the swing, I was almost certain I saw it swaying a bit in a lack of discernible wind. Then someone coughed, and it was not a little old lady cough; it was a big baritone hack.

Stepping silently up onto the front stoop, I slid sideways behind the rose trellis, across the front of the cottage and into the overgrown thicket of hazelnut bushes. As silently as a cat burglar, I slipped through the shrubbery into the next yard and made my way through shadows along the tree-lined street to my car two blocks away. I had backed it into the steep driveway of a house whose broken windows and collapsed porch roof declared it abandoned. With a spurt of pride, I silently opened my car door and slid inside, reflecting that I was getting good at this business of cleverly evading someone who was tailing me. As I released the brake, my car rolled silently down the inclined driveway towards the street. Before I made it to the street, however, another car drove up and stopped, blocking my exit. I felt no impulse to ask the driver to pull out of my way; I knew who it was.

Remy and I got out of our cars at the same time. He leaned on his open car door and I leaned on mine.

"You're not very good at this," he grinned.

"At what, minding my own business?" I replied.

"At evading the inevitable."

"The ego of the man who thinks he's inevitable."

"I'm not inevitable, but your path in life is."

"My path is my own business, Remy." (Despite the fact that I could still feel the shape of the man's fist imprinted on my chest, my occasional ability to get lippy in the face of a bully rose strong in me.)

Remy lowered his head to swallow some emotion, and raised it with a more amenable feeling. "I don't mean to intrude on your concerns, Dani. I just want you to reconsider what you're doing."

"What do you imagine I should be doing?"

"What comes naturally."

"I doubt you and I agree on what's natural for me."

"Oh, really? You don't think scholarship comes naturally to you? Finishing your Masters presentation, defending it before your masters committee, getting your degree; then teaching and writing and performing your one-woman shows—you don't think those undertakings are natural to you?"

"Not in the venue where I had hoped to complete those undertakings."

"Look," Remy said in his velvet-vested voice, "I've spoken to Professor Milton. He agrees that losing you would deprive the scholarly world of a bright new voice."

"Really?" I laughed. (Panic made me giddy.) "Has he decided he likes my rebellious ideas about the archetypal female character?"

"Come on, Dani, you can turn his opinion around by acknowledging that the changes made in the old maternal myths were part of the great social progress Mankind has made over the centuries."

"Except that I'm more interested in the even greater progress that could be made in the future by re-infusing the human story with values associated with what you call maternal myths."

Remy shut his car door and moved a step towards me. "What *values*?"

I moved behind my open car door and assumed a bold posture by putting one foot up on the threshold, unfortunately inadvertently trapping myself. What was I thinking, that I could launch myself from the running board up onto a convenient passing flying carpet? "Values of egalitarianism, protection of nature, creativity, and peace."

With a shout, he threw his arms in the air. "Those *are* Mankind's values!"

Slapping the roof of my car, I said, "Not the ones you use in everyday life. Whenever one power-hungry man oppresses a *peaceful* person or country, the system insures that the oppressor wins."

"Only for a while. How long was Hitler in power?"

"Add up the life-expectancies of six-million-plus humans. That long."

Remy took two bold steps towards me. "This is all very clever talk for someone who couldn't manage to stay the course to the end."

Seeing me pull my car door towards me as if it could protect me, he altered his tone to a sleepy wooing river of sound that slithered through the cold night air to my ears. "You need only alter your thesis a bit and defend it to reenter the collegiate world."

"Like you did when you read my Masters' thesis *without my permission*, and changed my conclusion?"

"May I remind you that, when I submitted it for review to Professor Milton, he liked your new conclusion-- that I helped you write!"

"*Your* conclusion, you mean. The moment I caught

the change you made in my paper, I changed the conclusion back to my own."

"Why?" Remy asked, looking truly shocked. "I made it make sense in the modern world. You and I are a great writing team. Your whimsy; my reason."

"Remy, you don't want me to be whimsical; you want me to be lenient, bend-over-backwards, spineless in the face of the status quo, and thus incapable of pointing out an injustice against females in storytelling that's been going on for time immemorial."

"Oh, for God's sake, Danielle, you belong in the world of the university, but it's a big place and you need to bend your ideas a bit to fit in there."

"Please, move your car so I can be on my way."

"I'll drive you home, Dani. We can have that talk we've been meaning to have."

"We talk, and I hurt, here (heart) and here (head)."

He thought about that, while the night rolled on, dew gathered on flower petals, and I wished he would go away. Finally he spoke, and his voice cracked with conflicted feelings.

"Why didn't you tell me you were in so much pain?"

"Why didn't you have the empathy to notice?"

By that time I had made my way around my open car door and eased toward the back bumper, with Remy tracking me like a determined sheep-herding dog. Unfortunately, I had parked so close to the ramshackle garage of the house that I got caught trying to squeeze through to the side away from Remy. Even though only semi-illuminated by the light of a streetlight blocked by trees, I was nearly hypnotized in place by his fierce eye contact, when, with a voice meant to becalm a lecture-room full of undergraduates, he said to me, "You belong in my bed, Danielle."

As scary as he was, and as lonely and off my path as I was, that was just too corny, and I felt a laugh about to punch its way out of me. But, through some odd twist on sympathy, or to forestall my laughter, he was the one who laughed. But laughing revived the coughing fit that had revealed him to me back at the cottage, and, while he was bent over recovering his breath, I jumped up onto the trunk of my car, slid across it on my butt, landed on my feet on the other side, and made a woman-sized hole through a laurel hedge. I got some scratches on forearms, and one pant leg got caught on a branch. But I was able to tear it free and run away. We had nowhere near resolved our dispute, but maybe I had managed to keep him at bay for another day.

~ ~ ~

The Underpass

I did not know the neighborhood at all, but on the way to Bibi's former home I had passed a place I did know well, and I headed for it, climbing over sagging fences and crashing through hedgerows gone to seed in this slightly frowzy part of town. I would have to cross the road that ran under the freeway, but it was late enough in the evening that I would be risking my life only a little bit.

I was recovering from running headlong into a birdhouse hanging on a tree in someone's yard when I remembered that one place to look for a homeless runaway was under an overpass. The Edsel had not followed me thus far, and, as the abandoned house where my car was parked was in a complex string of cul-de-sacs, it would take Remy a while to get to the freeway. I figured I had time to investigate the nearby underpass on my way to the place I was pretty certain Remy could not find me–if he still wanted to find me after I had failed to succumb to his ultimate seduction line.

Through three more cul-de-sacs lying along the freeway, over yards scattered with kids' toy cars, and, around (thankfully) empty wading pools, I made my way to the overpass. Fortunately there was a gap where some interloper had clipped and rolled back the cyclone fence along the freeway, or I would never have made it out of the last yard to the roadway. While squeezing through the hole, I snagged the coat I had stolen from Bibi's closet, but I made it through.

There was a steep ice plant-covered bank leading from the fence to the crossroad, and making my way down the incline I was tripped up by a cover of the thick creeping plants and sent rolling down the berm. Ice plant retains water like a *sumbitch*, as Lonny would say, and my clothes

132

were drenched with plant juice by the time I landed on the gravelly shoulder of the road. Before I could make my way down the freeway to the underpass, the headlights of a car came bowling down the freeway. Lying at the foot of the berm where dry leaves had mingled with newspapers and other detritus tossed out of car windows, I performed my most challenging acting role so far, *Pile of Debris*. With my head buried in a nest of the crumbled pages of last month's *County Journal,* I could not see whether the headlights had the distinctive Edsel grill between them. When the vehicle continued down the freeway without seeing me quivering in a pile of trash, I resumed breathing.

After my gambol through the ice plant, I warily approached the underpass, trying to get my eyes to work like a raccoon's. It was dark under there and smelled dark, like rat skat, rusted chrome bumpers and the dusty oil puddles that accumulate under old junker cars. Just when the cement pillars supporting the highway above were becoming visible, I heard the unmistakable sound of a helicopter flying along the freeway and coming my way. Was it about to poke its nose under this very overpass? But the copter clattered on down the freeway leaving me feeling strangely annoyed that it had failed to make a hazardous flight through the underpass to look for Bibi.

Feeling my way along the foot of the overpass, I realized I had dressed too warmly for my adventure. I was bumbling along like a big bear in a small cave sweating profusely under sweaters, jackets and Bibi's burly coat, Still mostly blind in the near-complete darkness, I scratched my hands on what must have been a nail semi-imbedded in the rough concrete of the freeway piers. I was scrabbling around in my pack for my flashlight to examine my wounded hand when the copter suddenly rose up from the tree-lined streets of the housing project; I did not dare turn on the light. Instead, I nipped in around the first cement pillar and waited in the underpass for the sound of the copter to ebb away towards town. When I lit up my hand to see how badly I was injured, someone or something grabbed my leg.

Shouting and jumping back, I took with me whatever had captured me. The light flew out of my hand and landed in a pile of something that obscured its light. I had the presence of mind to try to kick away whatever was holding on to me. Then magically the flashlight was resurrected from wherever it had landed, and, with one grand sweep, it flashed around the whole underpass. Desperately scanning the lit area, I saw in the wash of the flashlight the personage holding onto my leg. It was definitely a human being, though one obviously not as vicious as I had feared. The clinging hands belonged to a young woman whose face shone pale and remarkably clean for someone sleeping rough under a freeway. And, as the expression on her face suggested she was even more frightened than I was, I leaned down and began to pry her fingers off my leg.

"I'm not here to hurt you," I said. "I'm looking for my friend." I looked up at a second underpass resident, the one who was holding my flashlight. *Has not killed me yet, so probably not going to.* "Have you seen an old woman down here?"

The flashlight-holder directed the light to a third resident of the underpass who was rolled up in a wooly blanket towards the other end of what appeared to be a homeless lair. The young woman who had gripped my leg let me go. I made my apology for having frightened her and thanked her for releasing me. Then I approached the

134

flashlight person and found he was also young and clean of face. Young lovers running away from disapproving families? I would have liked to hear their story, but after making another apology for intruding on their rest and explaining why I needed my flashlight back, I gratefully received it and approached the third party loitering in the Underpass Motel.

He or she had not so much as twitched during my set-to with Romeo and Juliet, and, even when I stood over the unknown party and flash-lit him or her, I detected no movement. I could see clearly, though, that the sleeping person had white hair, and that it was straight, not newly permed. Also I could see that her face was no more lined than the face of any forty-year old who has spent half her life sleeping rough. The blanket in which she was wrapped was rising and falling over her chest, and, though I wished I could take the three lost souls back to my apartment and feed them hot soup, I knew that was not a good idea. For one thing, they had their reasons for being here, and I had my reasons for being elsewhere. Besides, the resourceful Remy would likely be glad to interfere with any such altruistic mission I might undertake at present. I walked on across the underpass to the far side to continue my long search for the much older person whom I feared needed my help far more than the young lovers or Sleeping Beauty.

~ ~ ~

The Arboretum

The freeway ran along the edge of town, separating most homes and businesses from the thinly populated area I was now approaching. Though I had never slept under or even walked under this overpass, I was more familiar with this side of the freeway than with Bibi's old neighborhood. The hilly area east of the freeway was wooded and mostly wild, but there was one place tucked into the wilderness I had often visited. It was a large estate, a legacy inherited from a wealthy donor who had designated it as an island of culture and art. It was duly called the Arboretum of the Arts. A college of arts and crafts was planned for the future, but, already there was a theater surrounded by an actual arboretum landscaped with flowers, shrubs and trees featured in literature worldwide. I knew my way around this woodsy campus just outside of town, because I had enjoyed a gig as actor in residence at the Arboretum Theater during the gap year before my graduate year at university.

While performing in plays at the Arboretum Theater, I had enjoyed wandering among the shrubs and trees featured in world literature. Because Bibi's memory seemed exceptional for a person of any age, I thought she might have remembered I had said there was a thicket of lilacs in the Arboretum devoted to the piece of historical fiction called *White Lilacs.* Chances of finding her hanging out there were slim to nil, but, other than in my grandma's garden and in the book I read as a girl, it was the only white lilac in my memory bank.

The berm on the Arboretum side of the freeway was thick with local types of brush: hazel nut, wild cherry, blackberry vines. Good thing my recent acquaintances had been kind enough to give me back my flashlight. Without it I could not have avoided the prickly blackberry vines, which in many places hampered access to the cultivated part of the Arboretum. There was no wall on the steep western side of the place, which rose high above the freeway, and making my way uphill through patches of blackberry vines, I reached the park proper with no more than a few scratches.

While I was standing under a wild cherry tree trying to figure out where I was in relation to the lilacs, the helicopter returned. Hugging the tree, I tracked the copter as it approached but it did not fly over the thick arboreal area. The helicopter followed the freeway again along the rim of the housing development, illuminating the yards and streets with its searchlight panning back and forth and then headed back towards the center of town. If they were looking for the missing centenarian, they must have figured she could not have made it past the populated areas. If I had any sense, I reflected, I would have figured the same thing. But I could not go home until I figured out how to deal with Remy anyway. And, unlikely as my proposed itinerary for finding the old woman was, I could think of nothing better to do at the moment than to follow my intuition.

Underneath a nearby hemlock (dedicated to Plato's account in his *Phaedo* about Socrates' demise, as I recalled), I paused to get my bearings. Shining my light on the placard next to a Japanese pine tree, I saw that it symbolized wisdom and longevity. I thought that was a good starting point for someone seeking a woman who had more longevity than any other person I knew. I hoped she was wise enough to have managed to find safety and shelter wherever she was, whether cuddled in the mulch beneath a lilac bush or–just as unlikely--sequestered in the home of one of her aggressive family members.

The Japanese pine was on the west side of the park,

located logically near a Japanese garden bridge arching over a small creek that ran at the Arboretum's edge. Realizing I could hear the creek babbling nearby, I turned in the opposite direction towards the eastern edge of the garden where I knew the lilacs grew. After stumbling through a swath of Alyssum–which I should have recognized by their sweet scent and avoided–and nearly falling into the koi pond, I found the meandering pathway and, at its easternmost curve, located the fragrant lilacs. Not that I really expected to find Bibi curled up under the branches of a bush waiting for me, but, on the off chance she was huddled under them and in need of immediate rescue, I shone my light along the base of the plants.

Before I could stride into the lilac copse calling the old woman's name, I heard a loud splash, coming from behind me in the vicinity of the fish pond. Either a very large koi had slapped the water, a turtle had taken a high dive off the observation platform, or somebody had fallen into the pond. I turned off my light and, continuing on the winding path–which luckily was paved in this part of the Arboretum–I crept to the opposite side of the pond from the place where the splash had occurred.

And there was Remy, lit by his own flashlight which had dropped onto an azalea bush, and, still shining bright, was aimed up at his face. I startled and unintentionally grasped my own light, which turned on. Remy looked right at me from across the pond. Fortunately, he was knee-deep in giant koi, and the fish, who were certain he had come to feed them, were leaping, flashing in golden arcs all around him. Before Remy oriented himself, I was able to turn off my light and run away along the paved path to the Japanese bridge.

The meandering walkway bent too close to the koi

pond, however, and Remy must have anticipated my course; for suddenly he was standing before me about twenty feet away on the path. Leaving the paved way, I ducked behind a huge rhododendron and ran to a gazebo where I had taken lunch breaks with other Arboretum Theater actors. I remembered that once, exhausted between long rehearsals, I had napped in a space under the gazebo where the koi pond's water pumps were housed. With a man way too clever at tracking his runaway girlfriend close behind me, I shoved aside the lattice cover of the door leading to the underside of the gazebo and slipped inside, pulling the lattice closed behind me. It was only a decorative door, but maybe my tracker would mistakenly think I would know better than to hide there. The sound of a man crashing through some very expensive landscaping was unsettling, but the sight of man-sized sneakers pussy-footing past the gazebo was terrifying.

Danielle, Danielle! He was calling to me in a whisper, which was odd. No one who might have heard him calling would come into the garden at night, so why whisper? I did not answer and was managing not to breathe any louder than necessary, when someone across the koi pond called in a loud stage whisper, "Is that the night watchman? I'm looking for a missing girl."

Even if there should be a sympathetic security guard in the vicinity, I did not pop out of the gazebo and volunteer to play the role of Missing Girl. I heard some more of the manly monologue, which receded to a distant murmur as the man wandered away through the rare plants toward the southern edge of the park. Only when I could no longer hear him at all, did I make my careful way to the garden bridge. I had just reached it when suddenly there he was, standing on the arched span. A noisy gasp escaped me.

How did he get there? Quickly I ducked under the bridge. Hearing his footsteps moving to the point where I had been standing, I crossed to the north side of the bridge, and, while he was peering over the south side, I snuck away along the creek bank as silently as I could go. He flashed his light up and down the creek bed, but I hid behind a boulder until the light and his footsteps went away. It took a while.

As I descended the rocky slope to the base of the creek bed, I began to cry. I was exhausted, scared for myself, sad for Bibi, and frustrated by my so-far thwarted mission to find her, which was going spectacularly badly. First, Remy's intrusive presence had prevented me from really searching for her among the lilacs, and, now I was as good as lost. *But Bibi is lost to everyone who knew her.* I had a nail wound in my hand and a bunch of blackberry vine scratches, but Bibi was out in the world somewhere, perhaps suffering purposely-inflicted pain, or neglect, or confusion. She might even be dying alone, like the dog Lonny had imagined she imitated. And here I was, traipsing around in the wilderness imagining I might find her where no one ever went. *But I have to go somewhere, hoping I will find her there.* I slipped on a wet boulder at the bottom of the creek bed and fell painfully on a bed of jagged rocks. I had reached a state where I could scarcely tell the difference between my minor hurts and the pain Bibi might be feeling, when, with a surge of heroic energy I stood up and strode onward. *I must find her. I will find her.* Instantly I stumbled over a thick branch and folded into a squat, whereupon the air went out of me all at once, and my grand image of myself as a heroine went with it.

After crouching crumpled on a bed of damp mossy rocks for a long moment while I recovered my breath, I was scrambling to an upright position when some animal screeched in the scrub near the bridge. I startled and fell flat on my face for the third time. Painfully rolling onto my side, I managed to sit on the only smooth boulder my rear-end could locate. Listening to track the path the shrieking creature might take in relation to my position, I was seriously considering that my idea of finding an old lady I hardly knew by using a brooch and a song about lilacs to guide me did not rise even to the level of whimsy. Not for the first time, I thought Remy might be right about me. Perhaps facing the music with him and the college was the only mission I ought to be pursuing after all. I almost turned back towards the bridge with the idea of finding my way to my car and home.

But a second horrendous screech from what sounded like a very large animal with probably pointy teeth and an appetite for whimsical young women sounded under the bridge. *Run away* were the only two words in my head, and I ran, stumbling over rocks and splashing through what was left of a seasonally diminished creek, away from a yowling varmint on the hunt.

~ ~ ~

Persephone

It was at that time of year just past harvest, the season when the corn stalks shrivel and rattle in the fields and frost tips the rims of the empty furrows, when the Great Earth Mother Demeter began to wander the earth grieving for her lost daughter. Persephone had that morning announced, "Mother, now is the time I must leave my childhood behind and go on a quest to the Underworld."

"The Underworld?" Demeter gasped. "What for?"

"I want to comfort the newly dead," said Persephone.

Demeter laughed, "What do you plan to do, just unlock the door to eternity and step right in?"

But Persephone knew in her bones the cipher that opens the door between life and death, and that night, between sunset and sunrise, she disappeared.

Demeter searched for her daughter through the fields and the woods, from lakeshore to hilltop, until at last in the depths of her own home, she fell to the ground, crying out in despair, "Persephone, your mother needs you!" And, when she spoke the code word, "Mother," the ground split beneath her, revealing a passage leading down and down and down into the Underworld. Demeter walked through the portal.

To her surprise, Demeter found herself in a large space without ceiling or walls. A friendly dog suddenly appeared and led her down a meandering path. All around her, she heard the voices of souls praising Persephone as "Queen of the Underworld," but she never caught up to her dauntless daughter.

When Demeter finally returned to the land of the living, the seasons had changed, and happily she found that Persephone herself had returned to herald a gentle Spring.

*The joyful reunion of mother and daughter foretold that a
bounteous Fall would be enjoyed by all. And every year
after that, when Winter came, Persephone made her trip to
the Underworld to ease the final transition of the newly
dead. And every Spring she returned to celebrate the
emergence of the year's new crops.*

*Until....somebody stole Persephone's story and
deliberately demeaned her character. And it is this revised
story that has come down to us. In the rewrite, when
Demeter followed Persephone into the afterlife, she ran
into Pluto, the god who ran things in the Underworld.
When she asked Pluto where Persephone might be offering
comfort to frightened souls, he laughed.*

*"Here's what happened, lady. Your daughter came
pussy-footing into my domain and was mollycoddling a
bunch of the newly dead. I saw right away that she was a
pretty young thing whose charms would be wasted on a lot
of sad sack stiffs. So I stalked her, captured her, and since
then I have held her in confinement as my concubine. So
get lost, lady. There are no visitors in hades!"*

"I'm no visitor," Demeter cried. "I'm her mother!"

Pluto shut the door to eternity in her face.

*The degradation of Persephone from comforting
earth goddess to sexual slave of the King of Hades has
titillated readers for centuries, blotting out the ideal of
empathy that Persephone represented. Christians went so
far as to rename her the Queen of She-Demons, to warn
people not to emulate the rebel's kind heart.*

*But Persephone's story may still arouse some hope
for whatever lies beyond the last door, be it joy, comfort, or
merely uninterrupted rest. You could say Persephone was
the Hospice of the ancient world, and that her great
empathy is still exemplified in the Hospice movement. ~ ~ ~*

Bibi's Itinerary

She was a silhouette beside a small campfire in the creek bed, weaving back and forth, maybe trying to keep her balance. She was uttering sounds, but I could not make out any words. I fancied she might be dancing and chanting *código* like Monte's *abuela*. Then the silhouette sat down on what I would discover was a moss-covered log. Fearing to startle her, I did not turn on my flashlight. But, as I carefully approached, I could see by the firelight that she was resting one hand on a knobby branch as if it were a cane, and with the other hand she was holding a pussy willow wand on whose tip was a roasting marshmallow. With fierce concentration she held the stick steady over the fire. Then I realized she was singing quietly. I could not tell if it was her white lilac song.

Remaining several yards away from her, I spoke. "Bibi, is that you?"

She startled, not only because of me, but because at that moment another scary animal in the bushes behind me let out a hungry shriek. It did not sound as big and ferocious as the one by the bridge--a feral cat, perhaps, or a coyote. Ferocious enough, though, to make Bibi jump up and point her marshmallow skewer at me like a fencer's foil.

"What you want?" she cried, waving her stick.

I was so happy to see her I would have grabbed her in a bear hug if I did not think that would freak her out even more than I might already have done. So I just smiled and joked, "Easy, Gramma."

"Not your gramma," she snapped, lofting her marshmallow stick over the fire. "Nobody's gramma." She added with a gurgly sort of laugh and focused her attention on her marshmallow.

"Do you know me, Bibi?" I asked. I'm Danielle.

144

Remember? From Safe Haven."

The old woman clucked. "Safe? Like nuclear war."

"Safer than a dry creek bed," I mentioned, looking around at the desolate locale.

"There's a trickle of water here year-round," she said, as if I had insulted the amenities of her palace.

"Impressive," I said, Looking around at the impenetrable tangle of brush and looming trees lining the dusty, rocky waterway. "I suppose the tree branches arching overhead keep off the rain."

"Guess I'll find out," she muttered, turning her stick to brown the flip-side of her marshmallow.

"How in the world did you get here?" I asked, venturing closer to the fire.

"Hitched a ride."

"You'd think a driver seeing an elderly lady wandering out of doors would report her to the authorities."

"Kid in a rusty pick-up. Gave him a few bucks." She chuckled. "Kids love to get a few bucks."

"How did you get through the brush to the creek?"

She shrugged. "He dropped me at the Arboretum entrance. Slipped around the gate. Followed the sound of the water."

A spasm of sadness shot through me, to think of her stumbling down this rugged creek bed. I'd fallen on my face three times. How had she managed?

"Did you get hurt on the way here?"

"Did *you*?" she said, peering at the bloody scarf I had wrapped around my hand.

"It'll be easier going on the way back, Bibi, because I'll be here to help you get home."

She turned towards me and, looking confused, let her marshmallow stick dip towards the campfire. "Home?"

she croaked, "Where's that?" Then a look of hope traveled across her face. "What's in that bag there?"

"Just some food. But now I've found you we can get you back for a real meal, Bibi. May I call you Bibi?" She looked doubtful; did she not remember me? "Or, do you prefer your formal name, Mrs. Bell?"

"Formality in a creek bed? Ha. Just plain Mrs. B. If you're the Old Lady Police, you can spell it *Bibi* on the rap sheet."

"I'm your friend, Dani."

"Old ladies got no friends, dear."

Seeing she was in a mood, I pulled her sneakers out of my bag and set them by her feet. She was wearing her roommate Bettina's fur-lined satin slippers. They were much too big for her and the toes had been shortened with shoelaces tied around them. They had seen some rough use in the creek bed. "I brought you these," I said. "You must have forgotten them."

"Meant to leave 'em," she snorted. Then she gave me a suspicious look. "Why you got my shoes?"

"Why did you leave your shoes behind?"

"Is there an echo?" she scoffed, then devoted herself to the task of rescuing her marshmallow from the fire.

The relief at having found her caught up with me suddenly and I reached between her fiery roasting stick and her cane to hug her. Her knit cap fell off. I plucked some burrs out of the weave and tried to put it back on her head.

"Made me drop my supper in the fire!" she scolded, pushing the hat away.

The old woman's anger was an odd consolation to me, in comparison to the confusing barrage of shame and blame to which Remy had recently subjected me. But, having succeeded in my quest to find Bibi--possibly to save her life–I was feeling too exhilarated to dwell on what a sad thing I was making of my own life.

Opening my bag, and pulling out packets of food, I said, "You're going to char your marshmallows, if you don't watch out."

She skewered a marshmallow that had fallen on a piece of unburnt wood, blew the fire off it, lifted the roasted glop to her mouth, and proceeded to nibble charred goo off the stick with the daintiness of a raccoon at dinner.

"Mind telling me what you're doing in my woodsy bower?" she said, cooly resting her stick on a log and sliding open the ziplock bag of veggie links I had brought.

"What am *I* doing here? What are you doing here? Was it something I said?"

"Don't wanna talk." She made herself busy slicing a link lengthways and slipping a slice of cheese into it.

"No, really, Bibi, was it something about my story of Daphne and Apollo? Did you really want to run away to the wild and become a tree?"

"Pity sakes," she said looking disgusted. "I may be old as a Sequoia--but a tree?"

"Maybe one of the trees in the arboretum? A white lilac, perhaps, like in your song? Did you come here because of what I said about the white lilacs in the Arboretum?"

"Songs aren't treasure maps! Songs just tell feelings beyond the everyday."

"You didn't leave your tree pin with the white beads on it as a hint you were going looking for a white lilac?"

"There's no getting back my white-lilac days, girly."

Blushing to think I had been searching under shrubs for the woman, I asked, "Then why did you come to the Arboretum?"

"Old man who ran away from Safe Haven that time told me about this place. Lasted five days here. I figured five days was long enough."

"Long enough for what?

"Shut up and let me eat my pig-in-a-blanket."

"What do you want me to tell Sister Pete and your family? They're very worried."

She stopped chewing and almost choked. "Don't you dare tell Sister Pete or my half-assed kinfolk I'm here!"

"Admittedly, your people are not going to be nominated as Family of the Year, but Sister Pete, for all her officiousness, has a kind heart."

"The nun would lock me up, and that wouldn't keep me safe from my loving grandnieces."

"Wouldn't being where you could be checked on regularly be preferable to dying of exposure, starvation or drowning in a creek bed?"

"The rains will come, but by then I'll be gone." She had roasted her cheesy link over the fire and chewed it neatly right off the roasting stick.

"Gone where? Is this just one stop on a journey to your true destination?"

"My itinerary: first stop creek, next stop eternity."

"You came here to die!"

"'Bout time, I'd say."

"To die? Even at your age, how can you say that?"

"My whole life is empty as a sock thrown on the floor. 'Bout time I let my life go where all empty lives should go. Into the abyss."

"Bibi, you are the least empty person I know. You hum while others make small talk or tell lies. You laugh when you are amused even if everyone else remains silent. You have the courage to speak up to a nun."

148

"Force of habit dealing with phonies–though, Sister Pete isn't *too* phony."

"And yet you left her to worry about you."

"I didn't leave her; I left my family. What do I care if they challenge the will? It's their father's will; they can do what they want with it. But the result will be that I'd be the poorest old lady in Safe Haven, dying slowly in plain sight like a neglected potted plant on the shelf. 'Druther disappear magically all at once, thanks."

"That's it, You just walked out of your favorite tennis shoes? When I saw them in your closet it was as if you had walked out of your own skin. Why did you really leave them?"

"I wanted them all to think I was defunct."

"But, why? Why walk out of your life?"

"My own family buried my nephew without taking me to the funeral so I could say a real goodbye. Do I need more reason than that? But, that same day, for a birthday present, they denied I had something to do with the songs that made my nephew well-off. Isn't having your contribution erased enough of a reason to disappear? The last person who really recognized my existence was my husband Roger, and they buried him across the sea where I could not even visit his grave. Now my nephew Wally's dead, the only person besides me who knows me. I felt like my family was about to stuff me live into a coffin to be clasped tight within dark walls until every tune that had ever entered my head, every song I ever sang would be deprived of the breath necessary for singing it. Well, little Missy, that was not going to happen to me. I could not stand to look at any of their faces--not one more time: my family, my jailers, my smiling torturers. If they could not feel my presence as I really am; if they could not know me

149

for what I created, they might know me by my absence. If they ask why I have gone, tell them *I had the character to reject them utterly.* Tell them I said, *if I die here, that is okay, because though I am dead to you, I am triumphantly dead to you. I am where you cannot hurt me anymore by discounting me!"*

The awful rush of self-immolation in her words nearly silenced me, but I had to say something. "You are where they cannot hurt you anymore, but you are also where you cannot protest their neglect anymore."

"Missy, if you think I'm going to walk back and forth on the sidewalk in front of their homes carrying signs of protest, you got another think coming. Kindly just go away, and let me be. You can't possibly understand what a burden a lifetime of disregard of a woman's actual function in the world can do to her."

After that long-suppressed deluge poured out of her, she folded herself in on herself closer and closer until she was a taut shadow crouching in a pile of leaves with her back to the fire. Although I had to respect her profound desire to disappear from the people in her life, if I did not say something to persuade her to let me help her, my own identity as a useful person was seriously at risk.

"Bibi," I said, "All I want to know right now is what to say to comfort you."

"Honey, some grief is too deep to chat about."

"But—"

"Have you told me what grievous acts made you dump your ex?"

"I told you, he stole from me."

"He steal your life, your soul, your good works?"

Something about that old lady made me feel it was time to face the music. So I told her in that wild forsaken place the thing I had tried to forget, how I had to break up with a great man, a brilliant playwright, a genius in my eyes, and a wonderful lover. I told her about the night Remy claimed he had created an idea I had shared with him. I told her how profoundly hurt and alone I had felt ever since. By the time I finished my tale, I was sitting beside her on her mossy log with my head in her lap crying the rest of the tears I had brought with me.

Bibi hummed a bit while I cried, then briefly patted my curly head. "Tears are for when you lose your best love," she said. "Though if you lost him over a little play that was never even produced–well, sobbing in the wilderness might be a bit melodramatic."

I sat up and wiped my eyes. "Your sympathy is overwhelming." Neatly folding my wet hanky in fourths and then eighths, I tucked it in my pocket. "He absorbed my idea as his own, and then asserted that it was I who was trying to steal from him. That was the death blow to our relationship."

"My dear girl, when he dies; *that's* the death blow to a relationship." She stuck another sausage on her skewer.

What was I to say to that? I just sat on that crumbling log, feeling wiped out from pouring out my grief to someone I had thought would surely understand but seemed not to. Then suddenly it occurred to me it might be okay to express annoyance at a willful old lady. "Come on, Bibi, I've bared my soul to you. What about your story, the one you hum about?"

"My story? *The very old person died: The end.*"

"Oh, no you don't! You promised to tell me about the song you hum."

"I've talked more words tonight than I talked in toto my whole life. What more do you want?"

"Telling me about the song called *White Lilacs* would be a good start."

"Never heard of it."

"But I heard you sing about white lilacs at your birthday party."

"No you didn't."

"I did, and it had the same tune that you hum."

"It's a tune I like to hum. What's it to you?" She poked at her campfire.

"I can't figure out why the melody is so haunting to me. My folks may have sung the song around their upright piano. If I knew why the song haunts you, maybe I could figure out why it stuck with me."

She snapped her willow wand over her knee. "Why is everyone always trying to take it from me!"

"Take what from you?"

"The song. Maybe I hum it to myself to *keep* it to myself. You ever think of that?"

"Bibi, I can't *take* it from you. I believe it was in my head before I even heard you humming it. Who else do you think tried to steal it?"

"You know who. My family."

"Yes, I remember your hinting that your nephew falsely claimed authorship of your songs. You must want to do something about that."

"I know the truth. Who cares what the rest of the world thinks?"

"Bibi, I think it's crucial that we don't ever let people take credit for what we create, at least not without complaint. You've said as much about yourself."

"My nephew's gone. Should I knock on ASCAP'S office door holding a pile of songs with my name scribbled on them?"

"You give up your creations very easily."

For a moment she looked as if she were going to hit me, but she crumpled between the log and the fire. "My god, you are cruel."

"Bibi, I know a little something about losing something I created to someone close to me, and it would be a comfort to me to help you reclaim what you lost to your family."

"You lost a little spin-off of a play from faraway Russia. What I lost...." The next word got caught in her throat and she stared down into the coals for a time as if she were viewing her past life illuminated. Then she began to hum, the lyrics of the song rising gradually out of the melody.

Once, when the moon shone bright above,
I gave to you my perfumed glove;
Today I ask the stars above,
What of our vow of lasting love?

Faded lilacs, tarnished ring,
The warring world wrecked everything,
And now what may tomorrow bring?
How shall I e'er again face Spring?

She sat with her back to me for long minutes before I dared speak. Tears had sprung to my eyes at the thought of my parents, singing that song together at the end of World War II. It was the first night he was home after his service in the Navy that they sang that song, harmonizing while my father leaned on the upright piano and my mother played, tears I did not understand at the time running down her face and plashing on the keyboard. "Thank you," I murmured to

Bibi. "Now I recognize the tune you're always humming! It was the one my parents called *their* song. They're gone now and, Bibi, I'm so glad you've returned their song to me. I'm guessing it must be of inestimable value to you too."

"Hummph. More than to your folks, I'm guessing. I wrote it the day some people came to my door and told me my new husband had died in the war."

"Oh. We were afraid that's what it might mean."

"S'pose you think I was a floozy whose sleazy lover dumped me?"

"Nothing like that. Although we wondered why you still have your maiden name, Bell."

"Oh, poo. My husband urged me to keep that name. Said the name Bell would sell. "

"How sweet. We didn't know any of that."

"You keep saying *We*? Does my family know my pain? And yet they act the way they do? That's monstrous."

"By *we* I mean Monte Diaz and I. You know, one of the aides at Safe Haven. We put our heads together to try to think where you might have gone."

"Oh. Monte's a good kid. I don't mind him knowing about Roger. He sang *Happy Birthday* to me in Spanish. I sang along in English. First time I sang with anybody since my nephew Wally."

She paused for a while, poking at the campfire with her broken willow stick, and, seeming to become mesmerized by the embers, she started talking about her husband. "When I sang one of my songs to Roger, he would harmonize with me. For years after he was taken, I kept my soul intact by humming that song night and day. I can still hear his harmonies echoing in my head."

The fire had all but died before she looked up at me.

"You still here?"

"I stayed to thank you for keeping your promise to tell me the story behind your song. My parents' song and your song with your husband. Bibi, I can't help believing Roger would want you to reclaim your rights to *your song*."

"Oh, poo. I only told you about Roger because I felt sorry for you and your little tiff with your boyfriend." She was dipping her broken willow wand in and out of the campfire's coals, and nodding along with it. "Roger's gone; you want your boyfriend gone. Presto! Bibi will soon be gone too."

"Gone back to Safe Haven?"

"Oh, no you don't. I like it here where I'm invisible to the world."

"*I* see you, Bibi."

She cringed as if I had hit her. "You ruined my plan to disappear. Now, if only you would disappear. "

Too long had I been sitting on a rock in the chill of the evening tying to convince an old woman to rejoin the human race. I was tired and cold, getting stiffer by the minute, and I probably needed a tetanus shot for my punctured hand. I played my last card.

"Bibi, I *am* going to disappear now. And the first thing I'm going to do when I leave here is to go home and make a big sizzling macaroni and cheese casserole with scads of cheese: Monterey Jack, extra-sharp Cheddar, Parmesan, Romano–"

"Stop it! You are a cruel girl!" she cried.

"Bibi, it's time to go."

She stood up. "I said stop!" She kept shushing me and waving her knobby branch towards the thick wall of trees on the west side of the creek bed. "You hear that?"

I had heard it. Something was moving through the

brush, and it was not the wind.

"Could be your exboyfriend."

"Could be a raccoon," I whispered. "Or even a mountain lion. Actually I would prefer that to my ex."

"Not me. I don't have enough energy left to fend off so much as a baby raccoon with my knobby stick."

"You will have to, because I'm not going to leave you here with no firewood, little food, and maybe a hungry cougar lurking nearby."

As if on cue, whatever animal was crashing about in the bushes beside the creek bed let out a shriek that made the hair on my neck stand up and made the old woman jump behind me for protection.

"That's a mighty big raccoon," she hissed in my ear.

"More like a mountain lion, I think." I hauled my sling bag strap over my head and started walking towards the bridge. "I'm going; you coming?"

"Dammit to Hell!" she grumbled. "I don't mind living the rest of my short life in a dry creek bed or dying for lack of food." Just then some wild thing shrieked right behind us, and Bibi jumped up onto my back, crying, "But I *do* mind dying to make a meal for a mountain lion."

With her on my back, I scurried along the creek towards the Japanese bridge, with the beast growling and crashing through the brush closer and closer behind us. As old as she was, Bibi had a pretty tight grip, and, as exhausted as I was, I could move pretty fast, with a cougar on my trail.

~ ~ ~

Monte to the Rescue

While helping the old woman struggle up the gravely scree to the bridgehead, I turned once to see how close the cat was. I was relieved to see it had not wanted to eat us but only to drink from the trickling creek. I did not tell Bibi that we were safe; I was afraid she would return to her campfire. I did feel eyes on us as we crawled up onto the Japanese bridge, and I assumed it was the lion contemplating having a meal with his drink. My plan was to hurry west across the bridge and make my way back to the place where I left my car. Turning towards the far end of the span, I realized with rising panic that I had left my car in a cul-de-sac far away on the other side of the freeway deep in a housing project. And that was not the only thing preventing me from getting to my car; for I could see a man-sized dark patch silhouetted against a nebulous spill of light from the city some miles to the west. Even if a man were not blocking our exit, I could not climb down the hill, crawl through the blackberry vines and scamper through a string of people's back yards to my car with an old person on my back. I would have to find help inside the Arboretum.

No sense whispering *Run away!* in the ear of a half-deaf woman. I just scooted her higher up onto my back and ran east through the thick of the Arboretum. I half-expected this one final task of the night to do me in, but, weighed against my burden, a bag of feathers would have tipped the scales. With Bibi clinging for dear life to my hips with her spindly legs, I ran off the wooden bridge and into the greenery.

Before I had gone six yards, the man-sized shadow I had seen on the bridge called out, "Stop! I mean no harm."

"I'll bet," I called back over my shoulder and kept

on running with my sack of feathers flopping on my back.

"Please stop, Dani!" the voice cried.

"Get lost, Remy!" I shouted, speeding towards the Arboretum Theater. I used to know a secret way in; maybe I could sneak in and use a phone to call for help.

Footsteps continued scrunching after us on the graveled path. "I'm not Remy!" he shouted.

Being nearly out of breath, I forbade to answer. But Bibi was gasping something in my ear. *Montana. Montana.*

Great Heavens! I can't run all the way to--Oh, does she mean it's Monte? I tucked in behind a laurel bush the size of a VW Beatle. "Monte? Monte Diaz?"

"If you know any other Montes, I'd be surprised," he said, suddenly standing right beside me. "Where on earth are you running to?" he asked.

"We're trying to go home," I gasped, allowing him to relieve me of my burden. As he helped Bibi sit down on a pile of leaves, I explained that she had been camping in the creek bed. "We need to get her back to Safe Haven."

"No!" snapped Bibi, bursting out of her leafy bed. "The place will be full of Bells, Bells, Bells."

Taking her hands and trying to warm them with my equally cold ones, I reassured her, "Don't worry, Bibi, I won't take you there until you're ready."

Then, to Monte–who I feared had opened his mouth to register a complaint– "We were going to my apartment. But I don't have my car. It's on the other side of the freeway, near one of the Bell properties."

"It's okay," said Monte." Then, lifting Bibi out of the leaves, he added, "We'll go to my place. He doesn't know where I live."

"He?" I asked. "He who?"

"Your friend, Remy. Obviously he's been trying to

get to you and just as obviously you have been avoiding him for some reason."

"Not just trying to get to me; flat-out chasing me."

Monte stopped me before I got very far into my sad tale."I know. I've already had a run-in or two with him. Tell you about that later."

Grabbing his arm, I stood firm and managed to keep him from running away with Bibi. "You know an awful lot about me for not knowing me very long."

"After you eluded Remy by the pond, he made a big fuss at Safe Haven. Seemed to me he had a bit too much to prove, you know? Tell you about it on our way to my car."

"Okay, but I must tell you, having been tracked by a man for possibly unfriendly reasons, I'm not totally comfortable having been tracked by another man, even for possibly friendly reasons."

"Understandable," he sighed. "Can we go now, before the possibly unfriendly man returns?"

Bibi Bell appeared to have fallen asleep in Monte's arms, but she perked up to warn, "Or before that cougar catches up and eats us."

In case fear of the big cat had been the tipping point for her agreeing to come in from the wild, I decided I would wait until we were safe indoors before telling her the lion had probably been thirsty, not hungry.

Monte's car was parked by the front gate of the Arboretum complex. I slid through the gap between the gate post and the fence and, after he handed Bibi through to me, he managed to squeeze through after her. I knew it was lucky for us that he had followed me, but, when we were in his car, I insisted he take us to my apartment.

"That would not be wise," Monte warned.

"Remy got my phone number somehow, but I think

we have some time before he manages to find my address."

"Look, I admit I followed you to the Arboretum because I was concerned about your going out looking for Bibi on your own. And I am sorry if I alarmed you when you took me for your ex by the gazebo. I stepped back when that happened and just kept watch until he left. I was going to identify myself to you then and tell you he had gone, but you got away from me at the Japanese bridge. I looked for you but could find no sign of you in the dark. Finally, I went back to Safe Haven, thinking you might have gone back there."

"Why did you come back to the bridge?"

"Remy and I must have given up trying to find you at the Arboretum at about the same time, because just after I arrived back at Safe Haven, his Edsel came screeching into the parking lot. He was looking for your car, thinking you might have come back there."

"How can you know that?"

"He nabbed me as I was getting out of my car and asked me if you had been there. I said,"I dunno. What's her car look like?" He described your car, then ran up and down the line of cars in the Safe Haven parking lot. When he did not find your car, he found his way into the building and barged into Sister Pete's office. She was not in at the moment, and I did not follow him soon enough to prevent his riffling through the office Rolodex. I fear he might have gotten a good look at your information card. I hurried out of the office to follow him. It is not difficult to tail an Edsel. I trailed him to your apartment."

"How did you know it was my apartment?"

Monte blushed. "He left your Rolodex card on Sister Pete's desk. Sorry, I sort of memorized it. And guess what, we're neighbors!"

When I failed to applaud, he blushed even redder.

"So, two reasons not to return to my apartment then," I observed.

"Could we go to *someone's* apartment?" Bibi groaned from the back seat where Monte had tucked her in with his car blanket. "I was warmer in the creek bed."

"Rather than go even to a friendly stalker's apartment, wouldn't you rather go back to Safe Haven?" I asked Bibi.

"I said no to that! Good grief, this is Montana, not some masher. If you can't tell the difference, I don't want to be your pal anymore."

Monte and I laughed and we headed for his place.

~ ~ ~

Monte's Place

When we got to Monte's apartment, we took a few minutes to look around the property before entering--just in case Remy's investigative talents had led him this far. By the time we finished, the old woman was so exhausted Monte had to carry her into the apartment. When they were safely inside and he was drawing the shades, I stood for a moment just inside the screen door to cast a final eye around the yard; I was still half-expecting Remy to pop up like a jack-in-the-box shouting "Gotcha!"

"Come all the way inside, Dani," Monte called. "There's a cold draft on Bibi."

"Just checking," I apologized, closing the kitchen door tight against any disgruntled ex-boyfriends who might have clung like burrs to our tail.

Monte was settling the old woman on his sofa, draping a blanket around her shoulders and lifting her feet onto a hassock. "Your stubborn fan could not have gotten my address from Sister Pete's Rolodex," Monte told me. "He doesn't know my name."

"He has eyes, and you wear a name tag," I said.

"I covered it on purpose with my lapel."

"Very resourceful, but he's resourceful too. He might have followed us when we drove here."

"I had my eye on the rearview mirror for his ridiculous Edsel grill."

"I did that too, Monte, yet Remy somehow followed me to the Arboretum."

"Let's assume he's given up resolving whatever his issue is–just for tonight, shall we?" Monte pleaded. "I vote we take care of Bibi for the present."

"You're right," I reluctantly agreed. "Would it be okay if I helped her take a bath, and if I followed suit?"

"Of course. I should have offered right away."

Monte showed us to the bathroom, where I was pleased to see a low cupboard heaped with a neat stack of fluffy bath towels. That was about as good a character reference as I might expect to find in a man's home. He also had bubble bath. I was planning to kid him about that later. I helped Bibi into a warm bath and kept her upright so she did not fall asleep in the water.

"Don't worry about embarrassing me," she commented while piling bath bubbles up and down her arms. "This body is not me anymore; it's just a thing I walk around in."

I helped her wash her hair and rinse it under the tub faucet, then I got her out of the tub and wrapped her in a man-sized bath towel. Monte found some clean pajamas that fit her as a toddler's clothes would fit a Barbie, and, after I helped her dress in them, he carried her back to the couch and wrapped her in the blanket again.

After I took a shower and put on a tee shirt and sweats Monte found for me, we reassembled around the sofa. As soon as she was safe and warmly wrapped in a thick blanket, Bibi took a little snooze. While she was napping, Monte and I quietly discussed how soon we should notify Sister Pete and anyone else who was worried about Bibi. But the old woman, who was somehow capable of eavesdropping in her sleep, grumbled, "Sooner walk the plank in an alligator swamp than go back there." She twisted herself and the blanket into a knot and began to snore softly like a kitten.

Monte whispered to me, "Looks like Bibi may not be ready to be reintroduced to civilization."

Leaning across Bibi's huddled form, I told him that I was fairly certain even I could not stand a Bell family reunion before getting a little R&R. He agreed, saying, now that he thought about it, he was absolutely certain he was not ready to see Bibi jostled around among her raucous relatives. "Also," he said, "You still seem to be concerned about your stalker intruding on our rescue mission. Do you think he's capable of arriving on the scene at an inconvenient moment?"

"If I need to do anything about that, I'll do it later," I said, "After we've made sure all is well with Bibi."

Monte half-nodded at that, and threw himself into making a fire in the fireplace, warming some soup and heating up some sourdough bread in the microwave. Bibi woke immediately at the aroma of tomato soup, and we all ate around the coffee table with the appetites of miners rescued from a cave-in.

Monte and I must have dozed in his twin Morris chairs, because the first thing I knew, the old woman was shouting at the top of her lungs, "Oh, no you don't! No, no, no!" She woke herself with her sleep-talking, poked her head out of her blanket pod and said, "Who's doing all the shouting?"

"That would be you," Monte told her.

"Bad dream?" I asked.

"Dreamed you two monkeys were up to something. What's going on?"

"Before too long, maybe we should let a few folks know you've been found and are all right?" Monte suggested.

"What folks?" Bibi demanded. "The newspapers, so they can compare my adventure to the wanderings of that Alzheimers' guy Sister Pete lost one time? Police, so they can throw me in the hoosegow for being naughty? My so-called family, so they can steal me blind?"

"I liked her better when she mostly hummed," Monte smiled.

"She's right though," I said. "Before we blow the whistle on her, we need to make a plan."

"Ha, my self-appointed guide-dogs," she said. "A plan to do what?"

"A plan to undo the thing that made you disappear."

"Oh, that," she snuffed.

"You do want to undo that thing, don't you?"

Bibi pulled the blanket tight around her shoulders. "Too old to tilt at windmills."

"Yet you felt strong enough to challenge Death in a dry creek bed?"

"Sarcasm hardly suits the young, Missy. Montana here is fairer spoken. So, I'd rather just stay with him."

"Great idea," I said. "But, of course, when the authorities find out where you are–which they will–they will think Monte kidnaped you."

She sat up. "That *is* the sort of idea my people would come up with. What do you think I should do, Montana?"

Tucking her blanket around her feet on the hassock, Monte said, "We ought to make a plan to counter your family's challenge to the will."

The old woman looked as if he had betrayed her. "Has Danielle been putting ideas in your head?"

"A few," Monte grinned at me, as he tucked some couch pillows around her. "We just want to make sure you have what you need to be safe and comfortable going forward."

"Going backward into Safe Haven, you mean. I do expect my family to contest the will, but I don't expect they will keep paying my nephew's allowance to me now that he's gone. And I refuse to be demoted to the butt end of the hall at that rest home, with all the other poor old folks."

"Then you agree that we need to do this?" I asked.

"You want me to spit in the faces of my family? They're the only family I've got left, you know."

"But they're something of a threat to your livelihood, yes? We can agree on that point, I think."

Bibi reached over, pinched my chin, looked me in the eye and said, "You're young. You may have a family one day. I wonder if you'll want to see your legacy dragged through the mud then."

"She *was* more likeable when she hummed," I said to Monte.

"Being a centenarian ain't no joke, Missy,"Bibi commented. "If you do spawn a dynasty someday, you may know what it's like to be a neglected matriarch."

The light finally dawned in my head. "Oh, you want your nieces to carry on where your children would have, if you....Oh."

"She doesn't want to hurt her nieces," Monte said.

"Because they're the nearest thing she has to daughters," I added.

"Some daughters! They wouldn't know me if they ran into me on the street and I wore a name tag the size of a pie plate."

"But, if you don't want to hurt them despite their treatment of you, I'm sure we can think of a way to reclaim your legacy without devastating them," I urged.

"Hell, devastate them to your heart's content; it's my nephew's legacy I'm worried about. You ever consider the possibility that I hum certain songs because I dare not sing the words without undermining Wally's legacy? I loved him like a son, you know–although I have nothing to

166

compare him to."

Hunkering down and leaning forward on the hassock towards her, I warmed to our task. "So, as long as you honor the wishes your nephew Wally set forth in his will, you honor *him*, right? And, if we fight his daughters' challenge of the will, we still honor him."

"Then, what we need to do next is to find you a good lawyer," Monte suggested.

He and I were sitting on the hassock in front of Bibi, who was still huddled on the sofa. For a moment, our urgency seemed to inflate her with hope, but then the air seemed to seep out, leaving her hunched over on the sofa. "The law was never my area," she croaked, "but I know this much: you need facts to make a case."

"Only one way to do that," said Monte, jumping up from the hassock and pacing around on the living room rug. "We find proof that she wrote the songs her nephew published under his name."

Enthused, I added, "Then we drive Bibi to a legal firm of her choice, and she instructs them to get the copyrights to her songs back."

"Which will prove Wallace Bell made no mistake in leaving her his fortune."

"So all we will need is the original copies of her songs." Monte and I shared a high-five.

Bibi snorted. "Good luck with that. All I have is some fusty old tunes wafting around in my memory."

Monte hunkered down beside me and looked in her eyes. "Oh, I think some of your tunes waft someplace besides in your memory. Dani found some slips of paper in your room memorializing the song you keep humming, words and music, signed by you. Seems like evidence of true authorship to me."

167

"And if they could be considered as real proof you wrote the songs Wally claimed as his, the family's challenge to the will would be moot," I offered.

"Moot," Bibi sniggered. "Funny word. Sadly, I have no official documentation of my songs to achieve mootness."

"Show her the notes," Monte told me.

I reached into my pocket for the notes from Bibi's cork board and her music box, and, with a flourish, waved them in front of her. "I only know enough music to guess, but are these your notations of the song you hum?" While she squinted suspiciously at the papers, I recited the lyrics Bibi sang at her birthday party and Monte accompanied me, humming the melody Bibi always hummed.

"Lilac blossoms of pure white/Shone like stars on our last night."

Bibi looked indignant. "You two monkeys been riffling through my stuff?"

"No. Well, yes, but only after you ran away."

"And it was lucky we did," Monte added enthusiastically, "because, look, Bibi, it's your handwriting, with some lyrics scratched out and changed. I have read that rough drafts can be proof of authorship."

"Oh, poo," she snorted. "I suppose you think this slip of paper's got mootness written all over it."

"You won't know unless you offer it in evidence," said Monte with an air of strained patience.

"Ha," Bibi sniffed, "You know why I wrote down these notes? Not to acquire fame or fortune, but just for me. I'm always trying to remember the exact notes and words of my songs, to weave an aura of music around me so I won't fly to pieces or evaporate into thin air. Sometimes I have tried to write them down, like the bits written on these

168

shriveled scraps of paper. But I don't have one sheet of official music with my name on it. Some composer I am."

She collapsed in on herself again like a life-sized rag doll. I patted her on the back and tried to think of something encouraging to say.

"Perhaps you composed mostly by ear?"

She pooh-poohed me, but her body seemed to regain its substance. "I could write music like a son-of-a-gun. I had sheets and sheets of songs I composed, all in proper notation like my music teacher drilled into me."

"That's great. What did you do with the song sheets?" I asked.

"As a wedding present my husband had them bound in silk–well, except for *White Lilacs* and one other; I added them to the silk notebook after...wards. The only person beside Roger I ever shared them with was my nephew. Wally was my singing partner from the time he was five years old. When his mama would drop him off at my place, his face would light up to see me waiting at the piano for him. He would sit on the bench beside me and sing along as best he could. Except for singing close harmony with Roger, my times with Wally are my happiest memories.

"When Wally was grown, of course, he did not come by as often to sing with me. Then came a time he said it was selfish not to share the songs. He offered to arrange them for me, to find an agent who would make them famous, and to get some of the studio musicians he worked with to sing them. I felt funny about sharing the originals, and as soon as Wally had copied them to work on them, I kept the silk-covered binder hidden away."

"Why was that? Did you suspect your nephew would steal them?"

"Heck no, that would never have occurred to me."

"But, if you trusted Wally to deal honestly with your songs,'I asked, "Why did you hide the originals?"

"Because they were mine!"

"Did he give you copies of his arrangements?"

"He said they were only for the agent who would get the songs produced and musicians who would play them. I never met any of those men. And, once they were in the hands of the professionals, I suppose, I lost track of the songs."

"How could you lose track of your creations!" I groaned.

"Well, *I* certainly had no idea how to get them published or performed."

"But you also kept them hidden, the originals?

"That was the plan."

"Where are they now?"

She laughed ruefully. "I hid them so well, not even I know where I hid them."

"Did you bring a copy to Safe Haven? Or do you have a storage facility somewhere?"

"Here's a piece of news for you: when you move to an old folks' home, you only think about where your body is going to be stored."

"Do you think one of the Bells stole the binder during the move?"

"Why would they do that?"

"To hide the evidence of the theft?"

"I think you read too many old myths," she snorted.

Monte leapt up and paced the carpet. "But, Bibi, to protect his claim to your songs, your nephew might have wanted to make sure no one revealed the originals."

"That's true," I urged. "And the paper your great-grandnephew Leon sang from at Wally's wake, was it your handwritten music or was it sheet music?"

"A copy. I know because Viola said she objected to the *Sweet as mother's milk* line and left it out of the version Leon sang at the party."

"To know about that line, Viola had to have access to your handwritten original," I burst out.

"Pfft! Or it was just a copy of a copy," Bibi said.

"And a copy has to come from somewhere," said Monte intently grabbing Bibi's hand. "Maybe we can follow it back to the original from which it was copied."

"Waste of time. If Wally had wanted to announce that the songs were mine, he would have had his lawyer hand my originals to me in a gift-wrapped package at the reading of the will."

"You mean the will in which your nephew in effect admitted to taking false credit for your work? Don't you think he must have wanted to correct the family history at long last?"

"Bibi," I insisted taking her other hand, "We have to go back to Safe Haven and challenge your family's challenge of the will."

Bibi burst off the sofa like a bird flying out of a cage. "You want me to drag my weary body back to that old folks home, tail between my legs and tell Sister Pete what: I got a little lost for a day or so and what's for dinner? And you just know she'll call the Bells immediately to tell them I'm back in captivity again."

"Aw, Bibi," Monte sighed, "I don't think they'll even ask where you've been; they'll be so glad to see you. "

"My great-nieces won't be glad to see me. They'll have me examined to see if I have come down with Whats-in-heimers and expect me to get down on my knees to beg them for more than the pittance they will allot me."

"But, Bibi, that's exactly why we need to find proof you deserve your nephew's bequest."

She pushed our hands away. "Why should I take life lessons from the two of you anyway? A fired auto mechanic with a piddling side business as a writer? And a college dropout, out-of-work actress with a stalker on her tail? Wounded fawns, both."

Monte and I sat there for a long moment, shocked at her rejection. Bibi shuffled to the fireplace where she huddled on the hearth and shivered like a waif selling pencils on the street. "All this talking, and I'm still longing to hide away in the woods somewhere, while you two keep dragging me back. I know you mean well," she sighed, "But, please understand, this hurts. Why do you keep at it?

"I can't speak for Monte," I said as calmly as I could manage, "but, I can't stand to think of you dwindling away cold and alone somewhere, dismissed and forgotten for who you are and what you have added to the world."

"Dani speaks for me, as well, Bibi," Monte murmured.

"But who speaks for Bibi?" she asked the fire.

For a long moment, her despair lay heavily on the room. Then Monte spoke in a clear positive voice, and, though Bibi was still slumped on the hearth, she raised her head to listen. "Wally spoke for you in his will, Bibi, loud and clear."

Taking Monte's cue, I said, "What would Wally want for you, Bibi?"

Her head swivelled towards me so fast it creaked; I imagined it might fly off her shoulders.

Before she could object, Monte said, "Can't you affirm the final resolve of a man you loved like a son?"

"Let his last act be what he meant it to be," I added.

Bibi was still shivering as if she were huddled cold in the creek bed, but she rose, walked toward us and stood in front of us with her arms folded over her chest. "You two make it seem like the first honest act my nephew ever performed was to name me in his will."

Monte and I just looked at her as if to say, *Well? What more could we say?*

Bibi set her chin and her eyes turned cold as marbles. "My nephew handed me a check every month. He paid for what he got."

"Is that what your husband would say, Bibi?" I asked.

The curls I had put in her hair seemed to shoot straight out from her scalp. "What would you know about what Roger would say!"

"You told me about your husband, Bibi."

"Me too," Monte nodded.

"If I did, you pried it out of me." She dropped to the sofa and wrapped her arms around herself. "Oughta be ashamed, taking advantage of a decrepit old lady."

"Maybe I could refresh your memory," said Monte, producing from his pocket the Safe Haven menu on the back of which we had recorded the words and music of *White Lilacs*. Without fanfare, Monte stood up and sang the song we had heard her hum so many times. Taking his cue, I stood beside him, and, while reading from our transcription, we sang as if we were obedient school children performing in a recital before their music teacher.

'Neath the lilac tree we laid,
Where our wartime vows we made,
Our life together lay ahead;
By spring, you would return, you said,

Faded lilacs, tarnished ring,
The warring world wrecked everything,
My dear, how shall I face the Spring?
How shall I e'er again face Spring?

Monte had a good voice, and when he broke into
harmony, Bibi looked up at him with what seemed for a
moment the reawakened delight of someone seeing the sun
rise after a long dark winter. But after we sang only a
couple stanzas, that sun suddenly set and Bibi cried out,
"Stop!"

We stopped in the middle of a note and stared at
her. Had we gotten the song wrong?

Bibi hastened to wipe the horrified looks off our
faces. "It pains me to admit you remind me of Wally's
singing, Monte. But I can't thank you for reminding me of
that. It hurts an old body to remember some things."
Suddenly, she leapt up as if she had seen something
horrifying. She poked Monte on the chest, crying, "O! He
knew! He *knew*!"

"Who knew what?" Monte said, holding her hands
palm to palm in his own.

Bibi gasped, "I felt the weight of his apology at the
reading of his will, but I refused to believe it. Then having
heard you sing....I see--my beloved nephew *knowingly*
cheated me of my identity as the writer of my little songs."

She shuffled past us and stared out the window at
the silver cap of the rising moon winking through the trees
in Monte's yard. She remained there while Monte made
more hot chocolate for all of us. Before saying a word, Bibi
drained her cup, then shook her head while gazing up at the
window framing the moonrise. Finally she set her cup down
on the arm of the Morris chair, folded her hands in her lap

and shrugged. "Would've saved a lot of time if you two had sung my song to me in the first place."

"For pity's sake, Bibi, is that a yes?" Monte erupted.

"As long as I am not going to be allowed to keel over and die out in the wild as planned, I suppose you think I ought to confirm Wally's one honest act."

Not sure whether or not she was agreeing with our plan, Monte and I said nothing but stood together facing her, holding hands behind our backs with fingers crossed for luck.

Bibi hunched her shoulders and, sighing a very large sigh for a such small woman, breathed, "If there's a chance I could see my original song sheets again in the silk binder Roger gave me...."

"A damn good chance, I'd say, Bibi," Monte said. "Something so valuable to the Bell family's very existence would not have, could not have been thrown away."

"Hell, if nothing else–the looks on Viola's and Rhoda's faces--," she chuckled. "Something to look forward to."

Monte and I looked at one another with mutual sighs of relief, "So, we're all agreed on a plan now?" Monte asked.

And I quickly added, "And I can let people know we're on our way back to Safe Haven?"

"Hell no," Bibi said. "We got business to finish here first."

Throwing up his hands, Monte exploded, "I gotta take a shower," and left the room.

Bibi sat stiffly on the hassock and folded her arms over her chest.

Slumping wearily into a Morris chair, I wondered why I had thought working with a centenarian in an old folks' home would be easier than working with academics in a university.

~ ~ ~

Idun

Long ago before books were written, the Morse code was invented, or the Navajo code talkers helped win WWII, someone came up with an alphabet ordinary people could use to write to one another. According to some early reports, it was Idun, a legendary Norse personage, who created the alphabet we all know and love so well, and who thereby became the Mother of our Mother Tongue.

The story is, she picked up a rock or lump of clay and carved some runes on it, thus inventing writing. Her runes were so potent that, as you probably know, a poem made up of them is also called a "rune." And this sublime instrument was Idun's gift to the human race.

But Idun is not generally remembered as the creator of writing. For her first thought was to share it with her beloved consort, a fellow named Bragi. And, because Idun wanted to communicate her gift to Bragi via a more personal method than by scratching runes on a boulder, she carved the gift of her runes on his tongue with a kiss. And could there be anything more loving than sharing your gift with a kiss?

But the first thing Idun knew, Bragi was out and about sharing runes with all and sundry–carving them on their tongues with a kiss, for all we know. And thus over time the story of Idun's accomplishment was altered so that the creation of written language was attributed to the man in her life, Bragi, who was given credit for his lover's invention (wouldn't be the last time that happened.) Today Bragi is sometimes known as the god of Poetry--all because Idun expressed her love in a poem without making sure she got her creation copyrighted before she blabbed about it to her significant other.

Sadly, the story of Idun's invention of runes was not

all that was stolen from her. Her very name was stolen and changed as well, from Idun to Odin. You remember him, the chief Norse god who took credit for physically giving birth to the human race. Tell me, what symbolic purpose was served by claiming creation not the province of woman but only of man? Was it to set an ancestral legacy that the male is all powerful and all female creation must therefore be delivered through him?

~ ~ ~

What's Good For the Centenarian

Bibi was sitting straight as an exclamation mark on the hassock, staring dispassionately at the fire. Monte could be heard singing some dolorous song in broken Spanish while he showered.

"*What* business do we have to finish here, Bibi?" I asked. "What plan to thwart the contesting of the will?"

Staring a question at the flames, she started to hum. I had always found her habit intriguing, but I found it pretty annoying at the moment. "Do you sometimes hum to avoid answering an important question?" I inquired.

"Sometimes," Bibi chuckled. "Or to consider a more philosophical question. Don't you wonder," she continued, twiddling her thumbs, "whether fighting for a right to your creation matters in the grand scheme of things?"

"Bibi, I believe not fighting for your due from your nephew helps continue an ancient system meant to deprive all women of credit for their creativity."

The old woman peered at me and smiled strangely. "I don't know why you ever left college; you talk more like a book than a girl."

That was a gut punch, but I had to answer it if I was going to help her. "You want the personal version? When Remy rewrote the conclusion of my thesis–unsolicited–I was tempted to let it stand, because I hoped by that dishonest inaction to save our relationship."

She whirled on the hassock to face me. "Then set your boyfriend straight instead of trying to set my dead nephew straight."

Jolted by her sudden change of subject, I answered with some irritation, "Setting straight the injustice you suffer at the hands of your family *is* settling my own injustice."

"Here's the deal, Missy," she declared, throwing her shoulders back and sounding like a woman half her age, "I'm not going to make my nieces feel like collaborators in their father's theft, unless you face up to the fella *you* call a thief."

"I'm not saying your nieces are thieves, Bibi. Female collaboration with the patriarchy's injustice is systemic in our world."

Bibi looked like someone who had just seen a puzzle piece fall into place. "Oh, yeah, like in those yarns you tell."

"Those *yarns* are based on ancient songs to the Great Mother's fairness and creativity, as you know; we talked about that."

"Great Mother. Yeah," she breathed, "I got it now."

"You got what?"

"There's another song I hum to myself; not just the one about my husband. One I don't ever hum when anyone can possibly hear me. It's about someone who would have been a mother as great as the ones in those myths of yours, if she'd had the chance."

Bibi seemed to stop breathing; I think she was deciding whether or not she actually wanted to share something more with me. Then she gulped a deep breath and began. "The telegram from the war office announcing my husband's death arrived not long before our baby was due to arrive. I allowed myself to grieve too much and lost his child. Her loss was not counted among the war dead."

"Oh, Bibi," I murmured.

"Don't *Oh, Bibi* me yet. Though my girl was stillborn, my breasts had not been notified that their efforts would not be needed after all. The hospital had no room in the maternity ward to separate a woman whose baby died from the women whose babies lived, and I had to lie there listening to the mother in the next bed bemoaning the infection that had developed in her breast. 'Just like a cow getting her udder impacted,' a nurse so kindly told her. The woman was given a bottle of formula to feed her newborn, but the child rejected it. After almost a whole day of her attempts to coax her starving baby, the woman turned to me and, saying nothing, let me see the anguish on her face.

"At first I turned my head away and wept into my pillow. Nursing another baby would be like cheating my own, it seemed, giving its milk to another. But the live baby cried so pitifully, and my own breast, at the newborn's call, clenched hard in pain soaking my gown from neck to waist.

"That is why I gathered myself up and turned to the hungry baby as if I were the Great Mother you talk about, the Great Gift Giver who held out her arms to embrace the whole hungry world. Then a nurse placed the poor woman's baby in the crook of my arm. I nursed that child day and night for three days, never knowing or caring whether it was a boy or girl. It felt like the moon over the ocean made all the waves bow to me in gratitude. Then the baby's mother's breasts were healed, and the nurse took away the wee life that had reminded me of my husband. Even today, recalling that baby's cry, or hearing any newborn cry, my breasts feel as if the milk is coming down. That is why I jumped as if I had been zapped with a stun gun when that animal cried out in those bushes in the creek bed. So much it sounded like a newborn crying I felt as if my milk came down. When I hear that sound, or even imagine it, I find a place to be alone and hum the secret song to my little girl. I know she can't hear me; but I can hear myself. And, for a moment, I am sustained by the remembered warmth of fulfilling a child's hunger for life."

Bibi cupped her hands over her ears, and, gazing past me at the high window over Monte's bookcases where the first streaks of dawn could be seen touching the treetops with light, she closed her eyes and sang.

The sea is hushed tonight
While I pace your shores so restlessly
Wishing to be blessed with one small sight,
But you do not emerge from the sea;

Never walk the sands,
Watch the gulls soar and dive,
Never laugh with the joy
Of being alive

Feel your skin flush with heat,
Your bones cry with cold,
Act neither silly and young
Nor solemn and old;

Perfect as a seashell
You are to me,
A tale never told
You will always be;

A tale yet to tell
You will always be.

Just as the last lines of the lullaby were reaching for the corners of the room, I noticed Monte standing in the doorway frozen in the act of drying his hair with a towel. Bibi leaned backwards and, rolling over onto the couch from the hassock, lay there limp as an empty sheath. Monte remained in the doorway for a moment, sharing a look with me from across the room. Bibi seemed to be sleeping when Monte tiptoed barefoot to me and breathed in my ear, "About her husband, I guessed. But her baby too!" That made me get all teary, and he put an arm around me, whispering, "No wonder she kept her lyrics to herself."

That did not make me stop crying, but Bibi was suddenly wide awake and ready to make a difference. She thrust out an arm, and, opening her fist, showed us the slips of paper I had found in her room. "These scraps you stole are all I got left of any of my babies."

"Oh, Bibi, I'm so sorry."

Bibi snapped to a sitting position fully alert and glared at me. "You feel sorry for my lost creations? How about *your* creations, your *little fairytales*?" Bibi let Sister Pete's minimization of my re-myths sink in before she shot back to me the words I had said to her about her songs. "How could you lose your creations?"

"It wasn't easy, Bibi. When I presented my university mentors my work, they ridiculed it, changed it to suit their values, or claimed parts of it as their own.

"Yes, yes, we know, your lover tried to take your little play from you."

"It wasn't little to me."

"Exactly," Bibi snorted. "Those stories you create are your babies, like my songs are mine. Some great mother you are if you don't defend them."

"I have years to reorder my life, but at one-hundred one you don't have much time to do right by your babies."

Bibi got very quiet."That's the second cruel thing you've said to me."

"Oh, Bibi, I'm so sorry."

Creakily, she pushed herself to her feet and got between Monte and me and the fire. "What do you know about babies?" she said. "You two may have housefuls of them yet–possibly together. Human babies. My songs were stillborn. And I've tried to cherish a couple of them just for myself. Now I've shared them with you. You, who have your own unfinished business--you gonna honor that gesture or not?"

Having thrown out her challenge, Bibi dropped back onto the hearth and closed her eyes. "Montana, tell this girl what's gotta happen here."

"She's right," Monte said. "Remy doesn't consider himself cut away from your life, or your work. I don't think he can let you go until you–It's your move there, I believe."

"Talk about *moves*," Bibi chuckled. "Half the reason you've been carrying me around like a papoose is you've got a crush on your partner in crime here."

Monte grinned. "That's true."

That was not the worse news I ever heard in a tight spot. But the thought of having a nice chat with Remy still left me weak in the knees, and not in a romantic way. With Monte and Bibi regarding me, I felt the first rays of the sun blaze through the window, spotlighting me standing there in the middle of the room like an actor with no lines to say. But no matter how lost I felt, I knew that, as inconvenient as Bibi's demand was, she apparently required that I stand up to my people the way I expected her to stand up to hers.

"Okay, Bibi," I said, "I'll do it after you deal with your inheritance."

"Oh, no you don't, Missy. I expect a pinkie promise from you, right now." She stuck out her little finger and waggled it at me. "You face up to this exboyfriend of yours when I face up to my people."

"Today?"

Bibi crossed her arms and stuck her chin out at me. "You want me to face my wrong-headed loved ones today, then, yes, today."

"Bibi, I don't know how."

"Watch an old lady and learn," she said, leaning back against the fireplace bricks and humming her signature tune. Monte strolled to the hearth and stood opposite Bibi. He leaned on the mantle and casually nodded in agreement with her. It was as if out-of-focus snapshots I had taken of my two new friends were swiftly coming clear: Suddenly I saw them as better influences on me than anyone from my so-called real life.

"All right, I will."

"Of course you will,"Bibi sniffed. "If not, what was all this for?"

"I'll get my jacket," Monte nodded. "Wouldn't miss riding shotgun on this stagecoach for anything."

"I can call Sister Pete now?" I asked.

"She's probably got her culottes all in a twist by now. Better call her before the day is out. But first!" Bibi added, holding up her cup to request one more cup of cocoa from Monte.

While Monte heated the milk, I picked up his phone and notified Sister Pete. "We found her and she is safe."

"Get her back here now!" she barked. "And don't talk to any journalists."

"Monte Diaz is with us," I said.

"Jesus! Tell him to keep his pen in his pocket until he talks to me, or else! And Danielle?"

"Yes?"

"I'll unlock the courtyard gate. Come in through the French doors."

"There's a courtyard gate? Oh, is that how Bibi got out?"

"Not now, Danielle. And for Pete's sake, the woman's name is Beatrice."

"Gosh, Sister Peter, don't you mean, for *Peter's* sake?" I said and hung up.

~ ~ ~

Someone's in the Kitchen

The Safe Haven lot was overfull of cars parked every which-way, and Monte had to park on a side street. When we came around the corner, it was immediately evident why Sister Pete wanted us to come in through the garden gate; the front doorstep was teeming with reporters and members of the Bell family. As if the closed door were sentient and could answer human requests for information, the lot of them were shouting questions on the doorstep about the location and well-being of Beatrice Bell. Hearing her name shouted by a gang of strangers, Bibi got a little hysterical. She did not stop giggling the whole time we snuck around the neighbors' hedge and found our way down their driveway to a spot where we could squeeze through the greenery onto the Safe Haven property.

By the time we got to the courtyard gate, several members of the crowd, hearing Bibi's laughter, had noticed us and crashed through the hedge to the garden gate. Monte and I evaded them by scurrying back around to Safe Haven's front door, carrying Bibi between us. A few vultures were still milling around there in great confusion, waving cameras and notebooks, but, just when they became aware of us, Sister Pete threw open the front door like a flaming Minotaur guarding the gates of the Labyrinth. I swear all her extremities were sticking out as if to electrocute the first persons they touched with the power of her rage.

"Get in here!" was all she said to us, and the camera-waving journalists parted for us as if the nun were Moses and the bothersome Red Sea were in her way.

Bibi pulled her blanket over her head and hunched forward, so that, as we passed the curiosity seekers, she looked less like the old lady they hoped to see and more like an oddly wrapped turkey carcass being carried to the kitchen for the residents' dinner.

The moment we were inside, Sister Pete closed and locked the door.

"My office!" was all she said, and, as if she were an even scarier version of the pied piper, we followed warily. Leaving Bibi leaning on me for a moment, Monte broke ranks to grab one of the wheelchairs stored in the cloak closet by the front door. He lowered the old woman into it and sped her across the dining and common room areas to Sister Pete's office. The old woman was reacting as if all the feverish activity surrounding her return was a comedy show staged for her entertainment. She giggled all the way, causing Monte and me to do the same. Sister Pete must have made sure the residents were all in their rooms before the return of the prodigal elder, and so, fortunately, they were not disturbed by our giddy entrance. Such was the power of Sister Pete's presence, however, that once we three truants were settled in her office and she had closed the door behind us, we became as solemn as three school kids caught playing hooky.

The first thing the nun did was to check on the old woman. She took Bibi's hands and turned her arms this way and that searching for wear and tear, and, while she was at it, she took her pulse. After sticking a thermometer in her mouth, she fished a cuff and monitor out of a desk drawer to take the runaway's blood pressure. Then she looked into Bibi's eyes for a long moment. "The doctor's on his way, but is there anything you need in the meantime, Mrs. Bell?"

"Nope. My two angels here have taken care of me."

"Angels?" The nun snorted.

"She usually calls us monkeys," Monte offered.

"Or fawns," I added.

"Or guide-dogs," we said as one.

Sister Pete glared at Monte and me. "Instead of playing animal charades, I would have thought the best guidance even a dog would have provided would be to bring her here immediately."

"We had matters to discuss before reentering the den of lions, as it were," Monte apologized.

"By delaying your return, you gave the media vultures time to greet you upon your appearance. I suppose they got a dandy picture of Mrs. Bell dressed in ridiculous men's pajamas with fluffy lambs all over them."

"A joke gift from my nieces," Monte apologized.

Sister Pete growled, "I can just see the headlines: *Runaway Oldster's Pajama Party.*"

Bibi giggled. "It *was* kind of a pajama party. A fun and profitable sleep-over, well, *nap-over.* I had many naps."

"And as for you, Mr. Diaz of the gamboling lamb pajamas, you--who are supposed to be gathering evidence for an article that will prove Safe Haven is actually a *safe* haven for the elderly--have somehow participated in an elder adventure that can have been anything but safe. After I make certain Mrs. Bell is truly safe again, I will be dealing with you."

Bibi fumbled to free the brake on her chair, wheeled a few inches closer to Sister Pete, and stared straight into her eyes. "These young people saved my life, Sister, and, believe me, neither one of them signed up for the trouble I gave them. Rather than scolding and threatening them, you ought to be giving them a medal for putting up with a difficult old woman."

"And for performing the miracle of restoring your speech, I suppose? Whatever. Next time you feel like playing teenage pranks with your young friends," sniffed Sister Pete, "kindly do not launch the caper from my place of business."

Bibi stiffened. "If you knew what the *caper* was all about, you would talk out of the other side of your mouth."

"That will become clear sooner than later, one hopes," said the nun. "So, until the doctor arrives, why don't you tell me what you have been up to for the past forty-eight hours, at the possible expense of the reputation of Safe Haven, the feelings of your family, and probably of your own well-being."

Bibi took a deep breath, smiled at us one at a time, and had just opened her mouth to confess her attempt to run away from her upsetting family mess, when the family in question burst in through the office door, with Viola Bell in the vanguard.

The Bells filled the office as sardines would fill a can if they were still alive and boisterously resisting the canning process. Their voices echoed around the small room so clamorously that none of their words could be understood. Sister Pete could make herself heard above the sound of a level 5 tornado though, and she blared, "How did you people get in?"

"The courtyard gate was unlocked," said Rhoda.

Before Sister Pete could quash the Bell's invasion, Viola trumpeted the family's official greeting to their truant relative. "Auntie Beatrice, we're so relieved you are here! We've been so worried."

Immediately, her sister Rhoda exploded, "We thought you had been kidnaped!" then added, "But no one even sent us a note demanding money for your return." She looked as if the lack of ransom note had disappointed her.

Viola hastily assured everyone in the room, "We

would have paid it, of course."

"Thank you," said her grandaunt, and, by her look, it seemed she might start giggling hysterically again. But she managed a solemn look before saying. "Any kidnaper would have found that I would not fetch much from...anyone."

"What do you mean by that?" one of the niece's husbands asked.

"Just Auntie's sense of humor," Viola assured him.

But Bibi thought it was a good moment to begin the conversation she had returned to the civilized world to initiate. "I meant," she said to Viola's husband, "I'm sure that, with me out of the way, your challenge to my nephew's will would have prevailed, and, once you all got your hands on my inheritance, you would not have let it go, not even if the kidnapers were Long John Silver and crew."

"No need to worry about all that, Auntie Beatrice," Rhoda smiled. "The confusing business of the will is going to be over... as soon as all the papers are signed."

"As soon as I've signed away my inheritance, you mean," Bibi said.

"*Your* inheritance!" Viola blurted out. "Why do you keep calling it that?"

" More like, *mistaken inheritance,*" Rhoda chortled.

"All right!" Sister Pete declared, rising up behind her desk like an avenging angel, "You'll have to take this discussion to your lawyers' office. But not until your aunt has been seen by a doctor and has had some rest."

"Don't mind me," said Bibi. "I rested up at Monte's. We can have it out right now and right here. I don't mind."

"Well, I do mind," said the nun, moving behind the wheelchair, turning it briskly and wheeling it right through a crush of Bells and out of her office. She was bowling across the living room area with her charge headed for the South hall leading to Bibi's room, when a gaggle of reporters burst in through the French Doors. Bibi pulled her blanket over her head again. Monte was grabbing cameras left and right and tossing them out into the courtyard, while the Bell family members frantically conferred with one another about what to do next.

One intrepid reporter called out over the heads of the gathering crowd, "Has anyone called the police?"

Sister Pete called out, "We've had enough police for the present!" then she whispered loudly enough in my ear for me to hear her over the havoc developing around us, "You didn't call them, did you?"

I turned to her, mouthing, "No!"

Then she turned to Monte and hissed, "Did you call these media people?"

"You crazy?" he said. "And let them scoop me?"

Recovering her usual unflappable manner, Sister Pete outflanked the interlopers, wheeling the old woman straight past them through the dining room and into the kitchen. As a vapor trail follows a jet plane, the Bells rushed in after her. Monte and I snuck into the kitchen with the family, and, while Sister Pete slammed down the metal shutters between the kitchen counter and the dining room, the kitchen staff skedaddled in alarm, leaving pots full of dinner steaming on the stove and two full biscuit pans the size of throw rugs in the great oven. Immediately the contest over Wally Bell's will between Bibi and her kinfolk erupted as explosively as if the deep fryer had splattered a volcano of hot oil all over the kitchen.

So many things were shouted at the same time, it would have been impossible to hear them all, let alone remember them, but I did hear Rhoda shout in her great-aunt's face early on in the mayhem, "You know Father would want his family to have his money."

To which Bibi laughed, "I was his family long before you were, Missy. 'Fact, I *was* his money."

All the Bell's hands were thrown up in the air at once in consternation. It looked like a choreographed moment in a revival tent. As if she were the evangelist at the revival, Viola leapt up on a kitchen step-stool to silence the Bells.

"Shut up, all of you. We promised we would let Auntie Beatrice give whatever testimony she imagines will convince us of her rights in this case."

Viola's command did not silence the Bells. "What about *our* rights?" more than one of them cried.

Sister Pete hopped up on one of the steel tables and rattled the pots and pans hanging on hooks, quickly convincing the unruly group to tone it down."In the name of St. Catherine Labouré, patron saint of the elderly, shut up, all of you, or I will have you thrown in jail for harassing an old woman." Such was the authority and dignity of the nun that, even sitting on a scullery table with her legs dangling in the air, she rendered the kitchen immediately silent. "Keep in mind that lurking nearby is a hoard of media people who can hear through metal doors when they want to. And, believe me, they are foaming at the mouth with excitement over the possibility of ruining your aunt's reputation, her family's reputation and the reputation of Safe Haven. As you have proven yourselves incapable of conducting your business at a proper time and place, be my guest and conduct it here and now. But if you do not conduct it with decorum and speak more softly than a sofa cushion might speak, I will have you all hauled away for disorderly conduct."

After a fitting moment of quiet appreciation for the nun's willpower, Rhoda tiptoed up to her and, holding what appeared to be a legal document for her to see, whispered, "We have this paper she needs to sign. That is all."

Sister Pete looked at it, then whispered to Rhoda. "Give it to her then."

Bibi's wheelchair was right beside Sister Pete's dangling feet, so she could have easily handed it to the old woman herself. But she made Rhoda do it.

Bibi refused to take the document, whispering loudly to Rhoda, "Viola said I get to give testimony before the Court of the Bells passes sentence."

After much sighing and tearing of hair, everyone finally shrugged their shoulders and with pretended patience folded their hands over their bellies and awaited the old woman's side of the case. Bibi told them how Wally had sat with her at her piano throughout his childhood, how the two of them had sung the ditties she made up and played for him. She told how, when he grew up, he had asked to sing her songs in public. In that steel-enclosed little room, her soft voice carried to every ear. "And then one day I heard Wally was singing at a club uptown. He asked me please not to come see him because performing before family made him nervous. 'Well,' I thought, 'If he doesn't know I'm there, I can't make him nervous.' And I snuck into the club where Wally was singing. He sang–oh, what he sang–one of the songs I had told him I wished to keep just for myself. He sang it anyway, in front of strangers. My world crumbled for the third time in my life."

There was a major eruption among the Bells at that statement, but it was quickly quelled when Sister Pete banged a ladle against a steel pot and demanded silence.

"Auntie can say whatever she wants," Viola said in

her indoor voice. "We have our answer ready."

The family settled into watchfulness as Bibi continued. "My beloved nephew Wally asked to arrange my songs for me. But he failed to mention to me–ever–that he published them under his own name."

"He published his songs under his name because they were his!" Viola hissed through gritted teeth.

"And we can prove it," Rhoda added. "Viola, show her the reason she has to, in all fairness, sign the legal document we brought today contesting the will."

Holding up something wrapped in a pillowcase, Viola pushed her way up to the steel table where Sister Pete sat like a judge overseeing a trial. Waving the bundle over her head as in triumph, Viola said, "We thought you might be reluctant to sign the document so we brought something that will prove our point."

While Viola held up the bulky pillowcase over her head. Rhoda impatiently grabbed the bundle from her sister, leapt atop a wooden crate, and, letting the crumpled pillowcase fall to the kitchen floor, thrust a notebook bound in white fabric into the air and cried triumphantly, "The originals of Father's songs."

Bibi had been standing ready to make her final proof to the family, but, seeing the binder, she fell back into her wheelchair and folded over like a paper doll.

"My songs," she breathed.

"Hardly," Rhoda snickered. "They were found under Father's mattress when we removed it to install a new one for our new roomer."

"Look at the title of the notebook," Viola crowed. "It's written in gilt yarn on white silk, and it clearly says, *MY ORIGINAL SONGS: White Lilacs and Other Bell Songs.* 'MY', it says. 'MY' means Father, because it was in *his* bed."

As if outraged by the Bell's revelation, the kitchen oven timer clanged that the biscuits were done. Monte reached over to the oven, turned off the heat, put on some mitts, and opened the oven doors to remove the biscuits. The Bells stepped away to make room for the open doors, throwing up their hands to shield themselves from the blast of heat coming from the oven.

"Who's this guy?" several Bells inquired.

Arranging the biscuit pans neatly on the counter, Monte whispered an apology to the visitors: "If the biscuits are left in the oven, they will get too overcooked for the residents to eat."

"Who are you anyway?" the Bells insisted.

"My staff, my kitchen, my biscuits," Sister Pete firmly asserted, quieting the family.

By then the oven had made the room so hot we might all have been friends sitting in a sauna together, except no one was looking friendly. The distraction allowed Bibi time to gather the strength to answer Viola's assertion. "*My* means *my* songs. Roger had them bound in silk as a wedding present for me, and I embroidered the title myself in golden yarn. Over my handwriting."

"No one writes in yarn," Viola sneered.

"And inside the binder," Rhoda warbled, ignoring Bibi's assertion, "The table of contents lists the titles of all his songs. You see?" she cried, shoving the open folder into Bibi's face.

Reaching out to touch the silk binder cover, Bibi murmured, *My songs.*

"Auntie," Viola explained as to a child, "These are all songs we have known as Father's all our lives!"

The stew bubbling on the stove started spitting in

apparent sympathy with the Bell family's vexation. As a result, the kitchen, a tight fit for the litigants, was becoming unbearably humid. Only Sister Pete stayed cool and watchful atop her steel perch.

Bibi was muttering something and looking appealingly at me.

"What is it?" I said, leaning down to hear her feathery voice.

She wiped the kitchen mist off her forehead. "Look at the pages. I am there."

"Could you show everybody the one called *White Lilacs*?" I asked Rhoda.

She shrugged and opened the folder, riffling languidly through the onion skin pages to the last song.

"Look at the name of the songwriter," Rhoda exclaimed when she found the title. Before she looked at it herself, she passed it around for everyone to see.

"*White Lilacs, by Beatrice Bell,* I read aloud when Rhoda held it before me.

"*Bell! Bell!*" Viola chimed as if she herself were an iron bell. "See, Father's name. Our name."

"We would have noticed if it said *your* name, Auntie," Rhoda snorted.

"You'd *think*," Monte muttered behind me.

"Bell was Bibi's name long before Rhoda's father was born," I offered.

"Your name isn't really Bell anymore," Rhoda insisted to Bibi. "You were married to Roger Rogers or something like that."

"Roger Blonk," said Viola. "Your real name is Beatrice Blonk." Every Bell in the room laughed heartily at the name *Blonk*.

Ah, Monte muttered to me, *Bibi–for love of Roger*

Blonk: Beatrice with a B + Blonk with a B.

Bibi's handkerchief was so damp from the humidity, she folded it carefully to locate a dry bit before wiping her face and defending her name. "Roger laughed at his name too. He insisted we would get my songs published after the war under my maiden name. 'Bell is such a musical name,' he said. 'Blonk is just a silly sound effect.'"

"So really you're just Mrs. B. Blonk," said Viola.

"Buh-buh-buh Blonk," Leon chortled.

"And these songs were written by a Bell, not a Blonk," Rhoda added triumphantly grabbing the binder from Bibi's hands.

The old woman moaned as if a baby had been ripped from her arms, but she swiftly gathered herself together and cooly explained to Rhoda, "*Legally*, my name *is* and always *was* Beatrice Bell. Your poor father must have felt so bad about erasing my name from my songs that he had to wipe away the lie with one final gesture."

I think the old woman would have wept then if defending her songs had not exhausted her. As for the Bell contingent, they became deathly quiet. It looked as if the contest about the authorship of the songs was winding down, but Rhoda, riffling through the binder one more time, cried out, "Oh, no you don't, Auntie! Look here. Father has added some kind of notation in pencil–all over some of these songs. It's his handwriting. And in *pencil!* You know Father always wrote in pencil, Viola."

"Yes he did!" said Viola.

"See here," Rhoda hooted, "here he has pencilled in *E♭,* and down here a *B♭*. Up here he wrote an *E♭,* and there a *G.*"

"Those are Father's scratchings," Viola cried. "I'd know them anywhere!"

198

"Of course they're your father's, Bibi snapped. "They would be notations made for the accompanist to read when playing for your father to sing."

"Notations Father made! So, you admit Father wrote the songs."

"I do not. Wally must have put in the chord notations in his key as he got older and his voice matured. Did your father teach you nothing about music?"

Rhoda was affronted. "Musical talent skips a generation. Leon has it from Father. Viola and I don't."

Viola objected to that. "I sing!"

Rhoda snorted, "Right. Everyone can hear you at church. But, look here at the very beginning of the song, Auntie. Father has pencilled in a whole line of little notes, climbing up the lines as if going up a little musical hill. I know enough about music to know that isn't just a key change."

"The little notes *climbing a hill* are an arpeggio. Your father loved to be introduced with the flair of an arpeggio. He was a singer, not a composer."

Suddenly Viola's musical son, Leon, piped up. "Great-grandauntie's right, Auntie Rhoda. That's an arpeggio. That's how Mr. Becker introduces my solos in Chorus at school."

Whether it was the accrual of evidence that Bibi had written her songs, or the traitorous concurrence of Leon with his great-grandaunt, the Bell contingent went silent.

In that quiet moment, Sister Pete reached down from the steel table and lifted the folder out of Rhoda's surprised hands. In her usual, uncluttered, authoritative voice, the nun read the title and songwriter of each song as written in Bibi's cursive atop each song's first page. The composer of every song was designated as Beatrice Bell.

While the Bells whispered among themselves trying to make sense of what had just happened, Monte whispered in my ear, *"That songbook--definitely not moot."*

Sister Pete closed the folder. "If no one minds, I will put this in the safe in my office. It might be needed as evidence, don't you think?"

No one had any objections at the moment. I think the Bells were too busy trying to add up zero and zero to make an inheritance with their names on it.

Sister Pete hopped down off the table and, making her way through the disconcerted Bells, was about to open the kitchen door when Viola stood atop the kitchen stool and shouted.

"We're not done here yet, Sister!"

"We're done shouting, however, and I am Sister Peter Mary. If you cannot speak in an appropriate manner, you can leave my kitchen immediately."

"You can bully me all you want, Sister Peter," said Viola climbing down off her podium and stepping in front of Bibi's wheelchair. "But I've got one more thing to say to Beatrice Blonk." She loomed over Bibi. "I know in the deepest place in my heart that my father wrote his songs, because he wrote one for me. He made it up to sing me to sleep when I was not three years old. Composed it sitting right by my bed. I never forgot that lullaby. I sang it to my own son when he was a little boy, didn't I Leon?"

Leon nodded. "Mama does like to sing."

"And I expect Leon will sing it to his children when he's a father, as my father sang it to me. You remember Father's lullaby, don't you, Leon?"

"Sure," Leon shrugged and sang in his sweet voice, *"Perfect as a seashell, you are to me; a tale yet to tell you will always be.* I never understood it, but once Mama's

200

sung a song–over and over--it's impossible to forget it."

Monte and I looked at one another across Bibi's head. He spoke first. "But, Bibi, those lines are from your...."

Bibi raised a hand to silence him. "No, Monte. It would be too cruel."

"From your lulla...," I whispered in Bibi's ear.

Bibi shushed me. "Poor Viola. Imagine taking that memory from her."

By then, the Bells were pressed up against Monte and me and the wheelchair, which was being rolled up against Sister Pete, threatening to squash her against the kitchen door. Obviously, she was not in the mood to serve as judge in the Bell kangaroo court any longer.

"I'm sure the lullaby your father sang to you was lovely, Viola, but it hardly changes the evidence of the notebook of original, signed songs, which you yourself put into evidence. And right now I must adjourn this meeting and make an announcement to the media people panting for news right outside this door."

With that, she burst out into the dining room, announcing in full voice, "Our resident, Beatrice Bell, is alive and well. She was caught up in a family matter that appears to have been resolved. Those of you who are not residents or employees of Safe Haven will please exit the premises so our residents can have their dinners."

With that, Sister Pete whispered to Monte and me to take Bibi to her room and await the arrival of the doctor who was to examine her. Then she made her way through the babbling media towards her office, raising her hands in the universal gesture meaning "Stop, Or Else!" The reporters stopped following her.

The Bell family had wandered out of the kitchen in

Sister Pete's wake, and, in a desultory manner, were meandering variously towards the front door and the French doors which led to the presumably still-breached courtyard gate. Monte and I, flanking Bibi's chair, ignored the gadflies and turned towards the residents' wing.

Bending down, I spoke quietly in Bibi's ear, "You were magnificent in there, standing up to your family like that. It's as if you were a different person. How did you find the courage?"

"I told you to watch how it's done," she said. "That's how it's done."

"And your lullaby?" I asked.

"Speak no more of it. Got to leave Viola something. Let her sing it to her grandchildren if it comforts her for the loss of her father. "

Before I could object, Monte began wheeling her chair towards the residents' wing. But, before we could escape the dining hall, two things happened almost on the same beat: Sister Pete commanded loudly, "Gloria, lock the courtyard gate," and two fellows new to the scene–having already breached said gate--burst in through the French doors, scattering Bells like kitchen roaches and knocking one of the fleeing reporters on her rear.

~ ~ ~

Some Academic Chickens

The chaos that Sister Pete had managed to calm erupted with even greater force when one of the new arrivals was accidentally shoved into Bibi's wheelchair and nearly landed in her lap. The other fellow was so busy bowing and apologizing to Bells and reporters that he did not notice his companion had collided with us. Though I had been struck by the man who tumbled into Bibi, I was able to remain upright and shove his shoulders to prevent his squashing the old lady. At the time, the dining room was such a riot of stumbling and bumbling bodies, some leaving and some arriving, that I did not register at first whose shoulders I was pushing.

For a second the man and I remained in stasis, almost chest to chest, tented over the wheelchair. He recognized me before I could bring his face into focus. It was someone who had barged in especially to see me, my exboyfriend Remington. And the older gentleman being buffeted around by exiting media personae was my thesis advisor, Professor Milton. My academic chickens had just come home to roost.

Only seconds passed after the latest eruption between persons with conflicting intentions, when most of the Bell family oozed out of the building and the remaining reporters scurried along after them asking impertinent questions about the missing woman.

Ignoring the hubbub, Remy loomed over the wheelchair and announced the reason for his third or forth uninvited and unwelcome appearance at Safe Haven–a location which regrettably was not proving as much of a haven as I had hoped. "The professor and I are here to bring you back into the fold," Remy announced.

The word *fold* struck me funny for some reason, and

I laughed. "What am I, a lamb?" Feeling a bit hysterical, I sang, *Bah, bah bah!* Then Monte, who was behind the wheelchair but unable, with all the bodies blocking the way, to push it to Bibi's room, laughed at my imitation of a singing lamb. I think being around the Bell family had left us both feeling a bit hysterical. The burst of laughter made Remy notice Monte standing right beside him, and he said, "You!" Monte turned his head, recognized Remy and responded, "You too." Feeling territorial under the circumstances, I suppose, the two men very briefly and somewhat indignantly reminisced about their recent encounter in Safe Haven's parking lot. Once they had voiced their respective reasons for being in the same place at the same time, Monte announced his intention to wheel Bibi to her room. As for me, I tried to ignore Remy, but, true to form, Remy would not be ignored.

To keep me from escaping him again, Remy subtly shifted his tall frame to block Monte from wheeling Bibi away in the chair, to which I was persistently clinging. He leaned over Bibi's arm to speak intimately to me–as if Monte were not there, as if the kitchen help were not passing close by on their way to rescue dinner, and as if Sister Pete were not leaning on the doorframe of her office with the aplomb of a cool private eye in an Edgar Award-winning mystery novel.

"Danielle Running," Remy formally asserted, "you can't keep running away from all responsibility just because you're through with our relationship."

When ambushed, I can, thankfully, sometimes mount a swift knee-jerk verbal defense, and, having my former boyfriend's face thrust suddenly into my field of vision produced one such occasion.

"Remy, it takes two to make a relationship, and I

vote not to be in ours anymore."

"Fine. But I would argue it also takes two to make a breakup. I have a right to demand you do not leave a mess in the space in which we were a couple."

With some interest, it seemed, and considerable amusement, Monte was watching this conversation going on right in front of his face. And, though Bibi's head was down, I could see she was smirking and not at all desirous of being wheeled out of earshot just yet.

Under such pressure, I continued to act as my own advocate for once. "What mess do you think I left behind when I left you?"

Remy raised his eyebrows halfway to the roof. "You left your MFA Thesis unfinished."

"That definitely remains a mess, but it's my mess, so why should it bother you?"

"Because I was your partner when you abandoned your work," Remy explained, as if pulling teeth. "That makes it look as if I might have discouraged you in some way, thus causing you to quit."

"Well," I said, "there might have been a discouraging word or two influencing my decision."

"As your supervising intern, I offered you some dispassionate criticism of your conclusions," he shrugged. "If people thought that was why you ditched the program, that reflects on me as your associate."

"You did more than criticize my conclusion: you rewrote it without my knowledge *and* took it upon yourself to turn it in to Professor Milton. And, yes, that made me very uncomfortable to work with you."

"Then forget me. I'm just someone abandoned along your blithe and careless path. Get a different supervisor. Think about yourself. Why would you give up a budding double-barreled career in theater and academia over the issue of a conclusion?"

Still agitated by Remy's waylaying me while I was caring for someone I valued greatly, I reflexively let loose on him. "Because my ideas are in it! When you've dismissed a person's ideas, you've dismissed the person. I was dismissed by academia so I left it."

"Ideas aren't people, Dani. Ideas are ethereal; *you* have substance." He took my head in his hands and squeezed my skull as if to make me aware that his hands and my skull were real and what went on inside my head was not. Monte watched closely.

"My ideas are not ethereal to me," I said. "They are palpable parts of me."

"Like babies," Bibi chimed in.

Remy snorted. "I don't see you cradling them in your arms."

"Just because you can't see them doesn't mean they aren't here. In a loving relationship, I expected my whole self to be seen, not just the parts you found acceptable."

Remy looked as if I had served him green cheese on toast and claimed it was a moon sandwich. "I know you," he proclaimed proudly, "I know you should be teaching in a university, not telling stories in an old folks' home."

I gasped. Monte gasped. Bibi nearly choked.

Remy drew himself up to his full six feet and sadly proclaimed, "All right, Dani, if I can't convince you to return to the university where you belong, maybe *he* can."

With that Remy stepped aside revealing, tucked in behind him, Professor Milton. Obviously my former mentor had prepared hastily to accompany his star intern on this quest, because his always impeccable satin vest was buttoned askew, and the portmanteau clasped in his hands was open with papers spewing out of it.

"You remember me, I trust, Ms. Running," he said, grasping the tips of his vest and attempting to tug them straight, "Although, you appear to have forgotten that your name appears on the list of my advisees and that you have a responsibility of loyalty to me and to everyone in the department."

With every word the professor spoke, a bit of my burst of courage evaporated. Immediately my mind leapt guiltily to the moment when I had crossed the street and put a faux hex on his daughter for shouting, "Man-hater" at me. "I didn't say a word to your daughter. Nothing at all," I dithered. "I had no idea she would run away screaming. It seemed so unlike her."

"That is not the reason I am here, Ms. Running."

"Though you did put a hex on her!" Remy put in.

"You two believe in pagan hexes?" I asked. The academic gentlemen shook their heads. "Then, um, we are agreed," I concluded, albeit apologetically.

"She's only a girl, Dani; you might have scarred her for life," Remy said.

"Never mind all that," the professor grumbled. "My daughter is very bright but she can be a little bitch. I, on the other hand, am your academic advisor. Have you forgotten that, Ms. Running?"

"I remember," said I in a voice a mouse would have found inadequate to its communication needs.

"Then perhaps you recall that you owe something to the university, your work, to be specific, the completion of your final project, and the defense of your MFA thesis."

He had me there. I could not think what to say. Caught red-handed in the midst of the most dishonest evasion of my life, and faced down by an autocrat of academia, I suddenly became so humble, I almost offered my wrists to be encumbered with handcuffs and willingly allowed myself to be dragged back to the university.

Safe Haven's manager, however, had apparently not appreciated my university colleagues' adding to the circus this day had been. Sister Pete had a way of standing aside and letting things play out as they would, but when she deemed it was time for an outside force to put a hand in, she did not hesitate. And, like a submerged iceberg popping up suddenly beside an oblivious luxury liner, Sister Pete appeared behind the two men who were looming over me and Bibi in her wheelchair.

"Pardon me," she said, "Since you two gentlemen are standing right in front of me in my dining hall, I could not help overhearing your intriguing dialogue, and I believe I can unravel a bit of the yarn you have been spinning."

"My name is Professor Milton," the esteemed head of the university's Drama Department announced, his deep voice resonating through the rapidly emptying hall like the call of a lustful bullfrog. "I am the advisor of this young woman, who has been a truant for some weeks."

Having stared at him until he began to wonder why, Sister Pete swept between the professor and me, smoothly shoving aside his portmanteau with the toe of her sensible shoe, and, with the utmost dignity, she got right in his mustachioed face. "I know who you are, Professor. You are one of the academicians whose literary sentiments have to some degree discomfitted an employee of Safe Haven."

"Employee?" I whispered hopefully.

Sister Pete gave me side-eye and would have continued, but Remy laughed in her face, *"Whose sentiments have to some degree discomfitted her? Did Dani give you that fancy phrase?"*

"I can come up with my own phraseology when pressed, young man," Sister Pete icily informed him. "And, by the way, nicknames are degrading. This employee's name is Danielle."

"Even if *Danielle* has been employed here," the professor explained, "she owes her first allegiance to her prior employer, the university."

"Oh! I thought we all owed our first allegiance to God," Sister Pete smiled. Then she turned to Monte, saying, "But maybe that's just me."

The professor, who obviously had his lines down pat, was not to be deterred by sarcasm, and turned to me to continue his speech. "You judged *Don Giovanni* rather harshly, I seem to recall, for his unfairness to women." To be fair to him, the professor's face turned red as he recalled my reaction to his admiration of rapists in literature. "I wonder how you justify your criticism of unfairness to females, Ms. Running, when you failed to complete the work paid for by a grant gifted to the university especially for a woman. How fair are you, a female, being to the females who might be denied the grant in the future because of your rejecting the university and the grant with it?"

Another of my rare bursts of bravery was trying hard to emerge, but, calling on my usual fear of authority, I tamped it down, nearly whispering,"I didn't reject the university; the university rejected me–my ideas."

The professor got all fatherly and explained to me in a more kindly voice than I had ever heard him use, "A university is the very place where scholars' differing ideas are meant to be discussed and weighed against one another, not run away with and hidden."

Though my feelings were in a hurly-burly of comeuppance, I stood like a scarecrow and said nothing.

"Ms. Running," he pleaded, with a look so uncharacteristically vulnerable that I could feel my objections to his opinions of women softening. "Think of all the future students you would cheat by continuing to receive your stipend while volunteering in an old folks' home."

Taking one step forward, Monte commented, "While being *employed* in an old folks' home."

"Whatever," the professor said with a grand sigh. "You have been caught in a fraudulent abuse of a generous grant, an offence that could damage the whole department. I therefore demand that you return and fulfill your obligation to the university."

"Fraud is a felony, you know," Remy put in.

The professor came so close our foreheads were almost touching as he intoned, "Do you want to be charged as a criminal and have that hanging over your head for the rest of your life?"

I really did not. In that moment, I decided that I would somehow return to the university and defend my thesis, even knowing I would be greeted with Remy's and the professor's scowling faces.

Sister Pete, however, was not going to let her newest employee go so easily. She smiled sweetly at my two gadfly scholars. "You perhaps do not know, gentlemen, that, against all odds, our Danielle rescued the venerable lady resident you see right here from a dangerous situation, and returned her safe and unharmed. And, as to Ms. Running's failure to complete her thesis defense, she has been practicing her presentation here at Safe Haven by performing for the residents the dramatic monologues which I believe are part of her paper. Though I am no university professor, I have found her takes on well-known ancient tales to be enlightening satires on the impact of classic character development on social gender norms."

Wow, Sister Pete got my idea in a couple weeks when my colleagues had not done so in a year. She may have gotten it better than I did.

Professor Milton raised his considerable brows. "Is that true, Danielle? You are still working on your Masters presentation?"

My mouth had dropped so far open at Sister Pete's understanding and praise of my academic work that I could not have spoken even if I had anything to say.

Monte whispered in my ear, *Sister Pete is a bad-ass!*

Unable to respond to the nun's monumental white lies about my work at Safe Haven, I was further dumbfounded when Bibi took up the slack. "Danielle could present one of the proofs of her theory right now, if you don't believe her."

Before I could catch my breath and declare that this was not the time or the place to defend my thesis, Sister Pete cried out, "Of course she could!" and, taking me firmly by the elbow, she escorted me across the room to the little platform stage.

"Of course I could *not!*" I said over and over again--but no sound accompanied my protests.

Meanwhile, Monte quickly pushed Bibi's chair into the living room area so she could join the audience. Rather than get run over by the chair, Remy and Professor Milton stepped aside to let them pass. With her usual deceptive grace, Sister Pete physically pushed me to step up onto the platform I had occupied so many times to keep the residents diverted before dinner. Meanwhile the two academics obediently lowered themselves onto the couch right in front of me, muttering things such as, "By all means," and "A pleasure, I'm sure," but probably thinking, "The little

211

renegade is about to flop big-time."

Sister Pete took her usual place in her office doorway, and I stood quivering downstage center reflecting that I had experienced many a terrifying actor's nightmare that was nowhere as dismaying as this. And to complicate matters, the moment I was to begin my dramatic take on one of the most maligned mythic figures in history, the elderly residents began appearing from whatever nooks and crannies they had been occupying while awaiting dinner. To prod myself to perform, I chose to believe the old folks had come to watch my performance not because the bar for entertainment at Safe Haven was incredibly low, but because they liked my renovated myths more than I had thought.

~ ~ ~

The Wise Woman

"Long ago our ancestors told a story about a woman so wise her very name meant"Female Wisdom." Today this wise woman is known by another name. We'll get back to that in a moment.

But first, I must tell you, there were once songs written about this wise woman, hymns and stories celebrating how beautiful she was, with her long swirling tresses falling down her back. It was said that when she spoke, wisdom seemed to flow from her mind through her hair into her listeners' minds. Guided by her, people wisely treated one another as equals, no matter which side of the hill they lived on, and they dwelt in peace with the wise woman's values of equality, empathy, creativity and reverence for nature as their guides. Their stories and songs celebrated her as a heroine to humanity and as the 'mother of all the gods.'

Until...some men came along who wanted to expropriate the wise woman's fame. To reverse her influence, they turned her biography upside down and her character inside out.

They knew it was not going to be easy to mess with stories celebrating the beloved wise woman, so they replaced the old heroine with an attractive young hero. In their revised script of her life, they claimed the young warrior was sent by the king to kill the beautiful wise woman.

The handsome warrior set out to find her, carrying a curved sword that could gut a rhinoceros and wearing only a loin cloth--in which he looked most appealing. He found and engaged the wise woman easily, for she was neither secretive nor combative. The people loved her, so she had no reason to think anyone wanted to murder her--even a near-naked fellow carrying a scimitar. So when the hero challenged her, she had no sword and would not fight him.

This is where the revision of the story of the wise woman gets really dodgy; for she was so innocent that the hero could not bear to look her in the face when he attacked her. So he tricked her by looking away, caught her off guard, and, with a single backhanded stroke of his sword, sliced off her head.

Of course, the revisionists knew if they claimed the peaceful, wise woman was murdered in such a cowardly manner, it would look very bad for him--and for the king who sent him to kill her. So, when the presumptive hero took the wise woman's head back to the king as requested, he made up the most outrageous excuse ever: that he was forced to look away when he killed her because to look in her face would kill a man instantly and turn him to stone. And, for millennia this revised tale of the wise woman has been handed down, depicted in statues and paintings galore showing a grotesque mockery of the female face frozen at the moment of her horrifying murder, her visage distorted, a hideous mask of evil--with snakes for a hairdo.

When proudly receiving the gory snake-infested head from the assassin, the king proclaimed, "We have slain the Destroyer." Now, this is the moment when the great lie about female wisdom was born. For 'Destroyer' in the ancient language, was pronounced ...Medusa.

Medusa, an evil gorgon invented by men who so yearned for power that they changed her name, her character and her story in order to claim all wise thinking belongs to men--the way Medusa's head and all the wisdom in it belonged thereafter to the king.

~ ~ ~

A Reluctant Invitation

The moment I was done with my bit and had taken an unnecessarily elaborate bow, Bibi began clapping wildly. Even Sister Pete was at my elbow applauding with uncharacteristic exuberance and grinning at the professor with an unspoken command to join her applause. When he did not readily respond, she strode between the two men clapping so energetically they could not fail to applaud-- which they did, in a gentlemanly if not enthusiastic fashion. Years passed while I stood dying a thousand deaths on the low platform awaiting the fall of their academic scimitars. The professor responded first. By snorting. Loudly.

Finally he spoke, while I cringed and tried to effervesce into the atmosphere. "Ms. Running," said the Professor, and it was a command. Obediently, I stepped off the platform and sat on its edge, hands tucked protectively under my thighs. Professor Milton slowly raised his whiskered face and took a good look into mine. "From the myth of Medusa, you conclude that men go around cutting off women's heads?"

Professor Milton's misreading of my presentation left me momentarily speechless, but a deep anger at his complete failure to comprehend my intention arose in me and I spouted, "That's not my conclusion!"

"Then just what is your conclusion about Medusa and her sibylline sisters?"

When I could not readily gather the courage to answer him, Sister Pete delivered me a reprieve by placing a hand on each of the two visitors' shoulders, saying, "If you don't mind, gentlemen, the elderly lady whom Danielle has so heroically rescued has been working out a complicated problem with some of her kin on an issue that has nothing to do with you. Ms. Running will need to stay at Safe Haven with the lady to help wrap up the details of her problem. Remain seated here in the living room area for a moment, if you like, in case Danielle wishes to make any arrangements with you. Montana, take Beatrice Bell to her room please."

While Sister Pete glided casually toward her office, I stood there like a stick trying to come up with a devastating comeback to the professor's disdain of my *Medusa*. It was like *going up* on stage, as it is called–forgetting your lines, your character and the name of the play in the middle of a performance. I was so far up, I could scarcely remember what piece I had just performed. Not for the first time, Monte rescued me by delaying the task Sister Pete had assigned him: picking up a water glass from one of the dining room tables, he called out to the room in general, "Let's toast Sister Pete tonight. Because Sister Pete makes everything all right."

Every elder in the room raised a glass, a hanky or a string of worry beads to honor the esteemed Manager of Safe Haven. But, the nun, who had reached the doorway to her office, stopped abruptly and, looking like a lowering cloud, turned towards Monte. "Sister *Pete*?" she thundered. "You *nicknamed* me?"

"Everyone nicknames you, Sister," piped up my second favorite old lady, Bettina, who was sitting at her table working on one of her dog montages.

"*Everyone?!?* " Sister Pete inquired of the entire room, which had filled up with the remaining residents awaiting dinner.

"We all call you Sister Pete," Bettina helpfully explained. "It's like when someone has a registered breed of dog officially called *Horatio of the Emerald Isle*, or something like that, but for everyday they call him *Hor*. You know, short and sweet. Here, Hor! Good boy, Hor!"

216

That was the first and only moment I ever saw Sister Pete absolutely flummoxed. She took a breath so deep I thought she might explode. Then she did explode,"Jesus, Mary and Joseph!" she bellowed, Then, shaking her head, she turned towards her room, muttering, "At least they didn't nickname me *Hor*." Stepping into her safe space, she shut the door, and, after a second or two, the sound of barking laughter, only slightly muffled by the manager's thick door, escaped from the office.

Having watched that moment of comic relief with puzzlement, the professor recalled his errand, and, rising to his feet with perfect professorial elan, he asked, *"Are* you ready to make some arrangement with us, Ms. Running?"

"Arrangement?" I mumbled.

Remy moaned wearily. "Professor Milton is asking if you are prepared to defend your thesis?"

"But you both find my conclusion indefensible."

"Again, I must inquire, what in plain words even I could understand would that conclusion be?" The professor clasped his hands over his badly-buttoned vest and awaited my answer.

Professorial sarcasm has always aroused in me a deep outrage at authority, but the only words I could come up with were: "I, uh, call for stories that dramatize a rebellion again the perversion of the Great Mother myths and the reclamation of roles that promote instead constructive female characters."

Bibi muttered, *Not like a book, child!*

Ignoring her, Remy shrugged his shoulders in the learned manner at which he excelled. "You damn men for plagiarizing female myths, but, in your retelling of them, aren't you plagiarizing both female and male-authored myths?"

217

Did he not know that the ancient myths are surely in the public domain by this time? "My thesis includes a bibliography--books about early myths mangled by later writers," I murmured.

"*Male* writers, I suppose you mean." The professor threw up his hands, shot his cuffs, and collected his portmanteau. "I don't know how you young women can bear to live in a world peopled with men, when you have such a low opinion of them."

Tears of frustration were threatening to reveal my utter helplessness at convincing him of anything, when Professor Milton uttered his umpteenth sigh of the day and took his parting shot. "I take your silence to be a refusal to fulfill your obligation to the Drama Department, to our benefactors, and to yourself, young lady."

Still stunned by the professor's failure to answer my thesis on its merits (or possibly the lack thereof?) I nodded to him with all the awareness of a dashboard bobble-head. Professor Milton and Remy stood shoulder to shoulder looking at me as if I were a hoped-for supply ship scuttling itself mere yards from a safe port. Yet I could not for the life of me think what I was supposed to say. Only Bibi, who was stubbornly tugging on my sleeve, seemed to see the great emptiness that had opened up where my nerve ought to be. I tried to brush her hand away, but she said, "It's time, Danielle."

"Not now, Bibi."

"I don't have that much time left," she hissed. "And you owe me." She pushed herself out of her chair, and, reaching up to where I stood stiff with fear, hooked my pinkie finger with hers.

I stuttered, "Well, I don't know if it's legally binding in *every* state."

"It's binding between you and me though, isn't it?"

The professor, who had waited about long enough for my answer to his appeal, demanded to know what was going on. Whereupon his dutiful sidekick, Remy, barked, "What's this crazy old gal talking about?"

Whether because Bibi invoked my pinkie promise to conclude my business with Remy, or because he had just disrespected a woman whose life lay behind her like a golden ribbon of unappreciated creativity, the words I needed to say to Professor Milton tumbled out of my mouth: "I will come back to the university, defend my thesis and hopefully receive my MFA, if you will accept my thesis conclusion, as stated."

"Are we to accept without discussion or negotiation the ideas of a woman who questions the worth of half the human race?" asked the Professor.

Bushwhacked by an attack of tears, I was too choked up to say a thing. But Bibi wheeled right up to the men and wagged her finger at them."Why, you have no idea how much she cares about you. She told me you were great geniuses the both of you. Was she wrong?"

"I think you must have mis-heard her," the professor mumbled and continued his march towards the door.

Remy, seeming struck by Bibi's words, turned towards her, murmuring a question. "Dani said I was great?"

"You were my hero, my exemplar, my champion," I babbled without thinking."

"Dani," he said and his shoulders sank as if in defeat, "I don't get what your hero would be like, if a hero could exist in your world."

Standing there looking bereft, Remy seemed to be hoping I could provide the answer to a puzzle about humanity he could not decode. I opened my mouth hoping words would come to take away his pain, but the professor had heard more than enough by that time and he was ready to leave. He grabbed Remy's arm and began to guide him towards the door. Remy, who seemed to be in somewhat of a daze, followed meekly after him.

But, before Professor Milton got out the door, he remembered what he had come to tell me in the first place. Staring at the door handle for a long moment before he let his hand fall to his side, he dipped one shoulder downward and used its weight to spin his body back towards me. Trudging across the dining hall he stood before me, head partly bowed, stopping not eighteen inches in front of me and regarding me through his shaggy brows. Then, turning pale as he reiterated the possible consequences of my shenanigans, he said, "Do you know, little lady, what will happen if you fail to complete your MFA? Of course the grant you accepted will be withheld from the department in future. And, when the other contributors who support the Drama Department find that a recipient of one of our grants was a scholar who only pretended to be researching her Masters Thesis, they too will withdraw their grants from the university forever."

Tears were still puddling on my lower eyelids from Remy's last words to me, but I did not dare dab them. Then, having failed to evoke the desired response from me, Professor Milton played his ultimate, hidden weapon: surrender. He stood in front of me for a long moment before he spoke, his shoulders humped like an angry cur deprived of its bone. "Since you apparently do not care about the vast damage you will be doing to the department by continuing to abandon the halls of academe, I have no other option but to say to you that, if all other perquisites are fulfilled, the conclusion to your MFA thesis will be allowed as stated.

And let this acceptance be a proof of academia's acceptance of your so-called Great Mother's beloved value of compromise."

My fickle tears transformed instantly to tears of gratitude and gushed all over the place, as I muttered, "You must mean her values of *cooperation*, not compromise, which would connote abandonment of her values."

"Whatever!" Professor Milton exclaimed, and, flipping the tip of his tie in the air, he turned on his heel and headed for the door, muttering, "My office, Monday morning."

Remy did not let me off as easily as the professor. Turns out when political issues enter the personal sphere, mingling ideas of power with powerful emotions, the tissues that hold the human psyche together can begin somewhat to fray. When Sister Pete appeared as always by magic and graciously opened the door to assist their escape, the professor gladly complied. But Remy did not.

~ ~ ~

Deep Waters

What a coward I am. Or at least I was at that moment. When my mentor accepted Sister Pete's invitation to leave, I gave a head-bob by way of agreeing to his proposal and bidding him adieu. Rather than making myself available to Remy to answer any further questions about my future, I readied myself to answered Bettina's usual follow-up questions about my *Medusa*.

But the excitable woman was hurrying towards me, and, as if signaling an impending train crash, she was pointing at my exboyfriend. Turning to look where she was aiming, I saw that something was very wrong. Remy was shuffling back and forth between the common room and the dining room with one shoulder hunched all funny. For a confident young man who had graduated from Harvard Magna Cum Laude to be suddenly slumping and shuffling aimlessly around a room seemed decidedly out of character. Even Professor Milton, whose academic eye was ever cast upon matters literary or fiduciary, and who was halfway out the door, noticed that Remy was going through something unusual. The old academician's knees seemed to wobble as he stepped up to his protégée and put a quivering hand on his back. By then Remy had wandered from the common room and was standing beside the staff lockers just beyond the archway to the residents' wing. He was shuffling forwards and backwards over a two-foot patch of floor, and, head-down, was banging his forehead against the metal lockers, rhythmically–shuffle-shuffle, bang; shuffle-shuffle, bang.

The residents waiting around for their next meal paid little attention to the young man attacking the bank of lockers with his head; possibly they had seen such behaviors before at Safe Haven. But I could not ignore the insistent rhythmic head-drumming of the man I had loved. Monte helped me out there, materializing suddenly in the hallway behind my ex, and, joining Professor Milton, he murmured something to Remy so softly that, though I could see his lips move from across the room, I could hear not so much as a whisper. The professor was saying things in Remy's other ear, and the two men took the troubled man's elbows and guided him to one of the couches in the common room, only a few yards from where I had been about to hold a discussion group with Bettina and a few of her peers.

Remy seemed blind to the residents and stared at the coffee table in front of him. Monte and the professor were still whispering to him, but suddenly Monte turned toward me and energetically gestured me toward the manly triad on the couch. Oh, my, I was supposed to do something here. Clearly I had to walk across the space between me and my ex and create some détente between the worlds of my past and my present.

Slowly I wove a path among the common room furniture, approaching Remy as one would a wounded animal who might either cower or bite an approaching stranger. As I neared him, Monte and the professor stepped away. I sat on a hassock across the coffee table from Remy. Immediately his eyes focused on me; though they seemed opaque, as if he had suddenly developed milky cataracts.

"I noticed something," he said. Remy always could get to the main subject. It was an academic talent of his. Or, I had to admit to myself, a life talent.

"What did you notice?" I asked. Or, mostly I whispered. He seemed to be a man who was skinless and that to be bombarded even by a soft voice might pain him.

"You are still wearing your ring."

We both stared at my right hand where a gemstone

shone in a simple gold setting.

"It was a gift from a friend," I smiled.

"More than a friend," he said, and the words seemed to burn him.

"Once." Hiding the ring in my palm, I slipped it off.

"Not anymore? Because you think I did an unfriendly thing to you?"

How could I say to him then--skinless as he was-- that, yes, I took it as an unfriendly thing, because he had hurt me, and because he could not believe that I could have been hurt by him. And because that did not bode well for me in our relationship. While I tried to think how to say that, the room nearly cleared. Only Professor Milton and Sister Pete stood at the far reaches, on opposite sides of the room. I also noticed that Bettina had evidently been doing one of her montage projects on the coffee table and had left there scattered bits of magazine pictures of dogs, along with a hefty pair of scissors. Thoughts tiptoed through my head: Disquieted man. Woman who hurt him. Scissors. *It's happening again!* I tried to cry out, but when I opened my mouth, all I could do was to raise a hand as if to shield myself from a blow. I was remembering the night when I had left him and he had punched me in the chest. I knew he had felt wronged by me. Could cultural indoctrination in the Man-owns-woman-he-loves-and-she-cannot-be-allowed-to-leave-him syndrome make him a physical danger to me? Right now? It became suddenly clear to me that, if he picked up those scissors, it would be an action bred of unbearable pain in him rather than from a desire to hurt me. Either way, I was in a risky situation.

Remy filled the silence with words that came out as a desperate cry. "I am not a thief!" With that, he lurched to his feet, grabbing the scissors from the coffee table on the way.

"You want to cut me out of your life?" I could only hope that was a metaphor.

Immediately, a hand appeared out of nowhere and grabbed Remy's scissors-holding hand. It was Monte, strong and quick, incapacitating the hand. But the hand did not drop the scissors. Then the professor's hand appeared and took hold of Remy's other arm. Presto like an apparition, Sister Pete game into view and, with Monte's assistance, wrenched the scissors from Remy's hand. Before Remy could take issue, my three angels conveyed him and me into the office of Sister Peter Mary, Manager, where she directed us to sit across the rug from one another. Professor Milton was seated just behind Remy's shoulder and Sister Pete just behind mine. I was still in a sort of daze arising from Remy's cry of pain, my fear, and my rescue from both. I had a sense Monte was standing close by, but, at that moment my blinders to everything but Remy kept me from seeing what else was going on.

Everyone said something, I know that–except for Monte. The only big surprise to me was that Sister Pete suddenly (and forcefully) took charge, getting us to sit in a close circle and talk civilly to one another. In short order, she got Remy to say, though haltingly, all he wanted to say. She got me to say all I needed to say in response. She got Professor Milton to say to Remy that he was safe; nobody was going to take away his academic credentials for brandishing a potential weapon. Then Sister Pete told Remy that what seemed unacceptable and treacherous to him now could be cleared up with further conversations like this one (with a good therapist, she murmured to Professor Milton.) She got me to say to Remy that I was not disappearing from his world, that I would follow his advice and return to the university to defend my thesis, although I was unable to be a couple with him. He winced at that, but she promised to find him a good counselor to make it work for him. Remy had his doubts, but Sister Pete had powers of persuasion way above the norm. She even told him she would meet with him any time he needed, until they had found a suitable counselor. She added, in her indisputable way, that the two of them would meet somewhere other than Safe Haven, because partners and former partners of employees must not interfere with the vulnerable elderly residents.

Her voice went on and on, though I could not make out the words after a while. All I heard were sounds that were as soothing and stimulating as hot chocolate on a snow day. Remy must have had a similar response to her voice, because his face gradually stopped looking pasty and gaunt. And, amazingly, his eyes seemed to clear and regain some of their characteristic look--as if he were on the verge of injecting a devastating witticism into the conversation, or a definitive theorem of art. All in all, Sister Pete was a deus ex machina in culottes. I thought, too bad Remy and I had not run into Sister Peter Mary six months earlier; maybe we could have made it. Now we could not try again, because he had hit me. (Though I have feared self-appointed authorities all my life, I do have a bottom line.) Having tracked every word Sister Pete uttered, Remy finally gave a sharp nod to her, and, with his chin set as if determined to hold on to her advice like a kid holding onto the handlebars of a bike for the first time or a non-swimmer holding onto water wings, he stood, leveled his shoulders, and prepared to step into an opaque future.

Much later I found out Sister Pete had been a clinical psychologist in an earlier decade and had successfully treated many a confused priest before the Church farmed her out to manage a rest home. She confided to me one time that she suspected the priests in her care would have preferred not to be helped by a female. She praised Remy as having been more amenable to self-improvement than any of those men of the cloth had been. As a lapsed Protestant and never-Catholic, I have no say in the matter, but I think the Church really missed a chance when they did not elect Sister Peter Mary as Pope.

There was a silence, for I have no idea how long–so absorbed was I in soaking in new knowledge of Remy's emotional life that had eluded me when we were together. Also notable was my realization of possible deficiencies in my own emotional involvement with him. Had I been blind to his feelings, or had he hidden as much of himself from me as I had failed to make obvious to him? While I was watching Professor Milton escort Remy from the room, the older, smaller man reached up to put a companionable hand on the tall, younger man's shoulder. I considered how the newly emerging bond between the two of them enlarged both men in my eyes. I did not flatter myself that I had enlarged myself in theirs.

As I watched the two people who had been so important in my life dwindle via the magic of perspective across the common room towards the outer door, Monte suddenly emerged from the margins of Sister Pete's office and stood beside me. "In a way I was kind of rooting for you two kids to make it," he said, then added, "And in a way, I wasn't."

"In a way I was too," I nodded, as I watched Remy disappear out the front door. "In many ways."

Monte placed his hand on top of my head, just for a moment. As he drew his hand away, I felt something go with it, as if a heavy and confining thing had been drawn up by his palm. He looked questioningly at his hand. I looked at him. Then, as one, we turned and looked at Sister Pete, who had seated herself at her desk, and, it seemed, had been watching us. Her expression was an encyclopedia of knowingness.

"Anything else I can help you two with?" she asked. Brisk. Acerbic. Back to her regular self. If she had worn invisible angel wings earlier, she had folded them up and put them back in a desk drawer.

Monte and I uttered our thank-you's as we left her. As we headed silently for the outside door, I saw Lonny wheeling Bibi to her usual table in the dining room. Bibi did not watch Monte and me go out the door. It was as if she knew we had done our parts to meddle in one another's lives, and she was ready to let the results spin out without further interference.

Monte and I were thoughtful as we exited to the parking lot. For a time, we stood looking at our cars, which were parked side by side.

"How did my car get here?" I wondered. "Didn't I leave it in a cul de sac about a thousand years ago?"

"Lonny and I went to get it for you," Monte shrugged.

I shook my head, "Wow, you don't miss a trick, do you?"

"I don't do tricks, Danielle," he said. He looked flat-out serious and maybe a bit insulted. Then, abruptly he changed the subject, reaching into his jean's pocket and fetching out a piece of paper. "Sister Pete asked me to give you this."

"What does it say?" I asked.

"Unlike Bibi's, her handwriting is legible."

"Can you just tell me? I've had a big day."

"She said when a tightrope-walking duo loses its

228

balance and crashes to the sawdust of the circus ring, it's not just the one who tripped up but both partners who need professional help to come out of the trauma without a limp. So, I assume it's a list of therapists' names."

"She thinks I'm nuts?"

"Now, that's as fine an example of overreacting as I've ever heard."

"Okay, how *traumatized* does she think I am?"

"You would have to ask her that. But I don't think she would mind if I told you she suggested that *Dani* is perfectly healthy, but that, when she ran away from her old life, she left *Danielle* a ways behind. She said you might want some assistance to close the gap until you catch up with yourself."

"Yeah, Bibi said something like that to me when we first met."

We stood there a while longer contemplating our cars' hood ornaments before I said, "That thing with your hand on my head...."

"That was something," he nodded.

"Maybe you inherited some of your *bruja* gramma's gift after all?" I smiled.

"Sadly, I don't even speak her language anymore, and she's no longer here to teach me."

"You do okay," I said. "As for me, I think I will go home and sleep for about three days before I check out the list Sister Pete made for me."

Monte stretched and sighed, "I don't know why I think I need to sleep for three days too; after all, I was not one of the principle parties in whatever just happened."

"If you don't know you were a principle party," I smiled, "Maybe you need to peruse Sister Pete's list."

"Just doing my job as a rest home aide," he said,

then, resting his chin on his open car door, he asked me one more question. "Speaking of names, Danielle, you once promised to tell me how you got yours."

So I told him about the gramma who told me old myths to get me to sleep when I was a child.

"Sort of a *bruja* herself, your gramma, eh?"

"How's that?"

"She planted a seed and years later you dreamed up a whole bouquet of stories."

While I was thinking about that, he said, "Drive safe," and slid into his car. Before driving out of the parking lot, he rolled down his window and called to me, "See you at Safe Haven, or at some other safe haven we happen upon," and drove away.

On my way home, I realized I was taking the straight-forward, not the devious route, because the fear that my stalker would follow me home had been lifted up through the top of my head and dissolved.

~ ~ ~

Dānu

Long ago there were stories about a very special person called Dānu. There were folks all over the world who called themselves "the People of the Goddess Dānu." Great rivers still carry her name: the Don, the Dnieper, the Danube. Did you know if you are Dan, Donna, Dana or Danielle, you are named after her? Apparently her qualities were not even gender specific: in Ireland she was called "King Don of Dublin, Mother of the Gods."

In early days, you could go to an elegant building, such as the Temple at Delphi where you would be greeted at the portals by one of the handmaidens of the Goddess Dānu. She would guide you to a quiet place where you would lie down to sleep with your ear to the cool stone floor, and, if you were plagued by dismaying nightmares born of the Great Untruths encountered in the waking world, you could envision helpers in your dreams or tools to solve problems or to get out of threatening situations. Upon waking, you would be more cognizant of how all parts of our lives could work together and thrive.

But some storytellers came along and changed Dānu's tale, describing a bloody takeover of the dream temple and claiming she was kicked out and her handmaidens were slaughtered and replaced with Apollo's own dream interpreters. It was sort of a protection racket, where thugs promised safety to the public in exchange for granting absolute power to greedy autocrats and suppressing Dānu's values of helpfulness and creativity.

But, though the mangled story of Dānu was meant to smother positive dreaming forever, the spirit of the dreamer lives on in some who avoid the Untruths of the waking world and create ideas about how to improve it.

~ ~ ~

The Last Bell Rings

The Bells did not easily give up on their attempt to get back the inheritance they thought was theirs. Sister Pete had some trouble preventing them from harassing Bibi at Safe Haven, but, when the nun had enough of their incessant phone calls, she strode down the residents' hallway and stood in the doorway of Room 17. The old songwriter was sitting up on her neatly-tucked bedspread, leaning on pillows propped against the headboard. She was reading a song from her silk-covered portfolio and humming along. Sister Pete cleared her throat.

"Well?" she said, reaching a hand out to Bibi.

Bibi Bell carefully closed the portfolio and held it out to Sister Pete, then suddenly jerked it back and held it to her breast.

"Not ready yet?" Sister asked.

"Ready," Bibi allowed, letting Sister Pete take the songbook, though her fingers clung to the silken cover to the last moment.

"I'll put these back in the safe for now," the nun said. "Just ask whenever you want to peruse them."

"I know," said Bibi.

"You're sure you're ready?"

"Now or never," the old woman sighed.

That day, for the first time since the big family skirmish in the kitchen, Sister Pete had answered the Bells' demands to see their Auntie Beatrice. Up till that time, she had made up some very creative excuses for refusing them entrance. Before she let them return, she made certain the doctor declared the old woman strong enough to deal with the sticky family matter. Then she arranged for a lawyer to come meet with Bibi, to work out a few details about her inheritance from Wallace Bell. The old woman and her counsel had been closeted in the conference room at Safe Haven for many days before the morning she declared herself fit to deal with her family.

When Sister Peter called to tell Viola and Rhoda that their grandaunt was ready to speak to them, she could hear their husbands harrumphing in the background, saying the whole family should be allowed to see Beatrice Bell. But Bibi wished to keep the next family meeting simple, and her wishes prevailed.

Monte was the one who let the sisters in and accompanied them to the conference room. He told me later that the nieces looked like a two-headed dragon ready to breathe fire on anyone who stood in their way. But, when they saw Bibi awaiting them at the conference table--not in her wheelchair but standing behind it with her freckled fingers resting lightly on its back--they shuffled like bucking broncos uneasy about entering the rodeo chute. Monte believed they were reconsidering their assumption that they had worn her down so far she would come around soon to their point of view. Apparently Bibi read their faces the same way Monte did.

"This is not about me," she said. "As you can see, there's not enough of me left to be the subject of anything. I'm only a chime the wind blows through. But if you listen, you might hear some music pertinent to the subject at hand."

The grand-nieces were not much for metaphors, and, businesslike as a pair of price tags, they took stances behind chairs directly across from their great-aunt.

"Be seated, please," a voice from the remote end of the conference table said.

When the voice solidified into the sturdily-suited body of Bibi's lawyer, Viola jumped a foot and Rhoda jumped a foot and a half. Being the more unvarnished of the two sisters, Rhoda talked back recklessly. "We'll sit down when she does!"

"It's my party; I can stand if I want to." the old woman reminded them.

You could almost see the dollar signs rolling past on the nieces' eyeballs as they calculated the power of their aunt's inheritance against the power of their longing for it. Smoothly they pulled out the chairs in front of them and, as if they were one being, sat down.

Sister Pete appeared instantaneously as usual, as if manifesting from the chalkboard or the philodendron planter. Then she stood one chair away from Bibi while the lawyer pronounced from the far end of the room, "Your aunt has a statement to read to you."

"We have a statement to make too!" cried Rhoda, leaping to her feet.

The lawyer and Bibi rattled their papers, just a riffle and a flick, whereupon Rhoda's fanny returned to its chair as if nostalgic for the time before the menacing paper shuffling occurred.

"When Beatrice Bell has read her statement, you may, if you wish, read yours," said the lawyer consolingly.

Spake the old woman: "It is my determination that my nieces, Viola and Rhoda, have received, via their father and my nephew, Wallace Bell, enough of the fruits of my labor--right into my declining years when he knew I could use it. I do not wish, however, to deprive my family of the totality of the estate which they have assumed they would inherit upon my nephew's passing. Unfortunately the estate assigned to me by Wallace Bell would not be enough to support me at the end of my life and also to make all his descendants rich as oil barons. There is enough, however, I am told, to set up bequests for two family members, and I have done that."

Viola and Rhoda perked up at the words *two family members* and *bequests*, but their responses became somewhat confused when their aunt spelled out what she had bequeathed to the family. For Leon, the Bell teenager who had rapped Bibi's song to her at her birthday party weeks ago, she had set up a scholarship fund to be used at a school where rap music is studied.

Since neither of the two bequest recipients mentioned was Viola or Rhoda, the two sisters exploded in a duet of volcanic gasps.

"If no such school exists,"Bibi continued, "the scholarship must be used for Julliard or some such educational establishment worthy of Leon Bell's very fine vocal instrument. I have no doubt his talent deserves admittance."

Viola rocked back into the conference chair at that, seeming somewhat mollified at the bequest or the flattery of her son. Rhoda remained alert as a Doberman pinscher on the scent.

"Sunday Bell, the family's passionate girl evangelist,"Bibi went on, "really should get something."

When Monte told me later of the bequest to Sunday, I bristled to think Bibi would grant anything to the opinionated and abusive little girl who had insulted and disrespected Bibi at her one-hundred-first birthday party. But when I heard the details of the bequest, I had to smile at the humor behind it and the possible practical improvement it might make on the girl.

"A bequest has been set up for Sunday, to pay for her education when she comes of the appropriate age, at an innovative liberal arts college. Such an education will not bend her opinionated ways, but it might broaden her thinking somewhat and soften her sharp edges. I will be hoping to live to one-hundred-twenty so I can see how the Bell grandchildren turn out."

Rhoda sat staring at the table for a moment, shaking her head back and forth as if weighing what one member of her family was going to get against what she had assumed they all would get. Viola had been experiencing similar financial calculations in her head.

The lawyer's sepulchral voice wended its way down from the head of the table. "That is the whole of Beatrice Bell's statement to her family." He fluffed his papers into a neat stack, but as he was slipping them into his briefcase, Rhoda jumped to her feet and shouted down the table at him.

"Viola didn't want to go to college, so Father gave her one of his houses instead of tuition. I was the one who had the ambition to go to college. Father paid my tuition, and gave me a small rental house he owned, a tiny cottage–which my husband and I generously shared with Auntie Beatrice for many years. Our little girl, Sunday, was born there. But I know Father wanted me to have a house as big as Viola's, as a special gift for graduating–almost graduating–college.

Steam was starting to stream from Viola's ears by that time, and her hand made itself into a fist all on its own and reached out to punch Rhoda on the hip. Rhoda was apparently accustomed to dodging her older sister's blows, however, and neatly hopped beyond Viola's reach, crying, "You know very well Father meant to leave me money to buy a house as big as, or bigger than yours. Where's the money for *my* big house?" Rhoda pounded on the conference table until the attorney's water glass danced around beside his briefcase. Promptly lifting the case out of the path of the puddling water, the lawyer, in his most conclusive tone, answered Rhoda's demand.

"I have no idea where such money may be, madame. I do know it is not in your father's will." Then, lifting his case in one hand and poking his pen into his breast pocket with the other, he strode out of the conference room, having given Bibi a tidy bow before he turned towards the door.

Rhoda and Viola stood and looked at Bibi.

Sister Pete stepped closer to her.

Bibi Blonk Bell looked at her nieces.

Viola and Rhoda opened their mouths a few times, somewhat robotlike, but neither seemed able to think what to say. Had they gotten more than they expected? Less? Or something so surprising they could not quite calculate its worth? They must have decided they got about as much as they were going to get, because, after that final meeting, they stopped calling to talk to their aunt. Except on her birthdays, of course, of which there would be a greater number than they could have anticipated.

Bibi also left money to a local homeless shelter, an animal rescue organization, and she set up a bequest for the Arboretum's Art School building fund, an action which she judged was none of her nieces' business.

~ ~ ~

Return of the Prodigal Daughter

As a beneficent result of Sister Pete kindly guiding
Remy towards a suitable counselor, my return to the
university was brought about with a minimum of drama. I
took up where I left off, with Remy overseeing my work as
he had before. But he spoke to me only when necessary and
with the restraint of a newly minted pastor counseling some
random chorus girl. The distance he maintained between us
made it possible for me to resist the frequent urge to run
away from the halls of academe again before I completed my
degree. Professor Milton also did his best to ignore me,
which was as great a gift as he could give me. In due time I
was able to complete my work and defend my thesis before a
panel which included both Professor Milton and Remy. In
my mentor's and Remy's official reviews of my work, they
managed to gloss over ideas that made them uncomfortable.
Remarkably, they also managed to find a couple aspects of
my work to praise; others on my defense committee were
even more cordial to my presentation. I was sure Professor
Milton would not recommend that I be invited to interview
for any of the many academic job opportunities that came
across his desk. But, though I did not pass with honors, I did
pass and received my MFA despite the temporary willful
escape I had made from the university.

Instead of the fair future Remy had once imagined
for me, I enjoyed performance gigs Sister Pete helped me
obtain in various rest homes, women's health care facilities,
and with services catering to special events such as
weddings and children's birthday parties. Eventually I had
original plays performed at the Arboretum Theater, and, for
a time now I have worked as its Artistic Director. Whenever
I can, I volunteer at Safe Haven. Sister Pete attends almost
every one of my performances at the Arboretum wearing

full-on traditional nun's regalia. She says it amuses her to face my pagan characters wearing the battle gear of the Church.

Looking back on such a checkerboard of employment opportunities has been more satisfying in the long run than a lifetime of academic squabbles and attacks on uppity females like me would have been. Some female scholars will need to beard the academic lions in their departmental dens, but I am mostly glad I am not fit to be one of them. Recently (out of curiosity) I made a search of grants and scholarships the university offers and found that the grant that got me my degree was awarded the year following my graduation to a male scholar whose thesis title was *Sounds and Rhythms of War in 21st Century Poetic Dramas.* I must reluctantly conclude that I have made not much of a dent in the status quo.

It is possible I made a bit of a dent in Remy's world view. After he completed his internship in the Drama Department, he accepted an offer for a position as an assistant professor at a college thousands of miles away from the place where we had come together and subsequently came apart. He published learned books in his subject, and, within a few years, he became a full professor and lived, I believe, as happily as he deserved thereafter. Before our careers had become established, though, Remy and I met one more time. He showed up at a one-woman show I was performing at the Arboretum. It happened to be the one-woman play I wrote in lieu of the Chekhov Noh play which Remy had "borrowed" from me. I could not bring myself to do the play we had argued about, but I am sure he recognized that I had transferred my original concept to another poignant Chekhovian moment. (I credited Chekhov, of course, as the source.) Remy waited for me after the performance. We stood regarding one another in that unsettling doorway between the house and the lobby. After a long moment, he waved his long arm towards the minimalist setting on the stage.

"It works," he said.

"The set?" I asked.

"All of it," he said. "The set. Your play. You."

That seemed a very big compliment coming from him. Then he added a sort of caveat. "I would have done it differently."

"I'm surprised you didn't," I said. "Do the *other* Chekhov Noh play, I mean."

He drew himself up grandly, being as always the good boy who truly never meant to do wrong to anybody. "I could *never* do that," he said.

"Why not do it?" I asked.

"I made a gentlemen's agreement with myself. Because you would have thought it a gross violation of a boundary, wouldn't you?"

I nodded, but I had to say something about that. "But, you would have made a beautiful play of it. In fact, now that you have said what you just said, I wish you would. If I have a blessing to give on the matter, you have mine. If you ever do write and produce that Noh play, please let me know. I would love to see it."

Remy just shook his head, regarding me with his deep-set eyes. "Sometimes doing what is right is not doing what is acceptable to...others," he proclaimed. Being a woman, I cannot judge whether a male partner might believe he must absorb his female's gifts as his own, to be right with the world. But I do know that, as two creative people brought up in a culture tainted by centuries of stories characterizing the female as evil, disgusting and, most importantly, parasitic, we had no chance. And I cannot say I miss him in my daily life enough to wish I had never had an idea of my own or the need to express it to others. But sometimes I do in my dreams.

~ ~ ~

A Safer Haven

Monte's article about Safe Haven turned out even better than Sister Pete had hoped. It was entitled *The Case of the Missing Elder* and was presented with such warmth, humor and convincing everyday details that retirees were falling all over themselves to be put on a waiting list to become residents. Monte got a full-time media gig out of the article, but he still volunteered at Safe Haven. He told me he felt he owed his new position to Sister Pete. And, besides, he liked to hang out with Bibi.

When her inheritance came through, Bibi could have lived in relative luxury elsewhere, but she chose to stay at Safe Haven. Sister Pete cleared out a cluttered storage space and arranged to have a nice single room set up for the old woman right next to the manager's office. Sister Pete remarked with one of her furtive smiles, "I need her to be located where I can keep an eye on her in case she takes it into her head to run away from home again,"

After Bibi had settled the legal battle, she declared that at last she felt almost right with the world. Then she closed the door of her new single room and spent ten days alone with her silk songbook. Sister Pete lifted the ban on closed doors and left Bibi's meals in the hall by her room. Bibi emerged on a Saturday when I was volunteering at Safe Haven. She wheeled herself from her room to the kitchen and handed her lunch tray over to the dishwasher before joining the other residents in the common room. As though her adventure had never happened, she lifted herself from her wheelchair and, as she always had, sat placidly in her favorite Queen Anne chair.

Monte and I were helping Bettina with one of her coffee table montages at the time. I whispered to Monte that I was glad to note that the big scissors had been exchanged for a safe snub-nosed pair. Monte confided that Sister Pete had spoken some sharp words to Bettina's nephew, who had smuggled the scary shears in to his aunt. Bettina showed us a basket of primate pictures she had cut out of some *National Geographic* magazines for a montage monkey she was planning. Leaving her to her creative efforts, we slipped away and sat in chairs on either side of Bibi. Without looking at us to acknowledge our presence, Bibi said, "I know you nosy Parkers will want to know what I've been doing."

"You weren't worrying about your nieces' welfare, were you, Bibi?"

"No, yes, maybe a little."

"Bibi, they got houses!"

"From Wally. No thanks to any grand expression of empathy from me."

"But Bibi," I said, "You gave Viola your baby's lullaby."

"And not without pain," Bibi acceded. "So I don't think Viola's and Rhoda's faces will haunt me. The face that comes to me at night is my nephew's. I have been grieving these last days for my Wally. I knew the will was a thing to be dealt with. But I had so much other stuff going on--the Bells, and you two buttinskis--I had no space to feel my loss of the little boy who sat with me on my piano bench and sang. Leon's voice is sweet, but Wally's was *dulcet*. When the rest of this whole business had been completed, the loss of that sweet boy caught up with me, and I had to be alone to deal with that. And you two will not say a word about an old woman's sentimentality! Now, what do you suppose is on the dinner menu? I could eat a cougar!"

As the latter days of Bibi's long life passed, when

Monte and I would hang out with her, she got a great deal of fun out of reminiscing about how I found her in the creek bed. "Chasing around looking for an old woman snoozing under a white tree! You might as well have been chasing rainbows."

The academic in me had to admit she was right. "I had less than a clue to go on, it's true. If people had not been chasing me around the Arboretum, I would never have stumbled on your location."

"I suppose Sister Pete says it was divine intervention that led you to me," Bibi snorted.

"When she heard I had tried to use your tree pin with the white flowers to find you, she gave me one of her pontifical mini-sermons. *If you took literally what I said when I was in a desperate state and lured an old woman home with some pagan symbol, you ought to be ashamed of taking advantage of me and of Beatrice Bell.*"

"And yet you still believe in your pagan heart that Artemis led you to me," the old woman razzed me.

Ever the gentleman, Monte spoke up in my defense. "Her search for Artemis's white tree got her to you, didn't it? As my *abuela* might have said, *It may not be magic, but if it works, don't knock it.*"

"And for your information, Bibi," I said, "Sister Pete is not as bound to theology as you might think. She calls me the girl who followed false signs and fell into the truth. That reminds me," I said, digging in my pocket for Bibi's white tree pin, "I borrowed this from your defunct music box. Sorry to have pilfered your room for nothing."

Bibi stared at the pin I laid on her palm. *Roger.*

After all she had gone through, losing her husband, her baby, her songs, it was the first time I saw her shed a tear in front of anyone. I thought to myself, Well, Artemis, at least I got one thing a bit right.

It took scarcely seconds for Bibi to compose herself. Plumping her pillow, she lay her head back on it with a sigh and closed her eyes. "Too bad you two are not my family-- now that I've trained you to keep your mouths shut so's I can hear myself think. Let this be one of those times."

"One more question, Bibi," I said.

She groaned without opening her eyes.

"Sorry but I have to know, when you ran away, how did you escape Safe Haven?"

Her eyes shot open. "You should be able to figure it out, being a runaway yourself."

"You can't have gone out the garden gate, because it was locked. The door to the garden is always open, but the fence is too high to climb. None of the windows open far enough for even a person as small as yourself to wiggle through. And the front door is thick as a prison door and is always locked. So, how did you do it? Is there a laundry chute, coal chute or garbage chute Sister Pete has kept secret from her guests?"

Relaxing back on her pillow and covering her eyes with her hand, she said "Someone opened the door to go out and I simply slipped out behind her."

"And she let you?" Monte was indignant.

Bibi's eyes popped open. "Not her fault. I had been watching for someone to be careless about the door. When I noticed her leaving all in a snit, I followed her. She was in such a tizzy, she never looked back to see if the door closed behind her."

"Who was she and what was she in a snit about?"

"It was Viola come back–maybe to bully me one more time about the will. She made it all the way to my room, but Sister Pete espied her and got there in time to put herself between my niece and me. For a moment I thought those two women would come to blows, but Sister Pete could turn an express train in its tracks. She chased Viola back up the hallway, spewing biblical oaths the whole way while my niece responded with some words a churchwoman oughtn't say. They spatted so long at the front door, I had time to follow them and hide in the coat room."

"But, Bibi, your wheelchair was left in your room, along with your cane. How did you get to the front door?"

"I may be old as the hills but I can walk unassisted when a cougar isn't on my tail," Bibi sniffed. "I only use the cane and chair to save energy in case of fire or whatnot. Left the chair and stick in my room to create a bit of a puzzle for any buttinski who wanted to follow me."

"It puzzled this buttinski, that's for sure," I grumbled.

"What you get for being nosy," Bibi chuckled. "Anyways, when Sister Pete finally threw open the door and invited Viola to leave, my niece headed out the door in a huff without looking back, Sister Pete headed for her office, and I slipped out the door Viola left open. My niece went her way and I went mine."

"Poor Sister Pete nearly worried herself sick wondering how you got out," said Monte.

"Oh, well," Bibi mumbled, "You two managed to shove me back into my cage soon enough. And here I am."

Our conversation had lasted much longer than usual and I could see Bibi was done for the day. Tomorrow she might be sitting in her Queen Anne chair laughing at one of my fairy tales as usual, but, having dismissed Monte and me, she nodded off before we could even tell her goodnight. Monte and I stood in the doorway for a moment holding hands behind our backs as we had on that day when we fought together to convince her to defend her just claim to her songs. And before we closed the door on her private room, Beatrice Bell was, as always, humming in her sleep.

~ ~ ~

Skadi

My remote ancestors held in their minds the idea of a personage called Skadi, a deity so beloved that all of Scandinavia and Scotland were named after her. Skadi was a Great Mother goddess of the Underworld, and, because all plants grew from the earth, all things created—whether crops, poetry, songs or funeral ballads—were thought to be gifts from her or inspired by her.

In Skadi's honor, an artist or poet-shaman who created songs or stories was called a skald. For my ancestors, a skald was said to stand with the gods in the hallowed shadow of Skadi. And, because a skald's works were divinely inspired, no one dared copy them, neither gods nor men. These days copycats would boldly stroll into the very shadow of the gods and snatch words from a skald's mouth while they were being spoken, and not even call themselves thieves.

~ End ~

Bibliography

Evidence or interpretation of changes made to early myths over time is gratefully acknowledged to have been suggested by the following books.

The Chalice and the Blade, by Riane Eisler. Copyright © 1987 by Riane Eisler. Harper & Row, Publishers, San Francisco.

The Once and Future Goddess: A Symbol for our Time, by Elinor W. Gadon. Copyright © 1989 by Elinor W. Gadon. Harper & Row Publishers, Inc., New York, NY.

The Women's Encyclopedia of Myths and Secrets, by Barbara G. Walker. Copyright © 1983 by Barbara Walker. Published in 1996 by Castle Books, Edison, New Jersey.

Lost Goddesses of Early Greece, by Charlene Spretnak. Copyright © 1978 by Charlene Spretnak. Originally published by Moon Books of Berkeley, California in 1978.

The Great Mother, by Erich Neumann. Copyright © 1955 by Bollinger Foundation Inc., New York, N.Y. Published by Princeton University Press, Princeton, N.J.

The Goddess Obscured. By Pamela Berger. Copyright © 1985 by Pamela C. Berger. Published by Beacon Press, Boston, Massachusetts.